Shakespeare IN CAMBRIDGE

A CELEBRATION OF THE SHAKESPEARE FESTIVAL

ANDREW MUIR

AMBERLEY

DEDICATED TO SARA

He's a coward and a coystrill
that will not drink to my niece till his brains turn
o' the toe like a parish-top.

Sir Toby Belch, *Twelfth Night,* act III scene I

First published 2015

Amberley Publishing
The Hill, Stroud
Gloucestershire, GL5 4EP

www.amberley-books.com

British Library Cataloguing in Publication Data.
A catalogue record for this book is available from the British Library.

ISBN 978 1 4456 4105 8 (print)
ISBN 978 1 4456 4114 0 (ebook)

Typeset in 10pt on 13pt Sabon.
Typesetting and Origination by Amberley Publishing.
Printed in the UK.

Contents

Thanks and Acknowledgements

So much pleasure has been brought to Cambridge over the years by the cast and crew. For them the joy has been accompanied by blood, sweat and tears. It is hard work in all kinds of weather and it takes months of planning and preparation. They deserve enormous praise and thanks for all they have achieved, and I hope they can accept this book as testament to my gratitude and with it my fervent wishes for a long future as filled with laughter and triumph as the festival's first twenty-seven seasons.

My gratitude is due to a number of readers and evaluators for their feedback on various draft versions. Many thanks, therefore, to Mick Gold for responding to my first steps and to Alan MacGillivray, Graham Hall, Chris Green and Robin Lloyd Jones for detailed feedback on an early draft. Extra thanks to the last two of these for also giving their expert views on the penultimate draft.

I am indebted to Abel Guerrero for unlimited access to his marvellous photographs. Much more from Abel is viewable here: *https://www.flickr.com/people/79167549@No8/*. CSF productions feature prominently under the link to his albums.

Special thanks also to Bob and Bill Wellman for being so generous with their time and for preparing a guide to the CSF based on their many years of attendance.

I would like to thank David Rowan for letting me refer to him as Dave, to avoid confusion with David Crilly.

Thanks for help and support are also due to Pia Parviainen, Lucy Guo, David Bristow, Joe McShane, the NAPP Co. in Cambridge, Craig Jamieson, the wonderful staff at the Cambridge University Library, the Cambridge Summer Programme at Churchill College and last but most certainly not least, everyone at Amberley who has been involved in the production of this book.

Introduction

The Cambridge Shakespeare Festival has changed my life. Not only has it come to dominate my every summer but, more importantly, it has challenged and refocused my views of Shakespeare's plays while reinvigorating my appreciation of them. This book celebrates its achievement in doing this and places it in historical, personal and educational backgrounds that illustrate the festival's importance in connecting us with Shakespeare's dramas as they were first performed. This, in turn, brings back to life what is often strangled to death in classrooms and by the pressures of written exams.

Although most obviously catering for those who attend the Cambridge Shakespeare Festival (CSF), this book is aimed at everyone with an interest in Shakespeare's work. It is not a scholarly textbook, but it should hold appeal for scholars as well as the general public who care about the theatrical conditions from which Shakespeare's plays emerged. The purpose of examining these, and other related topics, is to highlight the way they enhance our enjoyment and deepen our understanding of the plays today, and of how the dramas were conceived, written and received in their own time.

As the book is intended for a general readership, jargon and other unnecessarily obscure terminology is not employed. As the title and subtitle suggest, this book has two main parts. Part one concerns itself with Shakespeare and Cambridge connections. Part two, the bulk of the text, is an in-depth look at the annual Cambridge Shakespeare Festival. As the book progresses we broadly move from the historical to the general re-creation of authentic Elizabethan staging outdoors and then on to the specific management of the yearly summer festival in Cambridge. This event usually comprises of eight plays, with two sets of four plays running concurrently, performed by professional actors over July and August.

Chapter one covers three main areas, starting with a play put on by students in St John's College at the beginning of the 1600s in which Shakespeare is one of the many targets for satire. This is followed by a reflection on why the adult acting companies were compelled to tour the provinces, visiting both Oxford and Cambridge. The staging practices they employed while out on the road will lay the groundwork for a myriad of cross-references and parallel staging at the CSF. There is also an overview of famous Cambridge theatrical and scholarly contributions to the world of Shakespeare performance and study throughout the centuries and how some of these are directly connected to the yearly festival.

The main thrust of the following chapters is in examining the nature of the outdoor performances in the Cambridge college gardens and contrasting productions in these settings with those of other theatres. The festival founder and artistic director, David Crilly, nails his colours to the mast in the official blurb:

> The festival prides itself on an artistic policy which strips away unnecessary theatrical artifice and gimmickry, and the company exists to provide access for all to these marvellous works without assuming any prior knowledge of the author or the play in question. The productions themselves are vivid and spectacular, and are performed in full period costume with live Elizabethan music.

Chapter two looks particularly at the proximity of the audience to the stage and the interaction and intimacy this engenders. In it I suggest that there is two-way communication and from this a special kinship and communal feel develop.

Chapter three offers a discussion of the lack of elaborate scenery and props and the implications of performing in the 'bare stage' settings of outdoor gardens in Elizabethan costumes. The crucial connections to the symbolic theatre of Shakespeare's own time are much in evidence here.

Chapter four finds us moving more towards the Cambridge Festival in particular, though most of its content is applicable to any outdoor production. The venues are described with their interesting combinations of variable exits and entrances. The effect of performing in natural daylight, again just as in the sixteenth century, is another main section of this chapter, along with a look at the audience demographics and the effect of occasional animal intrusion.

Chapter five concentrates on the history of the festival and the practicalities involved in housing the casts, financing the festival and sourcing costumes and props.

Chapter six considers the various communities that have sprung up around the CSF over the years. It also includes a look at how the CSF manages the bawdy element of Shakespeare's writing as this is interlinked with the audience and it was felt that it sits better here than being exiled to the frozen wastes of appendices' land.

In the concluding chapter, comparisons with productions in other media, from radio to live cinema transmissions, are briefly considered. This is an intriguing subject, but one that stands outside my main concerns here and which would demand a full book of its own to be fully explored.

Tangential topics, along with future seasons' performances, including audience and cast responses, will be picked up in the supporting website: www.a-muir.co.uk/csf/.

The last part of chapter five, concentrating on things going wrong, provides a counter-balance to my otherwise laudatory tone throughout. That tone is deliberately adopted. This book is, after all, a celebration, and the driver behind it was the joy the festival brings to me. However, that is not to deny that it would be absurd to expect every night, or even every production, to be an unalloyed success. There have, in fact, been three productions over the years when I have expressed strong reservations. On each occasion I found that I was less scathing than the festival's actors and directors; they are their own harshest critics.

Generally speaking, however, my appreciation has been well merited and I want to celebrate the feeling I had when I first discovered the CSF. As will become clear when reading this book, it has brought a tremendous sense of liberation to me and a reawakening of the full extent of the wonder of Shakespeare's art. I felt like Charles Ryder in Evelyn Waugh's *Brideshead Revisited* when he first encountered the world of Sebastian Flyte. It is fitting to quote an Oxford story here as, just as happened with its University, Cambridge's Shakespeare Festival founders also came originally from Oxford:

> I went there uncertainly ... and I went full of curiosity and the faint, unrecognized apprehension that here, at last, I should find that low door in the wall, which others, I knew, had found before me, which opened on an enclosed and enchanted garden, which was somewhere ... in the heart of that grey city.

There are some naming conventions I have adopted that should be explained. I refer to the theatre of Shakespeare's time as 'Elizabethan' as to continually refer to it as 'Elizabethan and Jacobean' becomes too awkward. Nonetheless, it is important to remember that I am, unless specified otherwise in the text, using the term to refer to the theatre as it was throughout Shakespeare's career. After all, some fifteen plays, including a number of Shakespeare's finest, not least *King Lear* and *Macbeth*, were conceived in Jacobean, not Elizabethan, times.

Another avoidance of writing out the full meaning is more problematic – that of gender when talking of actors and actresses. I have reluctantly used the pronoun 'he' when gender is unspecified. This is for two reasons: firstly writing 's/he', which was my original intention, produced an overly fussy and ungainly look, as did repeatedly writing 'he' or 'she' and 'her' or 'him'. I found the recent convention of alternating between using 'he' in one chapter and 'she' in another to be hopelessly confusing, however well intentioned. In the end, picking either 'she' or 'he' as the standard term seemed the least unsatisfactory course and I was forced into adopting the masculine form as the term 'actor' has become accepted usage when referring to both genders. Most actresses now prefer it, because, as Whoopi Goldberg stated, 'An actress can only play a woman. I'm an actor – I can play anything.' To use 'she' in constant combination with 'actor' appeared even more off-putting than all the other options. Unfortunately, an ideal solution to this situation for books such as these has yet to be devised.

More straightforwardly, to avoid constant repetition of the phrase 'the Cambridge Shakespeare Festival', it is also alluded to as the 'CSF' or 'the festival'.

1

Shakespeare in Cambridge

Madam, it so fell out that certain players
We o'er-raught on the way: of these we told him,
And there did seem in him a kind of joy
To hear of it.

Hamlet, act II scene II

Back in the Day, Touring and Staging, Scholarship, Poetry or Drama

William rubbed his hands to warm them against the chill morning air. Autumn was beginning to turn into winter. The sun had yet to penetrate the Fenland mist that hung heavy over Cambridge. The fields by the river were completely occluded and even King's Chapel, which he was walking towards, had wisps of white attached to it, like string from a gift not quite fully unwrapped.

Still, it was a fine morning to be out and about. The cold, crisp air was a welcome antidote to the fog inside his mind from all that ale and wine last night. It was a remedy too, for the lingering after-effects of the foul, tobacco-laden air of the tavern, where they had celebrated the success of the *Hamlet* performance, at that wonderful hall in St John's College, long into the night.

It had been quite a party, spoiled only by that ruckus with the uppity St John's students who were so scathing about his background, manners, accent and, worst of all, his plays. They acted as though Ovid belonged only to them, the University graduates. Well, maybe that was too harsh, the men from Queen's College had been on his side and John Weever had even stood on a table to recite a sonnet written in his honour ...

A Shakespeare visit to Cambridge would make a splendid start to my book. However, we do not know if he ever was there or not. We know very little about Shakespeare's life with any certainty, most is speculation and most of that unfounded on any facts whatsoever. Contrary to popular belief, though, we know more about him, and especially his family connections, than one would expect about someone of his position and from his time. This is the result of painstaking and dedicated scholarly research from amateur and professional historians. Nevertheless, there is still very little in the way of hard facts on Shakespeare's life. On the other hand, and much more importantly, we do have nearly all of his plays, which is a near miraculous boon given that most of the plays from the many dramatists of the period are irretrievably lost. We also know a great deal about his working environment.

Needless to say, however, the insatiable demand for books on the life, rather than the works, of great artists, means that this has not deterred a steady stream, if not a flood, of biographies on the man. These all make claims as to where Shakespeare travelled and when. Unsurprisingly, as they can offer no firm evidence as to why these claims are to be believed, they all have him going to divergent places in the same years or months. If you were to take an hour or two in a library, you could find assertions that Shakespeare visited Cambridge in various years and in combination with a list of other locations of very varying degrees of plausibility. These assertions are not made merely by eccentrics. One of the oddities of Shakespeare studies is that extremely knowledgeable people will often make bold statements and startling claims without providing evidence to fully support them. This reaches its inverted zenith in the sad case of the 'Shakespeare was not written by Shakespeare' sub-industry, which is regrettably supported by some of the greatest Shakespearean actors of our day. The various opposing sides, Team Earl of Oxford, Team Bacon, Team Marlowe and so forth, build grand theoretical edifices on the slightest of foundations while ignoring the solid and manifold evidence that points clearly to Shakespeare having been who we always thought he was.

Many of the imagined life stories have Shakespeare visiting Cambridge, especially, and most plausibly, during times when his company of players was forced out of London. This happened repeatedly and meant that the acting company was forced to return to touring outside the capital. The causes were either the recurring outbreaks of deadly plague that brought an end to any large gatherings of people in the city, or the popularity of boy actors' companies making theatres in the capital inaccessible to adult players.

The eminent American Shakespearean scholar and biographer Joseph Quincy Adams Jr was the first director of the Folger Shakespeare Library. I based my whimsical opening on the following quote from him:

During the autumn of 1601 Shakespeare and his fellow-players closed up their London theater, the Globe, and traveled in the country. There is evidence that in October they visited Aberdeen, and a short time later, Cambridge.

Adams is careful enough to indicate that he is not stating these visits took place, merely that 'there is evidence' that they did. According to other biographical pieces, 'there is evidence' that the company went elsewhere in 1601. Indeed, if you add up everywhere that the claim of 'there is evidence' is made for, then hardly anywhere would appear not to have been visited by them. Evidence, despite so many volumes of (fictionalised) life stories, is sorely lacking.

While there are no certainties, it is nonetheless undeniable that, in terms of probability, Shakespeare most likely did visit Cambridge. After all, the companies really did have to flee the plague and were, for a time, replaced by boys' companies in the theatres. Additionally, even when they were occupying the Globe there was a need to supplement income out of season by touring the provinces. With its relative proximity and university, Cambridge would have been an obvious destination.

Furthermore, there is one piece of material evidence to bolster the likelihood: the first quarto edition of *Hamlet*, published in 1603 under the title, *The Tragicall Historie of Hamlet Prince of Denmarke* states, 'As it hath beene diverse times acted ... in the two Universities of Cambridge and Oxford, and else-where.' Shakespeare was himself an actor in the company at the time this would have been performed, and we can therefore suppose that he played a part in that production. (The part of the ghost is often attributed to being played by Shakespeare). We are still, I hasten to add, in the land of supposition as far as Shakespeare's personal presence is concerned. However, at least we know that his play, *Hamlet*, definitely was performed in Cambridge.

It is worth further speculating that it was put on in the imposing, hammerbeam-roofed Hall at St John's College. This is not just because it is one of the few feasible venues, but because if it was performed there it would form a satisfying and meaningful connection with an important Cambridge Shakespearean link. In a play written and staged at that hall, we have some of the most important remarks regarding Shakespeare made in his lifetime. As we have very few contemporary references to Shakespeare, these became very famous and have been much quoted over the centuries. However, they were unfortunately misrepresented as literal paeans of praise until relatively recently. Their true nature becomes apparent when they are read in full and in context.

Back in the Day

The comments came in a trilogy of plays, the first called *The Pilgrimage to Parnassus*, the second and third were entitled *The Return from Parnassus* (First and Second Parts). We do not know who wrote them, but we know that they date from somewhere between 1598 and 1602. They were put on as part of the Christmas festivities by students at St John's College, Cambridge.

The date 1601 is what most scholars think most credible for the third in the trilogy – *The Second Part of the Return from Parnassus*. In this play, two famous actors from Shakespeare's company, Burbage and Kempe, are presented as characters in a savage lampoon of the contemporary London theatre scene. Kempe is made to remark,

> Few of the university [men] pen plays well, they smell too much of that writer Ovid, and that writer Metamorphoses, and talk too much of Proserpina and Jupiter. Why, here's our fellow Shakespeare puts them all down, aye and Ben Jonson too. O that Ben Jonson is a pestilent fellow, he brought up Horace giving the poets a pill, but our fellow Shakespeare hath given him a purge that made him bewray his credit.

Until late in the twentieth century, partial selections of this quote were taken to show that Shakespeare was held in far higher regard than the group that became known as the University Wits (Christopher Marlowe, Robert Greene and Thomas Nashe from Cambridge, along with Oxford's John Lyly, Thomas Lodge and George Peele). Granted the comment 'Why here's our fellow Shakespeare puts them all downe' does seem like high praise, but the character making it is being held up to ridicule. So, while the actor portraying the Lord Chamberlain's Men star comedian is indeed hailing Shakespeare, his character is that of a buffoon and his claims are meant to be risible in the extreme.

This is obvious from a number of points within the quote itself, far less the larger context in which they appear. Firstly, 'Metamorphoses' was the name of Ovid's epic narrative poem that joined together an astonishing collection of ancient mythological tales under the unifying theme of transformation. It was one of the favourite books of the era, and the audience at St John's would have thought that anyone but a fool would know that the author was named Ovid and the poetry was called *Metamorphoses*. It was also, as were other of Ovid's works, deeply embedded in Shakespeare's output. From the evidence we have of Shakespeare's education and reading, he 'smells' more of Ovid than anyone else. *Metamorphoses* was most likely the greatest single inspiration on Shakespeare's writing; in it you will find Venus and Adonis as well as Pyramus, Thisbe, Titania, Perseus and Proserpina amongst others. It is a fountain of classical myth to which Shakespeare often returns. To act in his plays and not realise this is the sign of an idiot, an idiot presented as a target for the highly educated to laugh at and mock, for they were, as we shall see, exorcising some jealous demons in their Christmas satires.

To try and see the above quote in a modern context, it would be akin to an impressionist playing Elijah Wood playing Frodo Baggins and saying 'Tolkien is a good writer and *The Hobbit* is a very good one too, his books don't smell too much of fantasy like those of George R. R. Martin'. Kempe and Burbage, as they are portrayed in the Parnassus Plays, have as much credence as insightful characters such as Baldrick and Manuel from *Blackadder* and *Fawlty Towers*, respectively, were they to espouse on aesthetic matters.

You may be wondering just why there was such animosity and why Shakespeare and his companions were the targets for abuse. The rest of the plays make clear that the university students were extremely insecure at this time with regard to their future careers. They are studded with passages bewailing the lot of those who have apparently wasted their youth in studies because no proper employment awaits such educated gentlemen. The blame for this is pointed at education being available to those not born into nobility. These middle-class, educated *artisans* (you have to spit the word out to get the real effect) are seen as usurpers, as upstarts stealing what should be these Cambridge University students' future rights.

Shakespeare is singled out presumably because he is such a favourite. So, in this way at least, the passage turns out to be a testament to Shakespeare's fame and success after all. The recent Cambridge performance of *Hamlet*, which had been a success in London, would have exacerbated this exponentially. The eponymous, reluctant 'hero' is a university student, but the play was written by a mere commoner from the sticks in their eyes. That such a thing was put on in their university was obviously too much for the anonymous author(s) of the Parnassus plays. Shakespeare was an easy target in terms of class, upbringing and profession. While ranting against 'glorious vagabonds' (travelling players were considered tramps by the pampered university men born into luxurious ancestral homes), the ammunition is drawn directly to those who 'purchase lands, and now Esquiers are named'. This is a clear reference to Shakespeare's purchase of a coat of arms for his family. Such a procedure was one of the ways that the lesser born who had enough money could claim to be gentlemen. This practice was seen by gentlemen-by-birth as a horror brought on by the new, mercantile age. This final kick, from a verse lambasting Shakespeare and his acting company, was immediately preceded by a vicious dig against those who make a living by 'mouthing words that better wits have framed'.

The class-based jealousy and fear evident here was to be a feature of Shakespeare's dramatic career. He was often pitted against university educated dramatists. There was acute anxiety in the ranks of the old, landed gentry about the new world of broader education, exploration and innovation. The world was rapidly changing and the old order felt itself on very unsure ground.

There are two other direct mentions of Shakespeare in these plays that follow a similar path of having been quoted as praise when in actuality they were the opposite. A character named Judicio declares of Shakespeare's poetry:

> Who loves not Adon's love, or Lucrece rape?
> His sweeter verse contaynes hart throbbing line,
> Could but a graver subject him content
> Without loves foolish lazy languishment.

The first two lines pay homage to verses that were hugely popular at the time. Shakespeare was probably better known for his love/erotic poetry than anything else. However, the praise is immediately undercut by the following couplet which dismisses him as a lightweight, one incapable of tackling more serious subjects. The students howling with laughter at the sarcastic observations may well have had a copy of Shakespeare's love verse surreptitiously tucked away in their student rooms. This is a point picked up elsewhere when another character declaims, 'Let this duncified worlde esteeme of Spencer and Chaucer, I'le worship sweet Mr Shakespeare, and to honour him will lay his *Venus and Adonis* under my pillowe'.

However, the character in question is Gullio, literally a gull, which was then the word for what we would call a sucker. Once again praise is put in the mouth of a fool who is being ridiculed for preferring Shakespeare to 'real poets' like Spenser and Chaucer. Just in case we have missed the point, the romantic lines that are taken from Shakespeare to concoct a love plea for Gullio singularly fail to move the desired lady.

To be fair, nearly everyone in the plays is an object of ridicule. The customs and rules of Cambridge University and their enforcers were obvious targets in the plays that were also riddled with College in-jokes, drunken tales and bawdy asides – just as you would expect from such a student production today, or in any time. One can presume the performances of these plays were riotous rather than of the subtly debating kind.

There were many other Cambridge connections with Shakespeare in his lifetime, unavoidably so as it was the alma mater of such fellow playwrights as Robert Greene and Christopher Marlowe. There are also two connections with Gonville and Caius College. Firstly, Doctor John Caius, physician to Queen Mary and who founded Gonville and Caius in 1557, appears to have been the source for the doctor in Shakespeare's *The Merry Wives of Windsor*. Secondly, a master and vice-chancellor of Caius, Thomas Legge, wrote a play entitled *Richardus Tertius,* which was acted, again at St John's College, in 1580 – the year that Christopher Marlowe joined Cambridge University. Legge's play likely had a direct effect on Shakespeare's own *Richard III,* but, even if not, it would have had a general influence via its impact on the drama of Marlowe. It is perhaps worth noting too that the dramatist Robert Greene, whose path was to become entwined with that of Shakespeare, was at Cambridge when this was performed by a cast that included many of his classmates.

I have said that we have few contemporary references to Shakespeare, and having placed those we have looked at so far firmly in the camp of denigration it is pleasant now to turn to Francis Meres of Pembroke College, Cambridge. In his *Palladis Tamia, Wits Treasury* (1598) [1] he rhapsodises that 'the sweet witty soul of Ovid lives in mellifluous and honey-tongued Shakespeare. Witness his *Venus and Adonis,* his *Lucrece,* his sugared Sonnets among his private friends, etc.'

Ovid again, you will note, though this time used not sarcastically but as the very pinnacle of touchstones with which to equate Shakespeare. Meres is no less stinting in his praise of Shakespeare's plays, even before the Bard's mature years. The following quote is legendary for including the intriguing title *Love's Labour Won,* a play which has either been lost or which we know now under another name:

As Plautus and Seneca are accounted the best for Comedy and Tragedy among the Latines: so Shakespeare among the English is the most excellent in both kinds for the stage. For Comedy, witness his *Gentlemen of Verona,* his *Errors,* his *Love Labour's Lost,* his *Love Labour's Won,* his *Midsummer's Night Dream,* and his *Merchant of Venice;* For Tragedy, his *Richard II, Richard III, Henry IV, King John, Titus Andronicus,* and his *Romeo and Juliet.*

I placed John Weever, of Queen's College, Cambridge, in my mock opening scenario due to the following lines he included in a poem from 1601:

> The many-headed multitude were drawn
> By Brutus' speech that Caesar was ambitious.
> When eloquent Mark Antony had shown
> His virtues, who but Brutus then was vicious?

Two years previously Weever had, in *Epigrammes in the Oldest Cut, and Newest Fashion,* penned a sonnet on Shakespeare in what we think of as the Shakespearean sonnet form. This is potentially an intriguing clue in attempting to ascertain the sonnets' time of composition.

Intriguing though that is, we are concerned with the staging of Shakespeare's plays in his own time and how this is reflected in their yearly CSF performances. It is worth considering this in more detail before looking at other ways in which Cambridge has contributed in significant manner to the Shakespeare story.

Touring and Staging

Touring performances by travelling companies played a major role throughout Shakespeare's life and career as all-round man of the theatre. Their influence probably began in his childhood and almost certainly affected him deeply in his teens. They shaped his work as actor, director (to use the modern term), and dramatist.

It is these touring productions from Shakespeare's day that the Cambridge Shakespeare Festival comes closest of all to emulating, notwithstanding the impossibility of replicating an audience experience from a society so very different to our own. It is also worth stressing that many of the facets that underpinned the touring stage shows and are shared by the CSF were preserved when Shakespeare and his company put on performances at the Globe.

When Shakespeare was five years old, in 1569, the first recorded visit to Stratford by a travelling troupe of players took place. It is entirely possible that Shakespeare's father, John, given his position in the local community at that time, would have been given a private showing of what was to be put on public display. Whether Shakespeare saw any part of a private or public performance is, naturally, a matter of mere conjecture. It is almost irresistibly tempting, though, to imagine the child William imbued with an instant passion that would stay with him forever and cause him to later travel to London to become an actor and playwright, leaving his own children and wife behind.

Such fanciful notions aside, we can predict with a higher degree of probability that Shakespeare witnessed touring companies perform on various occasions as he grew up. It would be strange, indeed, if William had missed seeing any of the plays put on by the many companies known to have visited Stratford-upon-Avon during his formative years. These included six visits by the Earl of Worcester's Men and at least three by the Queen's Men as well as performances by the Earl of Warwick's Men, the Earl of Oxford's Men, the Earl of Essex's Men and sundry other touring groups. There would have been great excitement, in the town, at their much heralded appearances.

The young Shakespeare was probably also taken to Coventry, a mere 20 miles from home, to witness that city's famed cycle of mystery plays. These enactments of major episodes from the Bible were regular events until Shakespeare's mid-teens. If he did go to these, William would have seen, to our minds, a peculiar mixture of awe-inspiring spiritual drama intertwined with clowning and crude jokes.

The pageant wagons (moveable carts that could provide both transport and stage) that brought the players and their supplies to Stratford and Coventry were to become even better known to Shakespeare when they later became a part of his own working life.

Many scholars presume that Shakespeare left Stratford for London by joining one of the travelling troupes as it passed through Stratford. Details are, at best, sketchy guesswork. Both Leicester's and Warwick's men toured Stratford in the 1580s at dates that would fit in with the known chronology of Shakespeare's movements, but the fevered speculation most usually alights on a visit by the Queen's Men in 1587. Not only is the date convenient for those trying to erect the solid flesh of a biography on bones too thin to bear one, but the Queen's Men were reputedly a man short as they left Stratford and in dire need of hiring a new player. In addition, their repertoire included versions of plays that would later be rewritten by Shakespeare and elevated from blunt caricatures into artistic masterpieces. Versions of *Richard III*, *King Lear*, *Henry V* and *King John* featured in the performances of the Queen's Men in the 1580s.

It is a tempting theory and it fits well with the little that we know for certain. It would be particularly apt for this book, were it ever to be confirmed as the Queen's Men were impressive travellers. Their patronage stemmed from their usefulness as official propagandists and, as such, they were sent far and wide from London to the extent of even reaching the capitals of Scotland and Ireland. They were also known to have played in Cambridge while touring East Anglia.

Such confirmation is unlikely ever to occur; other biographies make cases for Shakespeare following the same route to London, but with other travelling companies. What is undeniable is that he arrived in London with some knowledge of theatrical life already under his belt and, it seems likely, was in fact already very well versed in such matters.

To whatever degree Shakespeare was personally involved at this time, such travelling companies of players were the cradle from which all his theatrical art grew, and they would be something he was forced to return to even throughout his successful years in London. The pageant wagons pulled in at all manner of places: at various halls in churches, country mansions, guildhalls; at inn yards and market squares; and in the gardens of the landed gentry and public fields. Basically, they would play in any building or space that would have them.

Even after becoming established at theatres in London, many of the same features that travelling players and the Shakespeare Festival share were still in evidence. Performances still took place under an open sky with shared, natural lighting; small casts were still the order of the day and the intimacy that comes from the audience being close to, and not separated from, the actors remained central to the experience. Theatres designed to emphasise separation by having an imposing arch between the stage and the auditorium, known as proscenium stages, later came to represent the conventional theatrical setting.

Back in Shakespeare's time, his company were often forced to go back on tour for a variety of reasons, prime among these being the plague, the popularity of boys' companies and the opposition to performances by the city authorities.

All manner of infectious and deadly diseases afflicted the people of the sixteenth and seventeenth centuries, but none were as fearsome nor feared as the Bubonic Plague – also known as the Black Death or Black Plague. It struck repeatedly throughout Shakespeare's life; indeed he was one of the fortunate babies who managed to survive a devastating occurrence in his hometown in 1594 that has been estimated to have killed as many as a quarter of Stratford's population. Shakespeare was to survive many other deadly outbreaks throughout his life. However, although the plague did not claim his life, it was responsible for most, perhaps all, of the untimely passing of family members. Shakespeare lost his sisters Joan and Margaret when they were infants, and another sister, Anne, who succumbed aged seven. In later life, Shakespeare's brother Edmund, whose acting career could contain fascinating information if only we had access to it, died at the age of twenty-seven. To top it all, Shakespeare's only son, Hamnet, contracted the Black Plague and died, aged eleven, in 1596.

In addition to inflicting repeated personal losses on Shakespeare, the plague also played havoc with his professional career. Public gatherings were outlawed to try and curtail the rampant spread of the disease, so, when it struck, theatres were closed once deaths reached a certain rate per week. In James's reign, this was set at thirty. Given the deadly virulence of the plague, the theatres were at the constant mercy of sudden closures. This could be for a brief time, but it varied greatly and there were major outbreaks in 1593, 1603 and throughout much of the three years between 1608 and 1610.

One of the most terrible of the occurrences of the plague in Shakespeare's lifetime began on 4 December 1592. By January, the theatres would close and not reopen until spring 1594, by which time over 17,000 Londoners had perished. This was too long a break for most companies to survive. Pembroke's Men and the Queen's Men went touring during this time and were never to return as the same companies. In 1603, almost twice as many people perished as had done so in the previous decade. Again the theatres were closed for over a year. Another epidemic struck in the summer of 1608 forcing the King's Men (as Shakespeare's Company now were known) back around the provinces, possibly including Cambridge, and to play in Coventry where once he is thought to have witnessed the Cycle of Mystery Plays. Although they were back playing at court that Christmas, the plague was to rage back into the city in 1609 and 1610. Even outwith the worst years, smaller outbursts kept recurring. So frequently were the theatres closed that touring the provinces in the summer became the norm.

To be able to do so with the same plays they performed at London theatres in winter and spring is a testament to the flexibility of the theatre companies and the malleability of their staging practices. Such outstanding versatility also shows how close they still were to their roots. It testifies, too, to an idea that some later Shakespeare scholars found hard to accept: that the plays were constantly being adapted. There is no final, fixed text; no one definitive version. The same plays, with Shakespeare appearing as an actor in them and presumably managing the changes, were constantly being revised, cut, and adapted for different audiences in different locations, under different political and social pressures, and run over varying timescales. Similar versatility and flexibility are also required by those putting on the plays at the CSF.

It is difficult for us to comprehend the popularity of the boys' companies where all parts in a play are performed by young males. However, they had been successful in the 1570s, more so than adult companies, and they were to re-establish this dominance during the years when Shakespeare had reached the full flowering of his abilities. Shakespeare seems alone in resisting the urge or need to write for them. All the other prominent playwrights, including Ben Jonson, wrote for these boy casts who swept all before them in the opening years of the 1600s. Adult companies were forced to rely on touring to keep in existence as the city theatregoers flocked to see the children.

As you would expect, Shakespeare did not take kindly to this usurping of his place in London's theatres. One can only imagine the frustration he felt when at the peak of his powers he found himself outshone in popularity by them. Or perhaps we do not need to use our imagination as, uncharacteristically, we have what would appear to be direct comments on this situation from Shakespeare himself. He brings the subject up, very deliberately, in *Hamlet*. There, Shakespeare used the arrival of a touring band of actors to Elsinore to comment on the enforced touring of his own company. Hamlet poses a series of pointed questions on the matter: 'How chances it they travel?', 'Do they hold the same estimation they did when I was in the city?' 'Are they so followed?' To which the answer is a flat negative: 'No indeed are they not.' As the conversation continues, Hamlet, one cannot but presume, outlines Shakespeare's position on the 'little eagles' ('eyases') that have taken over his nest:

Hamlet: How comes it? Do they grow rusty?
Rosencrantz: Nay, their endeavour keeps in the wonted pace: but there is, sir, an eyrie of children, little eyases, that cry out on the top of question, and are most tyrannically clapped for't. These are now the fashion, and so berattle the common stages – so they call them – that many wearing rapiers are afraid of goose-quills and dare scarce come thither.
Hamlet: What, are they children? Who maintains 'em? How are they escoted? Will they pursue the quality no longer than they can sing? Will they not say afterwards, if they should grow themselves to common players – as it is most

like if their means are no better, their writers do them wrong, to make them exclaim against their own succession?

Hamlet act II scene II

In the first quarto, Hamlet's question is answered perhaps less bitterly and more in weary recognition, if not resignation:

> Rosencrantz: I'faith my Lord, novelty carries it away for the principal public audience that came to them, are turned to private plays and to the humour of children.

It was at least partly due to this 'turning to ... the humour of children' at the Blackfriars theatre that Shakespeare and his company were forced to go on tour in 1601, which directly resulted in the comments made in *The Returne to Parnassus* that we looked at earlier.

As if the plague and the boys' companies were not enough, there was another feature of London at the time that meant touring was often the only viable route for Shakespeare's company to take, and that was the implacable opposition to the theatres from the civil authorities. A constant battle for survival was waged by the acting profession in London in the face of this antagonism. Royal and noble patronage was their defence against those who saw the theatres as centres for drunkenness, prostitution, crime and mob violence. The protection afforded the acting fraternity was forever being tested and it proved to be insufficient at times. For example, in 1596 London's authorities prohibited the public presentation of plays within the city limits for a year. In the words of the Privy Council, with the spelling modernised,

> Her Majesty being informed that there are very great disorders committed in the common playhouses both by lewd matters that are handled on the stages and by resort and confluence of bad people, has given direction that not only no plays shall be used within London or about the city or in any public place during this time of summer, but that also those playhouses that are erected and built only for such purposes shall be plucked down.

Strong stuff indeed, although mercifully the last threat was not carried out. This stern prohibition, in the Queen's name, is thought to stem from the performance of a play called *The Isle of Dogs* (which unsurprisingly has not survived) by Ben Jonson and Thomas Nashe at the Swan theatre in 1596. This play was immediately suppressed, as apparently it had gone too far in its satire and had caused outrage with its 'lewd' and 'slanderous' content. Imprisonments followed, and the theatre owner had his licence revoked.

The list of reasons to leave the city and hitch up the old pageant wagons were many, varied and persistent. Companies could be closed down; the plague could appear again at any time and fashionable trends in the paying clientele could alter. Touring repeatedly became the essential means of survival and the only way to avoid bankruptcy. This economic necessity was given a financial boost by the added value that plays already performed in London could be replayed to country and provincial audiences. This was more important than it may at first appear, due to the incredible turnover of plays in the capital during the decades surrounding the century changing. Touring allowed the reprisal of popular hits that, although much loved, had enjoyed only short runs due to the novelty-hungry nature of the London audiences of the time.

Much of our understanding and information of Renaissance theatre life in London derives from the existence of a diary of sorts kept by one Philip Henslowe, father-in-law to actor Edward Alleyn and an impresario of the day. He details as many as fifteen different plays per month, played every afternoon of the week bar Sunday, ten of which were only performed once. The pressure on the actors to deliver must have been immense. How they learnt all their lines is almost beyond comprehension from our perspective. Not only that, but they did not see the whole play their character would appear in, instead they only saw their own lines. Whether this was thought desirable or not, it would simply have been impractical. Even the minority of performers who could read would not have had time to absorb such a huge amount of material, notwithstanding the prodigious verbal memory of those from oral cultures.

In addition to this, you have to factor in the size of the companies at the time – there were fourteen to fifteen in a cast. A glance at the *dramatis personae* of Shakespeare's plays will show that there are many more characters than that in his plays. Doubling up on parts was therefore part of the Elizabethan theatrical set-up. The same actor undertook two roles in other words, and sometimes even more. This sets up all manner of resonances as we shall see when looking at the same trait, which exists out of the same necessity, at the CSF.

It would be an understatement to describe the actors' life in London as a hard one. How much tougher this became when they were out touring, however! With cast sizes even leaner, they would have been at the mercy of sudden injury or illness. As the practice of doubling was so prevalent, one missing performer could take out two, three or even four parts of a play. Covering this would be logistically difficult at best and impossible in most cases as any actor taking on the extra parts would likely be onstage already in one or more of their roles. Some very quick rewriting, cutting and adapting must have commonly taken place, and even then it is difficult to imagine how they managed. Yet, manage they did. Nearly every year Shakespeare's company had to tour; they played on improvised stages, in fields, at fairs or wherever they were afforded a stage before packing up and heading off to their next destination.

The CSF does not quite replicate the astonishing burn-through of material in the Elizabethan theaters, but it too has short rehearsal times, tiny casts, short preparation time, and multiple parts in different plays must be undertaken over a hectic seven-week spell. The differences from both of these endeavours when compared to putting on Shakespeare plays in the West End and at the RSC are striking. These latter productions boast casts that are carefully and expensively brought together, given extended rehearsal time and kept together for most, if not all, of the often extremely lengthy run.

CSF audiences are also presented with many other features of the staging of his plays in Shakespeare's own day. Similarities can be seen in the bare stages, the minimal props, the brisk pacing, of performer and audience proximity under open skies. All of these promote a non-representational theatre, where everyone is always aware that they are either presenting or witnessing an illusion where the stress is on the verbal and the auditory, and where improvising clowns play a central role.

Of all of these, as we shall see in the next major chapter, the proximity of spectators to the stage is the key element from which so many others flow. John Russell Brown has summarised these core elements:

> There was no gap between audience and stage in the Elizabethan theatre, so actors did not address the audience as if it were in another world. There was a reciprocal relationship; the audience could participate in the drama as easily as the actors could share a joke or enlist sympathy. The very fact that it is difficult to distinguish direct address from soliloquy, and soliloquy from true dialogue, shows that contact with the audience was quite unembarrassed. They shared a sturdy illusion of life.[2]

This 'reciprocal relationship' is key to the dynamics of Elizabethan and CSF performances. Mark Rylance, a major figure in the modern Globe's Shakespeare productions, has no doubts over its centrality. Talking of playing in such an intimate setting, he noted,

> You see the relationship of an actor to the audience. Normally, as an actor I play over these heads because you are busy reaching the galleries. These people it's easy to involve ... You are so close, I could grab an actor from here, you know, and it's fantastic. There is a thing Spencer Tracy used to do when he was shy, he would look down. Partly he was finding his mark on the floor, which you have to do in film acting, but he would look down. Well, you come

out here, you look down, you get a face looking back up at you again. There is nowhere you can hide.[3]

This is even truer when playing Elizabethan fairs or twenty-first century college gardens in Cambridge. This closeness to the action, combined with the mobility afforded by fluid spaces, brings a sense of being in it together. Additionally, it promotes improvisation as well as interaction between those on stage and those off it. By sharing the same space and lighting you get a dizzying sense of letting yourself be absorbed into the drama, where anything can happen. It is very liberating for directors, actors and audience members alike. These audience members were a variegated lot in the sixteenth century and still are in Cambridge in the twenty-first century. It is often claimed that Shakespeare's plays appealed to every strata of the society he lived in. We are regaled with tales of the Globe playing host to, in the oft quoted words of the poet John Davies, 'A thousand townesmen, gentlemen, and whores, porters and serving men together throng.'

Tradition maintains that everyone from lords and ladies, employers and employees, rich traders, craftsmen, apprentices, the unemployed and the low-born flocked to the Globe. Gentry were privileged enough not to have to work for a living, and students are mentioned so often in reports that they seem to have been very regular attendees. You can imagine, at a stretch, some of those at the low end of society, without any jobs, somehow managing to get their hands on the penny entrance fee to the ground area surrounding the stage on three sides. It is slightly puzzling, though, that craftsmen, manual workers and so forth are numbered among the habitual attendees. It stretches credulity to imagine them just walking out of work when the flag was raised over the theatre to announce that a performance would be put on that afternoon at two o'clock. Perhaps the advertising and scheduling of performances was more elaborate and reliable than we are often led to believe, and perhaps also long summer days allowed some flexibility in working hours dictated by daylight. Even so, the percentage of the audiences that are claimed to be taken up by craftsmen, tradesmen and shopkeepers has always seemed suspiciously high.

Notwithstanding my guarded scepticism on that one count, it is clear that members of all, or almost all, classes were in attendance. There were 'penny stinkards' as they were known, and as Hamlet refers to them, on the ground in front of the thrust stage. They were so called because they paid a penny to get in and, well, you can guess the rest. They are now commonly referred to by the equally self-explanatory term 'the groundlings'. Above this seething mass were the rows of those who could afford to pay more to get seats, which ranged up on three levels, with a concomitant hike in expense, all the way up to the nobility paying a shilling to sit high above, lording it over the lower classes and there to be seen as much as to witness the plays.

The CSF is even more egalitarian than the Globe. All manner of citizenry appear, from the distinguished don to the impoverished student, from the wealthiest to the penny conscious backpackers engaged in their own personal tour. At the Cambridge Festival no one lords it over anyone else; there are no special viewing areas, no reserved or elevated seating, no shelter for anyone and the same toilets for all, even if they be mere portacabins.

Scholarship

Cambridge has played in an important role in the Shakespeare story in the four centuries since his death. I will briefly summarise these before concentrating on an extraordinary man who brought Shakespeare to life for many and who had a profound influence on education in general (studies on the Bard in particular) and who directly connects both to the Cambridge Shakespeare Festival and the reasons behind me writing this book.

Cambridge University is world famous for its Shakespearean scholarship. Major critics have been students and/or lecturers at Cambridge, and their research, commentary and analyses have added an enormous amount to our knowledge and appreciation of the Bard's work. Much of their writing, and that of other experts in the field, has been published by the Cambridge University Press, which is also home to the Cambridge Shakespeare Editions. Historically important and hugely influential, these began in the nineteenth century with the initial edition aimed to coincide with the tercentenary of Shakespeare's birth in 1864 (which saw the publication of the accompanying one-volume 'Globe' edition). This first Cambridge Edition was a colossal work for its time. It brought together all of the important discoveries in previously completed research on the texts and became the de facto standard for published Shakespeare.

Beginning in 1921, John Dover Wilson led a small team of editors in producing the *New Shakespeare*, and these editions became the accepted touchstones for much of the twentieth century. However, the pace of Shakespearean studies had accelerated at an extraordinary rate even as these editions were being brought out. Consequently, in 1984, an updated series was begun entitled *The New Cambridge Shakespeare*. This series, currently being republished with dramatic new covers, contains in-depth scholarly introductions and annotations drawing together as much crucial information as they can hold. They also contribute vigorously argued and defended viewpoints on some of the more troubling cases of authorship and collaborations, and are the editions quoted herein.

The Cambridge college libraries contain treasure troves of Shakespearean publications and the city contains more than one of the precious, original

Shakespeare First Folio editions from 1623. Holding the University Library's copy in my hands in 2013 was nothing short of remarkable; I was expecting something more weather-beaten and fragile. Instead it is an impressive volume, just in itself, given its age, regardless of the priceless contents. I was profoundly moved. It is not a direct connection with the man himself, as he had died seven years before it saw the light of day, but it is our most comprehensive link to the precious words he wrote for actors to perform. It is impossible not to feel a sense of awe that his two friends and colleagues, John Heminges and Henry Condell, in producing this book, saved so very many plays from disappearing along with the lost, probably co-authored play, *Cardenio*. Similarly, no one can feel anything other than wonder at the genius that produced so much of such a scintillating standard. When you move from *Macbeth* to *Hamlet* and then realise that the facing page to the close of *Hamlet* is the opening page of *King Lear*, you just have to shake your head and marvel. It seems almost unfair. I confess that when I returned it, or rather just before I did, I placed my fingers to my lips and transferred a kiss on to that precious document. Our view of Shakespeare without this folio would be a very different one; apart from everything else it approximately doubles the numbers of plays that we would have in any form at all. In addition to gifting the world all these masterpieces that would otherwise have been lost, the First Folio preserves other, already known, plays in more comprehensive and comprehensible forms.

'A schoolteacher that can teach'

A Cambridge school, historically intertwined with the university, supplies another relevant link between the city and the Bard. The Perse School for boys in Cambridge, which became fully co-educational in 2012, has always had a myriad of connections with the university and, consequently, its Shakespeare associations. The school was founded when Shakespeare was still alive in 1615 by a W. H. D. Rouse, fellow of Gonville and Caius College. Rouse, the innovative headmaster in the period we are concerned with, also held a university appointment, as did Douglas Brown, who enters our story presently. Brown had the presumably tumultuous honour of being mentored by the hugely influential twentieth-century critic F. R. Leavis. Leavis was another 'Perse boy' who went on to Cambridge University both to study (Emmanuel College) and to teach (Downing College). The eminent and highly influential Shakespeare scholar, E. M. Tillyard, was another former pupil of the school.

An inspirational teacher, Henry Caldwell Cook, sparked something of a revolution at the Perse. Cook had been attracted by the school's relatively modern methods under Rouse's stewardship. In the years leading up to the First World War, Cook established and largely financed a mini-Elizabethan theatre which he called 'the Mummery'. The name stems from mummers – the travelling players who performed folk tales and carnival sketches in costumes and disguises from medieval times onwards. They form a significant strand of the background tapestry to Renaissance theatre in England and they would have had a profound effect on Shakespeare's imagination as well as his playwriting.

In the Mummery, Cook taught Shakespeare solely through the method of having his pupils act the plays. Indeed, this was the central plank of Cook's groundbreaking and influential approach to all education as detailed in his 1917 book *The Play Way*. Here, however, we are interested solely in his approach to Shakespeare performance and education. His Perse boys were enthusiastic pupils, and little wonder. Their Mummery could hardly have stood in greater contrast to the rest of the Perse school, far less the standard school accommodation and practices of the time.

Time and again Cook reiterated his simple yet profound philosophy in two words, 'Act it'. When asked by a visitor to the Perse, 'What do you do with a play of Shakespeare?' he replied, 'Act it. What else can you do with a play?' Meanwhile, the rest of Shakespearean education was, and would continue for many years to be, totally focussed on textual analysis of the plays. This incensed Cook who described it as cutting out blocks of lines from the text of plays and then 'proceeding to mince it into an unrecognizable slush'.

After Cook's death, the Mummery was neglected. Nevertheless, he had established a tradition whose light was not to be extinguished. Douglas Brown was to carry on Cook's work and the director Sir Peter Hall, founder of the Royal Shakespeare Company and leader of the National Theatre for fifteen years from 1973 onwards, joined the school in 1941 just as Douglas Brown was resurrecting the Mummery. Meanwhile, the educational theories outlined in *The Play Way* grew to become, by the 1960s, of considerable importance in selected schools and eventually became prominent drivers even in mainstream comprehensives. They are still influential a century after Cook began his work, particularly in the area of second language learning.

Cook's relevance to the history of Shakespearean criticism over the last century, and to the value of the performances of the Cambridge Shakespeare Festival, is considerable. The same holds true regarding his impact on the development of my own relationship with Shakespeare and, consequently, the impetus for this book.

To begin with my own Shakespeare story, this can be told as a classic tale of 'three steps to heaven'. However, step one would be more accurately described as a giant leap backwards. Had I been a beneficiary of the Cook method, the destination point of my journey would have been coterminous with its beginning. However, like the majority of schoolchildren in twentieth-century Britain, I did not attend the kind of school that was open to such ideas. Instead, my narrative went as follows.

Three Steps to Heaven

I am fourteen or fifteen and one of some thirty-five teenagers incarcerated in one of the many classrooms in a grey, prison-like block of stone and glass on the outskirts of Glasgow. Welcome to comprehensive education 1970s UK style. We are made to stand up, one after another, and read a block of ten lines from *A Midsummer's Night's Dream*. You pay no attention to the incomprehensible words that are being mumbled until the speakers get close to where you are sitting.

I realise with sinking heart that my 'turn' will come before the end of the class. It duly does, and I stand and stammer out the lines, to hoots of derision when I had to read out the names Titania (snigger) and Bottom (guffaw). I sit down red-faced and the inmate next to me stands up to recite their ten lines. It is one of the longest fifty-five-minute lessons imaginable; nothing else happens, nothing is explained. There is no rhyme nor reason to any of it and no one in the room, including the teacher, who is presumably catching up on marking, has a clue what is going on.

Two years later I am studying literature at university and glorying in the wonderful imagery of Shakespeare's poetic drama. The sweep, majesty and endless pleasure of his verse are overpowering; a journey of joy in his language that will last for the remainder of my life has belatedly begun. I write a long essay on the themes of reason, madness and identity in *A Midsummer's Night's Dream*. In that self-sure way of adolescents, I think I have finally 'got it'.

Some thirty years after that, I begin my annual visits to the Cambridge Shakespeare Festival and most years I see a performance of *A Midsummer's Night's Dream*. I am close to the actors, sometimes not only within touching distance but actually touching. They play it differently every year. There are variations from night to night. We are outside, so annually the weather, and therefore lighting, can change significantly from one performance to the next. The college gardens provide variable settings, and consequently each play is presented differently in order to take advantage of or to overcome the individual settings' unique layout. Each production brings new insights into how central stagecraft is to Shakespeare's visions and to how the language I had so adored for so many years is actually serving the performance, rather than vice versa. The text dovetails with, bolsters and embroiders the dramatic art which has to be experienced live, up close and personal, out in the open. Finally, I get it, I get it all.

The links to Cook are obvious. My first step illustrates the anti-education he so opposed. 'Learning how to move is of immeasurably greater importance than learning to sit still' is one of many apposite and prescient Cook quotes on my classroom experience. What I was forced to undergo was representative of that which millions of schoolchildren endured around the United Kingdom. The acclaimed actor, director, producer and screenwriter Sir Kenneth Branagh, from Belfast, remembers that, 'I was brought up in a school where Shakespeare was taught in the first instance straightforwardly and dully. We read it aloud and of course it made no sense to us because no connection was made.' CSF founder and artistic director, David Crilly, has similar recollections from his school in Birkenhead, Liverpool's port for the Belfast ferry: 'We didn't get it at all; the only thing we learned was crowd control.'

Step two takes us into another terrain that Cook illuminated, that of the divisions between literature and drama, text and performance, words and voice, academics and theatre people. Cook was a shining light for those who favoured performance over text and one of the inspirations for a twentieth-century revolution in how Shakespeare is studied and performed. Step three is the epitome of the benefits of productions in Elizabethan style where, as we shall see, even the onlookers cannot help but feel they are a part of the open-air stagings.

Cook abhorred the way Shakespeare was traditionally taught with 'the boys reading in turns while seated in their desks'. So, he would have been horrified to think that six decades later schoolchildren were still being forced to suffer in the same manner. Additionally, it was still standard practice to force-feed the plays as literary texts to be analysed for compulsory exam questions. It seemed that schools were intent on making Shakespeare as unpalatable as possible to their pupils. Nothing could be further from the experience of watching Shakespeare at the CSF than what is described here:

> It is doubtful whether there could be a more unsatisfactory way of approaching Shakespeare and his plays than the one suffered by generations of English-speaking people. Almost universally, our first experience at the man's work is in the classroom, where — often under the shadow of impending examinations — the once fair body is dismembered into forty-minute chunks of dreamy afternoons. It is hardly surprising that the vast majority of his compulsory readers never willingly open a text or go to see a play after they escape from the educational system.[4]

One of the influential Shakespearean thinkers who followed in Cook's footsteps was J. L. Styan. Styan, who was the Professor Emeritus of English Literature and Theatre at Northwestern University, Evanston, Illinois, acclaimed Cook and his work as a 'landmark in history'. One suspects that Styan would not have appreciated the word literature in the title of his professorship as he was against the way Shakespeare was taught in universities as well as schools: 'I believe students can hear the most brilliant sequence of lectures on Shakespeare and then, when they have left college, never pick him up or seek him out again'.[5]

I have to say that this was not the case for me, as some of the lectures I attended opened up the wonders of Shakespeare's poetics and certainly encouraged me to keep reading him thereafter. However, note the term 'read'. These were, admittedly, purely literature lectures, not drama. Herein was the division that lay like a chasm between the different approaches to the Bard's work.

Poetry or Drama

The question of whether Shakespeare is primarily poetry or play was entwined with that of how he was taught in schools and universities. As Moseley put it,

> the study of the plays as printed texts can be extremely interesting and rewarding, and indeed is utterly necessary, but what has happened to the plays as academic material could not be further from Shakespeare's intentions when he wrote them ... Shakespeare was a working dramatist in a very competitive world; he was writing highly topical plays to catch a particular market, and if he did not pull in an audience, the theatrical company in which he had a substantial financial share did not eat that week. What he and his fellows were selling was not a printed book but a heard and seen experience.[6]

The difference between 'a printed book' and 'a heard and seen experience' starts with the major physical and mental differences between reading a play and watching it being performed. A book can be read at whatever speed and over whatever timescale readers desire. It is they who dictate when the story starts and stops. A book can be put down and picked up again a few hours or days later. Furthermore, certain passages can be lingered over and reread. In the middle or near the end of the plot, a reader can return to earlier scenes to remind themselves of what happened, or to trace connections of character, plot or imagery. In complete contrast, a play occurs under others' control. As an observer of the unfolding action, you are part of a shared audience experience that follows events in a timeframe that is likewise outside your control. As a result, there are numerous problems with interpreting plays solely through reading rather than experiencing them live in the theatre. It is true, on the other hand, that one performance alone will usually only barely scratch the surface of a play's manifold depths of meaning.

The best way is undoubtedly to see as many performances as possible and also to read it in-between these visits to live performances. To read in isolation, while allowing one to revel in the majesty of Shakespeare's language, inevitably leads to misreadings of action that need to be witnessed to be properly felt and understood.

A few examples of how easily one is misled in this situation will give an idea of the extent of the problem when you imagine it being replicated throughout all the plays. Firstly, silent characters whose mute onstage presence is important are almost always forgotten about when reading. Even when remembered by a reader, they lack the effect their physical presence has on stage. Secondly, information that it is essential to keep hidden for plot purposes is often revealed in advance on the printed page. Thirdly, scenes that are intensely moving when enacted can seem forced, false or even risible when only read.

The denouement of *Twelfth Night* can exemplify all three of these points. Onstage, Antonio is yet another figure (along with Malvolio and Feste) who is unattached and left out of the traditional harmonious ending to comedies which sees everyone paired off into couples. However, if you merely read the play you forget he is there. Viola is only named at the end of the play, yet this climactic revelation, central to the plot, is known from the beginning of a printed text. This alone is a seismic change in how a reader receives the play as compared to someone seeing it performed. Shakespeare wrote for those attending the theatre, not the reader; it is a play, not a novel. Only on stage, with apt acting, can identical twins not recognise one another in a plausible manner. The long dialogue to confirm that they are indeed siblings is ludicrous when it is only encountered on the page. It is so tortuous to read that the entire feeling of the play is destabilised. Whereas when it is acted out, it can and has been extremely effective in stripping away the confusion of the previous acts.

Twelfth Night can also illustrate general points where reading the text gives a much more restricted, and often downright erroneous, impression of what is going on in the play. The electric sexual tension with the cross-dressing, gender confused and confusing frisson that lights up performances can seem contrived in print and is, in any case, an immeasurably colder and more distant experience.

These are just three of the many points that negatively affect our apprehension of the plays via text rather than performance. A further example would be that much of the slapstick and bawdy humour has no impact on the page but is exhilarating, and central to the overall experience of the play, when performed.

Shakespeare immersed himself in the live performances of his plays, but seems to have been unconcerned about their appearance in print, though we should bear in mind that there may be good reasons for this that are unknown to us. Still, the quarto editions appeared with a quite incredible amount of errors, many of which were glaring and ludicrous. In contrast to other such publications, they were bereft of any information such as *Dramatis Personae*. Furthermore, Shakespeare did not follow the lead of his friend and rival Ben Jonson in preparing and overseeing his own literary collection. The 1623 Folio came about without any input, or even apparent wish, from its now celebrated, above all others, author. Roland Mushat Frye remarks forcefully on this subject, stating that

> nor did he make any attempt to get his unpublished plays into print. When he died, he could not know that anyone other than theatrical directors, prompters, and actors learning their roles would ever read *Julius Caesar, Macbeth, Antony and Cleopatra, As You Like It, Twelfth Night, The Tempest,* and a dozen other plays ...

Mr Frye outlines a highly persuasive case that leads him to a conclusion over which he has no doubts, which is

> that every bit of our evidence indicates that Shakespeare was meticulously careful in preparing his plays for effective stage production before a theater audience, but that he took no care whatsoever in preparing them for readers ... if we are to understand Shakespeare fully, we should begin by approaching him in the milieu which he chose for himself – the theatre.[7]

The difference between reading versus hearing and seeing is basic and profound and the starting point has to be live performance. The feeling that this is natural and true is heightened exponentially by being part of intimate, outdoor, CSF congregation. This is just as well for those like myself who came through an educational mainstream that has resisted and delayed an acceptance of the idea of approaching Shakespeare as a dramatist first and foremost.

After my off-putting encounter with Shakespeare at school, I spent four teenage years at university with Shakespeare a major part of each of them. Never once did we go as a class to a play, or even a film version, nor study acting a scene in any way. We were 'reading literature' and, therefore, we concentrated solely on the text. Not that I did not appreciate this, after all the text is spellbinding and revelatory, and studying it changed my life. Yet, looking back, it seems inexplicable that Shakespearean studies were so totally separated into the two departments.

A counter swell of opinion had been forming, however, unbeknown to me. Cook's dictum of 'act it' was echoed by many later writers, critics and dramatists who also demanded that the way to study Shakespeare was via performances, not text. They did not walk an easy path and the closer they got to the university literature departments, the more the antagonism grew. 'The real crunch came when the universities had to reconsider their position with regard to the teaching of drama. And this, of course, is where the stalwarts of academe put up the strongest resistance.'[8]

One of many extraordinary things about Shakespeare is that he is both the foremost dramatist and the greatest poet in the English language. Academia has found this double mastery difficult to manage within its rigid curriculum categories. Another singular thing about Shakespeare is that, until education intervened at least, he was always a popular as well as critical favourite:

> He's always been a favourite, he's never stopped being a favourite with both audiences and actors. It's interesting that in early American history Shakespeare was the most read book. Even people who were illiterate would hire people to read to them from Shakespeare and Abraham Lincoln was very, very influenced by Shakespeare. Most cabins in the wilderness had Shakespeare and the Bible. Maybe Shakespeare ceased to be as popular with students when they started teaching it in the schools and part of it is that they began to teach it as a literary exercise. Shakespeare can be read on many levels but primarily he writes for the theatre, and he writes to be performed by actors and people using the words and speaking it aloud. It doesn't exist as deeply on the printed page as it does in the mouths of actors.[9]

The campaign to have the study of Shakespeare be a performance-based discipline has faced a long and rocky road in order to achieve its goal. However, from back around the time of Cook, there were always voices championing the idea. At first, there were only a few but their voices were heard. The Shakespeare biographer and critic Sir Sidney Lee wrote as early as 1907 that

> there are earnest students of Shakespeare who scorn the theatre and arrogate to themselves in the library, often with some justification, a greater capacity for apprehending and appreciating Shakespeare than is at the command of the ordinary playgoer or actor. But let Sir Oracle of the study, however full and deep be his knowledge, 'use all gently.' Let him bear in mind that his vision also has its limitations, and that student, actor, and spectator of Shakespeare's plays are all alike exploring a measureless region of philosophy and poetry, round which no comprehension has yet drawn the line of circumspection, so as to say to itself 'I have seen the whole.'[10]

The hugely influential actor, director and playwright Harley Granville-Barker grumbled, with considerable justification, that he suspected that most people writing about Shakespeare had never been inside a theatre. At the same time that Cook was having success with his pupils at the Mummery, Granville-Barker was stunning the Savoy Theatre by returning the stage as much as possible to audience proximity and absence of background scenery – the very things, indeed, that make the Cambridge Shakespeare Festival such a rewarding experience.

These early trailblazers found willing hands to carry on their beliefs. The idea that drama should be studied as drama was so overwhelmingly obvious that it became generally accepted in time. Nonetheless, resistance was fierce and still exists in some quarters.

This strong opposition led to a counter-reaction which caused some of the proponents of drama's primacy over literature to go too far on occasion. Styan builds up such a head of steam in his book *Shakespeare's Stagecraft* that when we read 'it is questionable whether the real advances in Shakespeare studies in this [twentieth] century have come through verbal and thematic studies', we feel he wanted to say 'any real advances' and only considerable self-restraint prevented him doing so. The innovative director Peter Brook felt no such compunction. Brook uses the terms pedant and scholar as synonyms in his classic study *The Empty Space*. He treats both with the same lofty disdain:

> ... there is always a deadly spectator, who for special reasons enjoys a lack of intensity and even a lack of entertainment, such as the scholar who emerges from routine performances of the classics smiling because nothing has distracted him from trying over and confirming his pet theories to himself, whilst reciting his favourite lines under his breath. In his heart he sincerely wants a theatre that is nobler-than-life and he confuses a sort of intellectual satisfaction with the true experience for which he craves. Unfortunately, he lends the weight of his authority to dullness and so the Deadly Theatre goes on its way.

And

> The theatre is not the classroom, and a director with a pedagogic understanding of Brecht can no more animate his plays than a pedant those of Shakespeare. [11]

In Al Pacino's 1996 film *Looking for Richard*, the playwright and director Frederick Kimball completely loses his temper, even at the mere mention of a scholar. This occurs when Pacino cannot fathom the motivation for Richard courting Lady Anne and does not want to accept Kimball's unconvincing attempts to portray the scene as Anne deliberately enticing Richard. Kimball is animated by something that has happened off camera and launches into the following tirade:

> You were gonna find a scholar to explain what really went down with Richard and Anne. I am telling you that that is absolutely ridiculous ... you know more about *Richard III* than any f***ing scholar at Columbia or Harvard. This is ridiculous because you are making this entire documentary to show

that actors truly are the possessors of a tradition, the proud inheritors of the understanding of Shakespeare for Christ's sake. And then you turn around and say 'I'm gonna get a scholar to explain it to you.' It's ridiculous!

Pacino tries to defend his actions by saying, 'A scholar has as much right to an opinion as any of us.' It is telling that he has already downgraded the sought-for expert view to being just another opinion of no more or less intrinsic value to that of anyone else. There is no surprise whatsoever when the following scene mockingly depicts a scholar being unable to come up with even the beginning of an answer to the question. It seems clear that many theatre people, even those who are themselves critics, see themselves as implacably opposed to academics.

Yet, appealingly straightforward though this attitude of disdain appears, it is far from being the whole story because directors were influenced by the scholars and critics they professed to despise. Brook had all but a creative collaboration of great minds with the Polish critic Jan Kott who wrote the profoundly influential study *Shakespeare Our Contemporary*. The existential, absurdist and sexo-psychoanalytic readings from Kott were clearly creatively explored in Brook's celebrated productions of *King Lear* and *A Midsummer Night's Dream*.

Nor were all critics merely dull pedants, closed to the fun of the theatre. That elegant writer and critic John Dover Wilson, in a chapter revealingly entitled 'Love's Labour Lost: the Story of a Conversion', describes how a live theatrical experience was not just a 'thrilling production' but 'Shakespearean criticism of the best kind', and that 'Granville-Barker was proved to be more right than even he can have dreamed possible'. Wilson was writing about Tyrone Guthrie's 1936 production of *Love's Labour Lost* and elaborated on the experience:

> I went, I saw, I was completely conquered; and I was not alone, for Alfred Pollard, my father in Shakespeare, went with me and was as completely conquered. I have had many memorable and revealing evenings with Shakespeare in the theatre – *Hamlet* in modern dress, *Othello* with Paul Robeson in the title role and Peggy Ashcroft as Desdemona, and so on, but none to equal this. For Mr Guthrie not only gave me a new play, the existence of which I had never suspected, which indeed had been veiled from men's eyes for three centuries, but he set me at a fresh standpoint of understanding and appreciation from which the whole of Shakespearian comedy might be reviewed in a new light.[12]

The other, somewhat obvious, point to keep in mind when reading their diatribes against education and criticism is that Caldwell Cook was a teacher and J. L. Styan a critic. While readily agreeing that it was both regrettable and absurd that

Shakespeare's dramatic texts were treated solely as poetry, it is equally unfounded to suggest that all the scholarly and academic work carried out on the poetics of the text has added little to our knowledge of the plays. That such claims were made, surprising as they may seem now, is more understandable when you recall that they came about in the face of what had for so long been a dismissal of the dramaturgy. Performing arts were overlooked in a way that is scarcely believable today. Styan notes, in his *The Shakespeare Revolution*, that the Shakespeare of the theatre, not the page, was 'often bitterly derided by the traditionalists'. The stark fact that a dramatist was being studied, taught and evaluated without a reference to his profession, nor being performed in circumstances even vaguely similar to those he wrote for, would have driven anyone to excessive counterclaims.

In time a rapprochement was established, perhaps not universally, but nonetheless there is a general acceptance now that the fact that Shakespeare was a dramatist, writing for a specific audience at a specific time in a theatre with defined conventions, should always be taken into account when studying his plays. Sir Sidney Lee and J. L. Styan had, to be fair, acknowledged this all along. Lee wrote that

> actor and student may look at Shakespeare's text from different points of view: but there is always as reasonable a chance that the efficient actor may disclose the full significance of some speech or scene which escapes the efficient student, as that the student may supply the actor's lack of insight.[13]

This feeling that there could be a two-way process of communication to mutual benefit between literature and drama slowly but surely built, and eventually some balance was achieved. The superb work of 'the theatre people' is now readily acknowledged from all parties. For myself, like so many others, the work of dramaturgy of Brook, Styan, director John Barton (yet another Cambridge man) et al has reinvigorated and expanded my pleasure and interest in Shakespeare beyond measure. This is especially so when I see all the ideas in action, annually, at the Cambridge Shakespeare Festival. Simultaneously, though, all of these benefits I see in conjunction with the love I have always had of the mesmerising poetical gifts the text of the plays contain. I have no need to support one area of study or approach to the detriment of the other; I prefer to embrace both.

Thus, we arrive at the end of my 'three steps to heaven' – my own reconciliation of text and performance at the CSF. As Cook tried to create at the Mummery, as Styan longed for, I have a symbolic, Elizabethan-style theatre on my doorstep every summer. This annual recreation of the essence of Shakespearean drama and staging and what it tells us about his artistry, achievements and working practices forms the remainder of this book.

Audience Proximity

According to the fair play of the world,
Let me have audience; I am sent to speak
                                    King John, act V scene II

Intimacy, Improvisation, Engagement, Interaction, Togetherness

Intimacy

Having actors within touching distance of audience members on an open stage, mostly in daylight, brings out the significance of facial and other gestures, such as eye contact, audience interaction, the two-way communication between cast and audience, and the intimacy that grow from these. As was alluded to in the opening sections of this book, these factors of closeness and involvement for the audiences at the CSF directly equate to circumstances in Shakespeare's own day. The Elizabethan theatre, and therefore Shakespeare's dramatic art, developed from travelling acting companies who played in a myriad of settings with the performances taking place on a portable stage in an open space. Crowds of spectators pushed forward, as close to the actors as they could get, to catch the action and make their feelings known.

Audiences today are equally enthusiastic when given the chance to be beside the performing space. Leonni Antono, a teenager visiting the CSF for the first time, wrote that seeing the play in a college garden gave her a sense of 'connection with the characters as we sit right in front of them', with the privilege of 'admiring the acting without any concealment'.[1] Gary and Susan, a middle-aged couple from London, said they visited each year and loved the informality and the actors being 'right there in front of us', with no barrier or separation. The speed with which the pegged-out picnicking areas, even closer than the seats to the actors, are occupied pays eloquent testimony to the desire to be as close as is physically possible to the action.

This proximity has effects ranging from the minor to the essential. To begin at a basic level, such closeness makes a practical difference. Detailed facial expressions can be witnessed by a large proportion of the audience at any one time. The actors strive to maximise this in every way conceivable that is appropriate to each of the varied and various venues. Similarly the extent of eye contact is remarkably high and all gestures are clear to everyone every time they are performed leading to a tremendously close feeling for the audience. We are sharing the same space with the actors and they are, in essence, 'right in our faces', unless they wish to withdraw for some dramatic purpose.

For the actor, the benefits of this closeness are immense. He apprehends immediately the effect that his wink, his stare, his hand movement and other gestures have on people. This two-way communication on a physical level is deeply embedded in what makes the CSF performances such visceral, communal and deeply felt experiences. It is a shared experience in all senses of that expression. The actors here do not stare out into darkness merely hoping that the audience are responding as they would wish. Nor are the spectators separated from the action by a large stage, or forced to look only where the spotlight dictates. Instead, genuine and thrilling communication is taking place out in the open between the two parties needed to make a play a success – namely those on stage and those right beside it.

We have already heard from Mark Rylance about how, in an Elizabethan setting, it is 'easy to involve these people, you are so close'. Talking elsewhere, on his role as artistic director of the reconstructed Globe Theatre, Rylance has noted that,

> I don't know how it works, but I find I can be in the story and in the audience making fun of myself in the story at the same time, in certain places in Shakespeare ... if we are all in the story, audiences and actors alike, then I found I could flip between these two seemingly contrary realities as if they were one. The actor and the audience are one group of imaginers somehow.[2]

And he further observes that, 'It became paramount to say to the actors, "Don't speak to them, don't speak for them, speak with them, play with them." Eventually, in my last years, I really came to feel it was not just about speaking, it was about thinking of the audience as other actors.'[3]

At the CSF actors are able to instantly engage the audience in this manner. Consequently, the relationship is much more familiar, and because of this the viewers become highly sensitive to subtleties and nuances that would be overlooked in other settings. As J. L Styan has noted, the pressure which intimacy puts upon an audience is a special factor in itself. The spectator is compelled to pay a closer attention to what is said and done on the stage. In intimate conditions he gives a wider range of attention to the actors, calling upon otherwise untapped sources of sympathy and response. [4]

Actors have enormous freedom and control. They can play up to the audience and the reality of their setting, for example, when they talk of a raging storm in *King Lear* and look out to people sunbathing, and yet, at the same time, they hold in place the character and historical situation they are portraying onstage. In the audience there is a similar stimulating tension between reality and the performed world of the play. You are simultaneously witnessing an Elizabethan drama, played much as it would have been in its own time, and you are somehow conscious of taking part in the whole experience, even contributing to it, in a college garden in the twenty-first century. It is a powerful, if near paradoxical, feeling and it is analogous to that felt by audiences over four centuries earlier. They too never confused the illusion of the play with reality as their theatre was similarly non-representational.

All of this allows the director and his cast to overcome over reverence and dutiful laughter which can bedevil theatregoers in more formal situations. Shakespeare's work is so powerful in itself, and carries such a monolith of cultural import, that an audience can keep its distance and be respectful rather than connected. Conventional theatre accentuates this distance and as time passed there was a steady movement of actors away from the audience. Almost every theatrical and technological 'advance' widened the gap. Over the last century, the error of this approach has been highlighted and attempts have been made to return to settings that bring those on and off the stage together. At the CSF a strong relationship between cast and those gathered to watch them perform has always been a given, and is one of the bedrocks of the festival.

The dutiful laughter I refer to is the live equivalent of TV's canned laughter, that deadening pre-packed laughter when an audience responds to something they are told is supposed to be witty by the release of carefully timed laughter at a given point. This never happens at the CSF. There, you laugh when something is funny or not at all, and when you do laugh, it is because you cannot do otherwise. In all theatres it is a natural reaction to join in when people all around you break out in laughter. Such group responses play a major role in the knowingly shared experience. However, it is much more keenly felt at the CSF because the other members of the audience are visible all around you and you are physically part of the whole experience. This heightens the group reactions to an extraordinary extent and they become part of the whole dynamic of the performances.

Oliver Ford Davis writes insightfully about this kind of experience:

Richard III talks to the audience so much that David Troughton felt he needed them to become an actual character, influencing and guiding his direction. Antony Sher likewise felt that they gave him new insights into the way of playing the character. This might suggest that the audience forms a cohesive group. While it's true that there will always be spectators who are bored, inattentive or even hostile, theatre at its best enables individuals to feel they form part of a group consensus. The effect of a neighbour's total concentration or outright laughter can be very potent. Group reaction helps the whole audience to become more uninhibited. The thrill of Iachimo emerging from his trunk or Benedick declaring that 'This can be no trick' can unite an audience in gasps or laughter. Both reactions can actually make an audience breathe together, and there is no more exhilarating feeling than an audience holding and releasing their breath at the same time.

Improvisation

Actors at the CSF can be very quick to play on an unexpected occurrence. It is a major strength of the CSF, this electrifying effect of improvisation. Once, the explosive opening of a champagne bottle led to a slightly retimed line about cannon fire. Another time, Benedick, in a matinee of *Much Ado about Nothing* that had been assaulted throughout by a steel band at an adjacent wedding, pointedly delivered the line 'I cannot woo in festival terms' in that direction. The audience loved this multiply punning, quick-witted refocusing of the line.

Davis's comment, 'Iachimo emerging from his trunk' recalls a favourite personal occurrence of this off-the-cuff yet completely apt ad-lib. On the opening night of the first ever CSF performance of *Cymbeline* (2013), Iachimo, played by Ethan Holmes, was slowly and quietly extricating himself from a laundry basket to creep up on the sleeping Innogen [the *New Cambridge Shakespeare* uses this name rather than Imogen]. Alas, the basket wheels were misaligned and his foot got caught as he tried to work his way out. As the audience sat or lay in a collective hush, the laundry basket toppled over with a crash. The noise it made seemed astonishingly loud because it happened just at a moment that demanded total silence. Innogen was lying, supposedly asleep, close beside him.

Ethan/Iachimo froze for a second but then, with tremendous presence of mind and quick thinking, he turned to us, and, putting a finger to his lips, fiercely whispered, 'Shhhhhh' as though it was our fault. This funny reversal of what had actually occurred released the tension of the pent-up audience in an explosion of laughter. Then, in a brilliant touch, just as he was about to examine her bosom to see if there was 'On her left breast/A mole cinque-spotted ...', he glanced up at us again and put his fingers to his lips to warningly 'shush' us again, as though he could not trust us not to make a noise 'again'.

When I recounted this to director David Salter, he responded,

> That's what I love about it, complete interaction between the audience and the actor. You wonder too how much of the work, the comic monologues particularly, were improvised in Shakespeare's day. I like it when that improvisation works and stays within the world of the play.

Acting in an outdoor environment demands that the cast be alert to the need for constant improvisation. Indeed, so key is this element in the festival that its importance can be felt throughout the remainder of this book, primarily when discussing audience interaction below, but also when looking at the implications of playing in the open air with the changing weather, animal visitations and other facets of the live, outdoor experience.

Audience Engagement

Shakespeare, as a man of the theatre, was very much in tune with what his audience needed and how to engage them. He always ensured that the audience was involved, and his plays insist on a genuinely creative partnership between actor and spectator.

Two of the main ways they do this are via soliloquies and asides. Both directly address the audience ensuring, when Shakespeare is staged in the spirit and style of his own theatre, that everyone assembled is absorbed in the action. We are part of the drama both individually, as we feel we are being directly addressed, and communally, as part of the crowd responding to this interaction.

Soliloquies are among the most loved passages in all Shakespeare's work and there is no denying the thrill of being taken into a character's confidence. *Richard III* and *Hamlet* famously take us by the hand and guide us through the action while Viola in *Twelfth Night* has no one except us to whom she can talk truthfully. Thespian Harriet Walter observed that

> soliloquies come to life when you involve the audience. That sounds obvious, but people do ignore that. A very good acting note is that, though on the page there may be twenty-six lines, you must always start as if you've only got one, and this one line leads to another, and another, etc. If the actor argues with him/herself through the audience, with one thought leading to another as if

coined in that moment for the first time, it can be thrilling and the audience get caught up in your dilemma, or secret or whatever. With Viola, your main protagonist is the audience, and you only find yourself through them; with everyone else onstage, you're lying. In a soliloquy you can confide in the audience things you can't say to anyone on the stage. Rather than being the 'boring bit' where we all sit back and let the character rant, a soliloquy can be the most dangerous and involving moment in a play.[5]

The involvement and also, therefore, the thrill are heightened dramatically when the staging is as informal, close and personal as it is at the CSF. The actor Adrian Lester was struck by the relationship he had with the audience when playing Hamlet in a cut-down chamber production by Peter Brook at the Bouffes du Nord in Paris in 2000. The non-stop two-and-a-half-hour performance was presented with little scenery or other distractions, and so, as at the CSF, the relationship in the soliloquies was especially close. In reply to Oliver Ford Davies' question of how much he felt he was talking to the audience in the soliloquies, Adrian replied,

Completely. I find it difficult to do soliloquies unless I am looking at someone and see a face. Sometimes I would ask for the house lights to be touched up a few points so that I could see individuals, and perhaps refer back to them. It stops me doing it just for myself, because every face has a different expression.[6]

For the CSF audience, watching in daylight, there is an electric charge created by sharing the thoughts and the same space as the speaker of those thoughts. It is so direct and personal that it really is someone talking straight to you. This must have been how it was at the time of the sixteenth-century travelling troupes and at the Globe and the other theatres. Mark Antony, Hamlet, Viola and all the others speaking to you, questioning you, haranguing you, pleading for support or help, looking for information you had and they needed. Alas, you cannot warn Othello to stop trusting Iago, though one suspects that this may well have been cried out on more than one occasion from the assembled throng.

The asides that pepper Shakespeare's plays further this cosy relationship, as do improvisations. Asides, whether in or out of character, bring an energetic edge to the actor audience interchange. Each audience member feels a privileged participant in the ongoing drama when they occur.

It is crucial for both actor and audience to feel this dynamic and it benefits to an extraordinary degree by being, as we say, up close and physical. J. L. Styan once wrote that 'the ideal is to see the whites of the audience's eyes from a stage, so that you know what is happening to your words, to Shakespeare's words, as you speak them'. Andrew Stephen spoke to me about being so close to the crowd at the CSF as to 'see the whites of their eyes' and recalled revelling in the boost the immediate feedback from such close encounters gives: 'When you get that buzz, you can tell, you get feedback immediately. At the interval, for example, there's this hum that comes up, it's always very exciting, and I always like to listen for that.'

This proximity and the lack of any physical barrier results in actors often directly and physically interacting with spectators. Wherever we are situated in the audience, we are always close to actors, whom in any case are often encroaching into or emerging from audience positions. While I was watching *A Midsummer Night's Dream*, in 2013, Charlotte Ellen playing a mischievous, cockney-accented Puck ran into the audience while escaping from a grumpy Oberon. As she passed me, she cheekily, and perfectly in character, knocked my hat off my head. The year previously, Alan Booty as Falstaff in *The Merry Wives of Windsor* ran towards me as though to steal my apple. For whatever reason, he changed his mind at the last moment and instead resorted to lifting his skirts in my face as he ran shrieking from Mistress Ford's house, disguised as her servant's obese aunt. These are the kind of personal moments that festival audiences live for and never forget.

Similar contact was made in Shakespeare's day, not only by touring acting companies but also at theatres like the Globe whose pre-proscenium stages allowed the majority of the audience to be in close contact with the players. This makes an enormous difference. The spectators can pick up on the slightest gesture while the actors can feel the audience and can communicate with them in sounds ranging from quiet whispers and asides to booming declamations. Perhaps even more than all of this is the cumulative impact it has on audiences. There is an overwhelming feeling of being involved, of being part of the event that is making Shakespeare's word and dramaturgy come alive in each instant you are there.

The CSF casts feel this strongly, as Daniel Simpson told me:

A good actor has a relationship with the audience, it's funny because as an actor the thing you crave is to be completely absorbed in character but it's a lie, it's a myth to suggest the best actor will be; because the best actor will be that person without ever losing the understanding and the relationship and communication with the audience. You have to have ninety per cent character, ten per cent audience and environmental, awareness.

Director Simon Bell once had to cover in an emergency in the role of Mercutio and he was struck by this awareness:

I am fine on stage but it should be professional actors. But what was interesting from a director's point of view was how aware you are, onstage, of the audience. The movement; you can sense when they want something. Although you are fully committed to the scene, you have another eye that is watching all those faces and how they are reacting and you read body language and everything.

A relationship between creators and performers on the one hand and their audience on the other is a basic starting point for all art. It is often claimed that all creative work requires someone to hear or read it in order to exist as art. There has to be a communication between artist and audience, otherwise the creation itself is unfinished, incomplete or even non-existent except in some abstract sense. If Kafka's books and papers had all been burned, unread after his death as he had stipulated they should be, then they would as well have never existed other than for the self-contemplating creator. To what extent the now burned novels would have constituted art is a point for philosophers to ponder. Such abstruse questions aside, an audience can probably be taken as almost always necessary for all expressions of art and definitively so when talking of the theatre.

For actors, it is absolutely essential that they be watched; it is necessary for every line they say, every gesture they make. Rehearsals are one thing, but they are merely practice for the real thing, which is to communicate your director's vision to an audience that reacts to what you are doing or saying. Naturally, this is true of all acting. Nonetheless, it is only so to a lesser degree in standard playhouses where the actors project out to an unseen audience clothed in darkness, or when they perform to a camera which records their performances for later broadcast to TV or film viewers. The difference at the CSF is that it is all so immediate and physical because the audience is not at all separate from the actor. This looks back to the tradition we observed in the opening chapter about staging in Shakespeare's own day. It was one of performing outdoors, at fairs, in town streets and squares, in village greens and the courtyards of inns designed for stagecoach stops. Anywhere the actors had space to perform and where they were always hemmed in, playing not only to, but also off, the people right in front of their faces. All the drama of the stage, the wooing, the loving, the fighting, the wars and the dying, all of it was performed so close that the audience felt totally involved.

At the CSF, the actors are similarly near enough to engage the audience's senses. This keeps us hyper alert and invokes that special extra sense of the magic of creation. We all share in this; the audience has the added bonus of feeling it has helped create the event. Not only do actors and spectators feed off each other as they always do, in this case they do so with a familiarity that is simply not replicable in the regular theatre experience where separation rather than kinship is stressed. I keep emphasising this because the difference is elemental. As regular CSF attendees Bill and Bob Wellman wrote to me,

We tend to take it for granted and forget that so much of the action is in the audience and very close to the audience. You tend to forget that if you come often and, thinking now of recent productions we've seen outside the Cambridge Festival, that doesn't apply ... We feel part of it. Once, in *A Midsummer Night's Dream* the actors playing the viewers of the play-within-the-play were sitting in the audience to watch it.

Time and again CSF actors and directors stressed to me how they were always learning from the audience. This is only natural, and it seems reasonable to assume that Shakespeare, as an actor, also did so, and we must surely suppose that he edited and reworked plays after seeing them performed. There are clear signs of this in the texts that have survived, inasmuch as anything can be clear about those precious documents, of plays that were also tailored for different settings. It is only by trying things out in front of a live crowd that you discover what works and how best to play it. Actors have always known this, but again it is something that seems even truer at the CSF. There is a wonderful quote from Michael Pennington that always makes me think of the CSF relationship as it highlights the physical nature of the experience:

> The audience will never desert you, bringing you every enthusiasm for the event; and you now learn everything from them. You and they are carried by the prevailing winds: everyone wants it to be special, and everyone, including you, waits for lightning to strike. This animal relationship is a wonderful thing, like champagne to tiredness, and more than makes up for the sniffy reservations of a hundred experts.[7]

In a more explicit sense, the live audience will let you know if your timing is right and if you are putting the correct emphasis on the lines to elicit the reaction you and your director are seeking. The alertness of an audience, sitting on plastic chairs or grass, in the same lighting and weather as you, the cast, means that every nuance, gesture, every word and every movement is immediately picked up on and elicits an instant, unfeigned reaction. This is especially true for comic lines. 'The audience can teach you so much,' says Judi Dench,

> sometimes it's only in performance that you make discoveries about a line. In *Antony and Cleopatra* there was a line I knew should get a laugh, and I couldn't get it. We did the hundredth performance and that night the laugh came. That's why the theatre wins over film and television every single time: *you* get more out of it, and the audience teach you so much. You rehearse

something for weeks on end, and then at the first preview they tell you so much about what you should be doing ... Everything finally depends on what the audience are going to get out of it.[8]

Helen Meadmore pinpoints an exact instance of this at the CSF. Helen played Titania/Hippolyta in *A Midsummer Night's Dream* in 2013, and recalls that

> you learn from the audience. One night Thisby fell down near Bottom and her hands happened to touch Bottom and tickled him. Eddie Beardsmore, playing Bottom, instinctively reacted, with a 'woo-ooo-hoo' sound and the audience howled. So we kept it in to see if it would work again and it did, so that has stayed and always gets a good response.

Furthermore, the audience does not merely passively receive. That lovely feeling of contributing to the overall event is only available to those who put something into the experience. We need not doubt, as an audience, the part we should play, as no less a figure than Shakespeare himself spells this out in the prologue to *Henry V*:

> And let us, ciphers to this great account,
> On your imaginary forces work.
> Suppose within the girdle of these walls
> Are now confined two mighty monarchies,
> Whose high upreared and abutting fronts
> The perilous narrow ocean parts asunder.
> Piece out our imperfections with your thoughts,
> Into a thousand parts divide one man,
> And make imaginary puissance.
> Think when we talk of horses that you see them
> Printing their proud hoofs i'th' receiving earth;
> For 'tis your thoughts that now must deck our kings,
> Carry them here and there, jumping o'er times,
> Turning the accomplishment of many years
> Into an hour-glass.

As this makes clear, CSF attendees, if they wish to experience the full delights enacted for them, must, like their Elizabethan forerunners, strive to help in the creative effort supplied by directors and actors in attempting to embody the actions and visions of Shakespeare's texts. When I discussed this with Simon Bell, he enthusiastically agreed: 'I tell the actors this in audition, I say to the actors in audition, "That opening speech of *Henry V*, we are restoring actors to the text, that's exactly what's going on."'

When faced, and faced closely, by such absorbed witnesses, the actor will feel both inspired and obligated to draw on all his resources and give of his very best. Styan continued on from his earlier remarks about Elizabethan audiences with the following, equally astute, observations:

> In his turn the actor must satisfy the range of effects such an audience asks. He will be required to use his voice in every shade, and his body with great flexibility: there is no better test of acting ability than a mature play by Shakespeare and, conceivably, no more exacting playhouse than the type of open stage theatre for which it was written. There would be many moments when the Elizabethan actor would be working as if under a microscope.[9]

Clearly, these comments are also especially relevant to the Cambridge Shakespeare Festival, as well as the Elizabethan stages.

I do not mean to imply that the audience needs to work in any negative sense of the word. The CSF performances, in their delightful garden settings, are the antithesis of drudgery and the 'work' of using your imagination is a pleasure in itself. Pleasure is one of the guiding principles of the CSF. The feeling of unity between performers and audience encourages much laughter and irreverence alongside rapt attention. Indeed, even the word 'watch' seems inappropriate, as it is too passive for an activity in which you feel you are partaking.

At the CSF, as in Shakespeare's day, the spectators are very alert to what is being said because they feel a part of it all. Time and again, I received feedback that confirmed this. Regular attendee from Germany, Ute Hienze, told me, 'I really like the natural surroundings, they make it so much more relaxed. By being much closer to the actors, you feel a part of the performance.' Natalie, a seventeen-year-old from China wrote that 'As the stage is in the garden, audience members like me feel more involved in the play'.[10]

Audience Interaction

I hear more laughter at the CSF than I do anywhere else, even than at the Globe which, due to a stage that is welcoming rather than a barrier to the crowd at its feet, also enjoys more of it than conventional theatres. Mark Rylance, talking about playing at the Globe, stressed how important he felt this and how fascinating he finds the close-to-the-stage audience:

> They laugh in this theatre, much more than I've ever found in other theatres.

You'd think it might be a very reverent place, wouldn't you, but it is not, it's a very irreverent place. And they go very quiet at times and that's an incredible thing in the theatre. We have videos of the audience, they speed up, and then they are still again and then they move around and shuffle around like that and then they're still again. In speed, it's fascinating how you see the story grip and release them, grip and release them, grip and release them.[11]

Yet, even at the Globe there is still more of a separation than in a college garden and consequently the laughter is less prominent than it is at the CSF. The marvellous thing about the CSF laughter is that it is real and spontaneous. It is, as alluded to earlier, far from the respectfully rehearsed guffaws and sniggers of well versed patrons showing off that they know a particular line was really funny in Shakespeare's time. Rather, as in those days, the performances are alive with witty asides, improvisations and interactions. Again, as in the original performances of Elizabethan times, the clowns are central to these activities and in engaging the spectators. Again, this is even more pronounced in the CSF settings, where there is nothing to hinder the dialogue between stage and audience.

Long-time CSF director Simon Bell is keenly aware of the important parallels between his stage settings and those available when Shakespeare created all his masterpieces,

It is a gift for directors, you can unleash the clowns into the picnic area – this year [2013] after *Comedy of Errors* neither Dromio had to be fed for a week, they had stolen so much wine and food – and the audience absolutely loves it. I don't like ad-libbing, I always think it is a kind of a cheat, but in *Comedy of Errors* I said 'you can't put in extra lines, but you can flesh it out by slipping in the odd aside', and this has a lovely spontaneity and freshness which is part of the spirit of the festival.

You cannot help but think that it was also part of the spirit of Elizabethan productions which undoubtedly would have been peppered with asides. We can also readily imagine that the topical references that have survived in quarto and folio versions are but the tip of the iceberg. Many more would have been 'slipped in' to 'flesh it out' back in the day. This is especially likely as the clowns were stars in their own right in Elizabethan theatre; they drew in customers by their reputations and routines. As a result, they were afforded freedom to improvise and perform what and how they wished to, depending on how that day's audience were reacting. They were both permitted and expected to clown around, as it were.

In the opening part of the book, we considered what kind of travelling entertainments the young Shakespeare was likely to have seen when growing up in Stratford. One of the most probable forms of these that he would have witnessed were the strolling players, based on the traditional Italian *Commedia dell'arte* companies that toured England in the 1570s and 1580s. They performed a comic mixture of music, dance, gymnastics and theatre that relied heavily on improvisation and clowning. These performers were extremely popular and had a considerable influence on the theatres of the succeeding decades. Their spirit of exuberant improvisation was passed on to the clowns of the Elizabethan stage. It has also been passed on to the CSF. Dr Edmond Wright wrote to David Crilly after the wonderful *The Two Gentlemen of Verona* in 2013. Among the many things he had enjoyed, the fun of such clowning stood out:

> I cherish so many moments of fun - I thought of the staid Hamlet rebuking clowns for adding material not written down for them, but all your additions worked splendidly – particularly when there was interaction with the audience. There was one moment when all your outlaws were on the stage together and one made comments immediately improved upon by another – I can't recall an example, they came so thick and fast, one burst of laughter tripping up the next to the enhancement of both.[12]

In all eras, if the clown is on a roll and the reaction overpowering, he is likely to play up to it for a little longer than on an occasion when, for whatever reason, the crowd is less responsive. I was curious as to how they could control these incidents. They are so spontaneous and engender such positive audience reaction that it seemed to me almost inevitable that the temptation to overplay them would prove irresistible.

At the same time another, almost equally inevitable, thought occurs and this is that the playwrights themselves would not approve of this. There is a wonderfully dry, surviving remark by a Renaissance dramatist on watching a performance of a play he had written. He liked it well enough but, alas, barely recognised a line of it. Some scholars attribute the disappearance from the framing character of Christopher Sly in *The Taming of the Shrew* to a reaction against the dominance of this clown figure playing a drunken buffoon, whose comic plot was originally intended to surround the main story. Whether or not this is true, and it seems at the very least a plausible theory, there is no mistaking Hamlet's words on the worth of restricting clowns from over-playing their roles and ad-libbing to an unpalatable extent:

> And let those that play your clowns speak no more than is set down for them, for there be of them that will themselves laugh, to set on some quantity of

barren spectators to laugh too; though, in the meantime, some necessary question of the play be then to be considered: that's villanous, and shows a most pitiful ambition in the fool that uses it.

Hamlet, act III scene II

However, every actor and director from the CSF that I quizzed on this matter has maintained that there was no danger of such interplay going too far. All the performances I have attended support their claim, and Bill and Bob Wellman were adamant that they have not witnessed excessive clowning around at any of the hundred plus productions they have attended since 2001.

This admirable restraint is explained by various factors. While the clowns may swipe food and trade banter, the main actors consciously do not. Tessa Hatts said,

> I know the audience love the interaction but I try not to speak, I don't like talking out of text. Food is difficult as there are not always picnics on a wet night. And you can't easily eat it if you have a speech to do immediately afterwards. But people always take their shoes off so, as Puck, I'd take a shoe and put it on the next blanket, and they always laughed at that. There was no danger of this going too far as I only moved shoes when the fairy was getting changed and she didn't take too long.

Daniel Simpson recalled one incident that he felt went too far, but stressed it was very much the exception to the rule:

> I remember in *Love's Labour's Lost*, Don Armado took someone's wine and basically emptied it over his own head. It was a really good wine too! I am not sure that's right, but, in general, I don't think that there is a danger of overdoing it. You've got to trust that the play will continue. The play will happen in its own good time, if the audience are enjoying themselves, you let them ride that out. Something that happens a lot in theatre that is terrible, and I've been guilty of it elsewhere because it can come on you unexpectedly, is when an actor tramples on that. It is the audience's right to react as they react, that's their right and if they are laughing, you let them laugh and you don't trample on it. If they are enjoying themselves then you go with that, you've got to celebrate the moment, the play will look after itself.

Jamie Alan Osborn explained that 'in rehearsal you probably do go too far, but in performance you probably don't have time, it happens in a moment, you've only time for that one funny, improvised bit.' Thérèse Robinson said,

It's a difficult one; I don't really like it when someone is not speaking the text. It jars a little bit. If I hear certain words, they turn things away from what was written. I would always feel awkward about being in a Shakespeare play and ad-libbing too much, because obviously I don't want it to sound like I am speaking in the twenty-first century.

David Salter provided an insight into how in tune he is with his actors and how far he trusts their judgement. He commented on the incident where Falstaff, in *Merry Wives of Windsor*, almost grabbed an apple out my hand as he was running past me, but had refrained at the last moment:

In that split second, he must have evaluated practically whether he could do it at all, what he would do with it, what your reaction might be. If he knows he has to go and get changed then he can't do anything with the apple. All of that is going on in his mind. And then there is whether it is true to the integrity of the play, integrity to the production, integrity to the piece. So, I think it is taste and integrity. Also there is the thing that you have to trust the play. Directors and actors like to be creative and sometimes we might be tempted to push too far, so what you have to do is keep within the structure of the work.

Rory Thersby gave me an example of such situational awareness and the importance of paying attention to the integrity of the piece from a CSF actor's point of view:

I don't mind engaging audience when I've got a basis to do so. When I was training I did a lot of improvisation, I was always good at it – but when it is Shakespeare I want to get the lines right. I don't want to speak modern-day English, I don't like stepping out of character. I do engage, in character, in non-verbal exchanges, though.

He remembered one successful piece of improvisation, in *Much Ado about Nothing* (2008), where he brought a modern touch to an Elizabethan play, but in full cognisance of the audience's current mindset:

I was playing Benedick, it was not a very good summer and a downpour started just as I was coming out to do the bit where he is writing his song for Beatrice and he's trying to sing the song that starts 'The god of love/That sits above' to whatever tune you are supposed to pick. So I sang it to the tune of 'Singing in the Rain' and I got a round of applause which is jolly nice. But the audience had already been taken out of the sixteenth century because they were putting their umbrellas up and their jackets on, so I didn't feel I was breaking any barrier that had not already been broken.

The clowns, as we have seen, are much freer to interact on their own terms and so the closeness between actor and audience applies most of all to these picnic-foraging, rapid-fire, ad-libbing comics. Nevertheless, its impact is everywhere, from moments of farce to those of the highest dramatic expression. Helen Meadmore remembers, while she was playing Bianca in *The Taming of the Shrew* (2012), watching Fleur Shepherd's portrayal of Kate:

> Kate went into the audience every night and she'd always find something to pick up and eat – she would select something and say 'Ooooooooohhh Scotch egg/Pringles/sausages' or whatever. Then one night she could not find *anything* until she saw somebody was eating rice cakes and she jubilantly grabbed one and yelled, 'Yaaaaaaaaaaaay, rice cakes!' She made it so much more enthusiastic because she couldn't find anything else. 'Yum, fantastic!' The audience loved it and roared with laughter.

Such improvisation can strike at any time and adds to the special festival ambience. It really is a joy to behold when it does not overstep, as it so very rarely does, the boundaries of that particular play in that particular night's production. More fixedly, and as already alluded to, Shakespeare's prologues and epilogues are addressed to the audience to underpin this two-way relationship between stage and audience. The *Henry V* prologue is an outstandingly famous direct address to the audience and the epilogue spoken by Prospero, in what many believe to be Shakespeare's last solely authored play, is another. It is also a speech that most find irresistible to think of, regardless of any signs to the contrary, as other than Shakespeare's own farewell to the stage when 'he' asks the audience, 'As you from crimes would pardon'd be/Let your indulgence set me free.'

This final speech is the very essence of being personal with an audience. As everyone else leaves the stage at the play's end, Prospero kindly bids the audience 'Please you, draw near'. At the CSF productions you are compelled to strain ever closer towards the actor in front of you. He no longer appears to you only as Prospero but more as a combination of various men. As he beckons us close, he seems to be the magician who has just divested himself of his powers, the actor playing the character and Shakespeare himself, the creator of this and all the other, many and multifarious characters in his plays,

With the help of your good hands.

> Gentle breath of yours my sails
> Must fill, or else my project fails,
> Which was to please.
>
> *The Tempest,* act V scene I

There are no barriers between audience and actors at times like this. Instead, a feeling of kinship radiates around the college garden. It is worth reiterating here that, with the exception of Robinson College, we are merely referencing different areas of the same shared piece of grass and the empathy this evokes between those on stage and those off stage has a multitude of benefits.

When Styan concluded his thoughts above, by writing of the Elizabethan actor that he 'was at all times vulnerable, and compelled to communicate with the audience, provoking it and provoked by it. This lively tradition of two-way traffic was part of the actor's art', he could have been accurately summarising the position of those performing at every festival production.

It is a deliberate and vigorously enforced policy of the CSF to strengthen this relationship between watchers and performers wherever possible. Artistic director David Crilly told me emphatically, 'Separate stage? We never wanted that. It is engagement. It is breaking down the barrier between audience and performance.' The way they work to promote the special festival bond is shown in all kinds of ways from the seemingly trivial to those directly impacting on the performances themselves.

So free from barriers and reverence are the CSF productions that occasionally a well-timed piece of wit from an audience member enhances the performances. On one memorable occasion, director Dave Rowan had to cover for an actress with no time to prepare, or even shave, but merely to put on a dress and go out on stage. The audience, aware of what had happened was indulgent and Dave's performance was, as ever, a winning one. Nevertheless, when Orsino spoke the line, 'when I see you in your women's weeds' someone could not resist calling out 'Oh God, not that *again*' with perfect timing and to general hilarity. While few of those in attendance will ever forget a six-year-old boy's contribution to *A Midsummer Night's Dream* one summer evening. Unimpressed by Bottom's long-drawn-out, hamming up of his death scene in the play within the play, put on by unskilled Athenian artisans, the young lad jumped to his feet and shouted, 'Just hurry up and die, won't you?' Audience comments, as you would expect and hope, seldom feature, but I think these two illustrate how comfortable everyone is with each other at the festival.

Togetherness

The togetherness of those on and off stage has begun to be built even before a play starts. Prior to every show, we have a few words from the night's director or someone standing in for him. There are practical reasons for this, such as pointing out the toilet facilities or reminding everyone to switch off their phones. Additionally, the long-term directors are very aware that it also instills a feeling of camaraderie. Simon Bell has a routine that has been repeated so often that it has become part of the CSF furniture. He implores everyone to raise a clenched fist to the sky and exclaim 'Thou Shalt Not Rain!' If the response is not uniform or enthusiastic enough, he asks again. It may seem a small thing but it engenders a communal spirit as well as reminding us that rain may come; it is an ever-present possibility in a British summer after all.

Good summer weather calls for a slightly different approach. As Dave Rowan put it,

> quite often in the Cambridge Shakespeare Festival if the weather's great, you suddenly get this massive surge of people coming in. And if it's far more than you expected, you cram them into the audience. You inconvenience them, you move them about five times and then they're sitting there some times feeling a bit grumpy that you've shoved them back and you've pushed them and somebody's sat on their picnic. And then, when you make the announcement, you've got the power to make that better and get them in a good state of mind. And so you can pick them up, you can thank them, you can explain to them, you can tell them, 'you're the biggest audience we've had so far', and they start cheering. And actually that to me is part of the performance as well, how you tee up the whole mood of the evening is important.

It is appreciated by the actors. Daniel Simpson enthused about this aspect:

> Especially someone like Dave Rowan, who does stand-up comedy, he's so good at working with the crowd in this setup. In one second he's got the whole audience ready, electrified, excited and they are clapping before you come on because he builds it to such a point in introducing the show and doing the daft announcements and everything that you do right beforehand. It's a really nice feeling for the audience and for the actors because they can feel that warmth and that generosity; the people clapping before you've even come on, it's just a really nice feeling.

When talking of breaking down barriers, above, David Crilly continued by saying, 'Every night at *Dream* we get small children dressed as fairies (splendidly including a woman in her forties the other night). We engage with the children; when we talk about the fairies we are addressing the children in the audience as fairies. And the actors go over and give things to children and stuff like that.'

Sometimes, when attending performances of *A Midsummer Night's Dream*, you can sense an unofficial competition for the best audience outfit of the night.

From the actors' point of view, it is easy to involve the audience as there is almost no hiding place. You can, depending on the venue, hide behind bushes and trees (particularly good for the many eavesdropping scenes in Shakespeare) and there are other physical features of the colleges' gardens that can be utilised in all kinds of special ways. Nonetheless, this is only if the actors wish to temporarily set aside the feeling of being all together in the same garden.

Small touches can emphasise this feeling. Actors waiting to take part will sometimes make their way through the crowd, or even sit in with the audience before reacting to their cue. Newcomers to acting at the festival can feel a little self-conscious of this at first. Dave Rowan recounts that 'some actors, waiting to come on, hold back on the shoulders of the audience and say, "I need to hide from the audience." I tell them, "No, no, it's fine, they know it is a theatre, they quite like the mechanics of it, the actors dashing behind them to make a quick change."'

You can see that people are interested in the mechanics of the production at the end of performances. Then, any props that are still around are touched and examined and what had been hiding places are explored.

The informal set up also encourages post-performance words to be exchanged. I always make a point of thanking any actors I see milling around the gardens afterwards, as do many others. This may read as unimportant and trivial, but it all adds to the special relationship engendered each year. It is not every night you can have a few words with, and bid goodnight to, Cleopatra, Falstaff or the sweet Prince of Denmark.

I can still clearly recall bumping into Tessa Hatts after watching her marvellous performance in *Twelfth Night* (2006) in torrential rain. As she passed near me, I wanted to stress my gratitude that the cast had played on. I could scarcely get the words out because she was already telling me how grateful she was that anyone had managed to survive to the end under the deluge from the skies. If you had caught her wonderful portrayal of Feste that year, you would know why the moment will stay with me forever.

Another boon of the festival, then, is that actors can be the recipients of the most amazingly direct and immediate feedback. Actor Andrew Stephen remembered an encounter with an audience member at the end of a performance that deeply touched him:

> I remember doing Prospero in 2005 and this young man made for the tree that concealed us just after the curtain call. We were all under the big tree in Woodlands Court in Girton College. Simon Bell stopped him initially but he was looking for me and I said I would speak to him. He was so nervous, he was shaking and stuttering. He said that he just wanted to thank me and explained that he had developed a love of Shakespeare following his attendance of *Macbeth* ... It's easy to get jaded about things but here you can change someone's life. You can change the way people look at Shakespeare, their perceptions. Looking at the children there last night, they might think of Shakespeare as something dusty and badly taught but you can change their view of that, and so you change their view of everything. It's an extraordinary experience for everyone potentially, when it works – when it is done with commitment and belief.

In the *Comedy of Errors* mentioned above, a clever double bluff was employed. Knowing how often audience members are involved in small ways, we all sat back to enjoy the usual banter when two young ladies were reluctantly enticed and dragged on to the ground-level stage at the purpose-built outdoor amphitheatre at Robinson College. After that, however, the relief that it was not you who had been selected and the *schadenfreude*-tinged pleasure you were enjoying was stretched to breaking point by the length of time the two ladies were left, nervously fidgeting and looking lost, on stage. The pressure was intensified when the hapless victims were repeatedly teased by imminent threats of water being thrown over them. Then, suddenly, they were drenched unexpectedly with a large amount of water. We all gasped – this had really gone too far. They were, of course, actors whose parts were to come later in the show, and in a mixture of relief and embarrassment, but mainly in humour, we all roared with laughter and delight. I asked the play's director, Simon Bell, about this and he told me that

> we spent a lot of time debating that. I was uncomfortable, which is why I added the line 'Don't worry they are actresses' after the water was thrown over them. I wanted the audience to go, 'oh my goodness they have gone too far ... ' but later when they appeared as actors, I didn't want the audience to feel deceived. We spent lot of time rehearsing that and I was ready to cut it after the first night if it didn't work.

He need not have worried; it all worked perfectly. So well that it tricked me even though I thought I recognised one of them and began by suspecting it was a deception. They played their parts very convincingly, growing ever more uncomfortable and self-conscious during what seemed an extremely long period of inactivity, as though they had no idea of what to expect next. As this was exactly how I know that I would have looked in the same situation, I was seduced, by their apparent anxiety, into believing they were part of the audience. Their screams when the water hit them were also totally persuasive.

Utilised at its best, this combination of on- and off-stage participation, this oneness of cast and audience, can be extremely effective. During 2013's *Romeo and Juliet*, when Juliet was impatiently calling for the nurse to run to her with news, the nurse was going round and round the dispersed audience. She sat down now and again but mainly was expending quite a bit of energy going around and through the rows of seats and picnickers. By the time she got to Juliet, who teased her about being slow and out of breath due to tiredness, Emma (Emma Sylvester played the nurse) really was tired. We had an actress who was tired from running about playing a character pretending to be tired to tease Juliet. I mentioned how effective this had been to David Crilly and he enthusiastically explained,

> Yes and again this means the audience are completely engaged in what's happening. Because if you've got the nurse walking through the audience, or around the back of the audience, the audience are looking at the scene but they can also be perfectly aware of the character, the movement still going on around them. And they are really at the centre of everything that is happening. It is a more immediate and intimate experience.

These instances give a flavour of the interaction and togetherness that make for a more cherished Shakespeare viewing experience. One which stands in stark contrast to that of an indoor, evening theatre with the spectators physically separated from the stage and plunged into darkness, with their gaze determined by stage spotlighting as they listen passively to well-known lines being recited from afar.

3

The Bare Stage

This green plot shall be our stage,
This hawthorn-brake our tiring-house
A Midsummer Night's Dream, act III scene I

Bare Stage, Props, Costumes, Symbolic Theatre

Bare Stage

The Romantic poet and critic Samuel Taylor Coleridge wrote in his *Essays &*
lectures on Shakespeare & some other old poets & dramatists that

> the very nakedness of the stage, too, was advantageous, for the drama thence
> became something between recitation and a re-presentation; and the absence
> or paucity of scenes allowed a freedom from the laws of unity of place and
> unity of time, the observance of which must either confine the drama to as few
> subjects as may be counted on the fingers, or involve gross improbabilities,
> far more striking than the violation would have caused. Thence, also, was
> precluded the danger of a false ideal, – of aiming at more than what is possible
> on the whole. What play of the ancients, with reference to their ideal, does
> not hold out more glaring absurdities than any in Shakespeare? On the Greek
> plan a man could more easily be a poet than a dramatist; upon our plan more
> easily a dramatist than a poet.

Coleridge here notes, among other things relevant to this book, the strange
paradox that informs the following pages: the more real you try to make a play
appear, the less real it feels. Conversely the more emphasis that is given to the
fact that it is all an illusion, the more real it feels.

We can explore the heart of this matter by examining the 'very nakedness of the stage', props, costumes and the nature of theatrical illusion and what Coleridge describes as the 'willing suspension of disbelief'.

In fact, neither in Shakespeare's day nor at the CSF are the stages totally naked. In both cases props feature, sometimes prominently. Nonetheless, these are minimal when they are compared to conventional theatre and its heavy reliance on, often spectacular, scenery and props. Acting mainly took place in Shakespeare's day, albeit with significant degrees of difference in whether it was a travelling show, at the Globe or at Blackfriars Theatre. In what Peter Brook famously refers to as 'the empty space'. Probably the most common term for both the Elizabethan and the Cambridge Festival stages would be 'bare', which is what will be employed here. In both cases, though, this does not mean a total absence of props. The implications of this and the natural and theatrical props that supplant this 'very nakedness' are what we look at in this chapter.

As we saw in the opening chapter, Shakespeare's plays were originally performed in a variety of settings: inns of court, the rooms of royal palaces or noblemen's mansions, on the road, as well as in the London theatres. His art had grown out of the drama of the medieval mystery plays and the peripatetic acting ensembles. All the companies prior to, and in, Shakespeare's time were obliged to change their productions to suit whatever locations and conditions they found themselves in. It was very much a day-to-day existence, and all manner of physical or personnel exigencies arising from venue layout and cast availability would result in a play being altered due to the prevailing conditions.

With its almost total lack of scenery, other than what nature provides, its varied venues and its small casts, the CSF is at the mercy of the same exigencies. One actor falling ill in 1593 in London, or 1993 in Cambridge, necessitated rapid improvisation from casts where doubling or tripling were commonplace. Likewise a performance could be under sun-split skies one day and torrential rain the next. Even without such uncontrollable factors, stages were also often open to change in size, layout and location.

Understandably, in such circumstances scenery was kept as sparse as possible. If Shakespeare's stage was not always as bare as it was when he started out in touring companies, it remained close to being so even in his London theatre days. This was why Caldwell Cook, as we saw previously, insisted on his plays at the Mummery having no scenery and minimal props, and why Harley Granville-Barker insisted on a bare stage in his groundbreaking productions of *The Winter's Tale*, *Twelfth Night* and *A Midsummer Night's Dream* at the Savoy Theatre in 1912 and 1913. Granville-Barker, did, however, employ dazzling curtains with abstract, symbolic designs and other startling visual effects. At the CSF, the approach is even more authentically raw and more akin to what it must have been like originally.

The emphasis is very much on being able to move fast, roll with the changes and be flexible in your approach. The trick that needs to be mastered is to do all this while staying true to the spirit of the play, a spirit that may change not just due to external pressures, but also to the ever unpredictable mood of the audience.

It sounds from all of this as though the productions, both back then and now at the CSF, suffer from terrible constraints but, paradoxically, the opposite is true. The release from any obligation to provide naturalistic stage productions is liberating, and the absence of such cluttering distraction affords a total concentration on the words. These words, the greatest ever written, are designed to paint in our minds, if we let them guide us, all the scenery necessary for this and other worlds.

This liberation is boundless: the plays can move anywhere or any time via words, gestures and symbols. They are not restricted by the need for representational scenery and props. The actors move, and the audience with them, simply by someone saying, 'we are in a forest', or an orchard, a castle, or 'we are in Rome', now Egypt and now Rome again. They can go from room to room, upstairs to downstairs, inside a house to out in the street, they can cross the street to enter a tavern or be held deep in a dungeon, all through language only. Even though, in reality, they are physically occupying the same bare stage, be it the thrust stage of the Globe, an Elizabethan courtyard inn or a spot of grass in a Cambridge college garden.

Not only is 'all the world a stage' but all the world is available, instantaneously, on this stage. Our location is identified in a few words, often accompanied by a gesture. Suddenly, we find ourselves in a specific setting. A few examples will suffice to demonstrate this. In act II scene III of *Much Ado about Nothing*, Benedick instructs the boy, 'In my chamber-window lies a book, bring it hither to me in the orchard.' In *Henry VI Part One,* act II scene IV, Suffolk orientates us with the lines, 'Within the Temple-hall we were too loud/The garden here is more convenient.'

So it is, time after time and in scene after scene; the language tells us where we are and very often where we have been and are going next. In *Much Ado about Nothing*, Ursula warns Hero, in act III scene IV, 'Madam, withdraw: the prince, the count, Signior Benedick, Don John, and all the gallants of the town, are come to fetch you to church.' Or we are told which country we are in, 'This is Illyria, lady' Viola's sea captain famously tells us in the opening lines of act I scene II of *Twelfth Night*.

Some of these location lines have double meanings, perhaps to highlight the theatrical nature of what we are witnessing, perhaps to poke fun at representational theatrical depiction (the rude mechanicals' rehearsal in *A*

Midsummer Night's Dream is an extended and complex example of this). In *As You Like It* Rosalind exclaims, 'Well, this is the forest of Ardenne' which she can exclaim in a variety of tones to convey one of many emotions ranging from delight to ennui. Yet whichever one is chosen, the comment always performs the same basic function of letting the audience know where we now are.[1]

One of the most extraordinary and complex instances of this technique comes in act IV of *King Lear*. The blinded Gloucester is led to believe he is climbing a hill. Both in the play and in actuality in the theatre, Gloucester/the actor is walking across flat ground. The described climb is a theatrical illusion that is played out on several levels simultaneously, in both physical and mental senses:

> Scene VI. Fields near Dover.
> Enter Gloucester, and Edgar [dressed like a peasant]
> GLOUCESTER: When shall we come to th'top of that same hill?
> EDGAR: You do climb up it now: look, how we labour.
> GLOUCESTER: Methinks the ground is even.
> EDGAR: Horrible steep.

A few lines later, Edgar depicts an entire panorama from this doubly imagined perspective. The blind Gloucester must imagine this scene just as audiences of plays on a bare stage must always imagine every vista. This masterly use of stagecraft is suited only to such stages, and so it works perfectly at the Cambridge Shakespeare Festival, whereas it can seem contrived, affected and unbelievable in a regular theatre, TV or cinema production:

> EDGAR: Come on, sir, here's the place. Stand still. How fearful
> And dizzy 'tis to cast one's eyes so low
> The crows and choughs that wing the midway air
> Show scarce so gross as beetles. Half way down
> Hangs one that gathers samphire, dreadful trade!
> Methinks he seems no bigger than his head.
> The fishermen that walk upon the beach,
> Appear like mice, and yond tall anchoring barque,
> Diminish'd to her cock; her cock, a buoy
> Almost too small for sight. The murmuring surge,
> That on th'unnumber'd idle pebbles chafes,
> Cannot be heard so high. I'll look no more,
> Lest my brain turn and the deficient sight
> Topple down headlong.

In scenes that have garden settings, the CSF has an inbuilt bonus set of double allusions, as would field performances have benefitted from back in Shakespeare's day. The word 'garden' takes on an extra resonance when one is actually in a garden. There are numerous instances of this throughout Shakespeare's work. Here are two examples that should illuminate the point:

> What sport shall we devise here in this garden
> To drive away the heavy thought of care
> > *Richard II*, act III scene IV

and

> Should not in this best garden of the world
> Our fertile France, put up her lovely visage?
> > *Henry V*, act V scene II

Words like 'orchard' can benefit in a similar manner if the venue has sufficient trees. When the Second Lord in *All's Well That Ends Well* pronounces 'He can come no other way but by this hedge-corner' it can be very convenient to have a hedge-corner to hand. Those hiding from Malvolio, to eavesdrop on his behaviour in act II scene V in *Twelfth Night,* always have a convenient box-tree at hand in whichever college garden is representing Olivia's garden at the time.

The trees, shrubs, arbours and hedges at the CSF are real, rather than scenery pretending to be real, but they can be so convenient that artistic director David Crilly was once, at the end of a play, approached by a spectator who asked, of an ancient, large tree, 'Did you build that tree?'

Time is just as flexible, as there are no lights to dim or brighten on a stage that is under the afternoon or early summer evening sky. Hours, days, months and years are similarly signified by what the actors say and do or carry. Everything can be fluid, flexible and capable of unlimited range. Actors in Shakespeare's plays are always telling us what they see; they are constantly describing where they are/have been/are going to because there was little or no scenery to indicate this. They tell us the season and the weather too, painting the scenery in our minds with their words and actions.

It is no wonder that Shakespeare's words have to be so radically cut in cinema translations. He had his actors verbally prompt us towards what we were supposed to imagine, whereas the camera has already filmed what we will see. The implications of this are obviously profound, as we all imagine differently, in our individual way, whereas the camera shows the same picture to all. We will glance at the contrasts between watching plays at the CSF and watching them at the cinema or on television in the conclusion. However, it is worth noting radio at this stage.

That Shakespeare so often begins a scene with a discussion of location means that his plays are much more amenable to radio adaptation. On hot summer days in Cambridge you will see various attendees lying at the back, either with their eyes closed or staring up into the blue sky, luxuriating in the sun on their outstretched bodies as they listen, as though to a radio dramatisation. I think they miss too much, as seeing the actors is so enriching and central to the experience. On the other hand, one can easily see the attraction and far from being disturbed by it, David Crilly views this practice as being 'perfectly fine'.

The freedom of time, place and pace which Shakespeare allows and fully exploits in his drama is all the more extraordinary, as Coleridge notes, when compared with the Classical unities of time and space. These rules were attributed to Aristotle but in reality they were the result of later, restrictive extrapolations that partially reflected Classical views but had been transformed into codified rules that distorted the views of the Greek genius. Nonetheless, they were in both Shakespeare and Coleridge's times, and still are in many people's minds, thought of as authentic Aristotelian instructions.

These held that a play should have one central action without sub or divergent plots, the action must occur in one place, and finally, the action may last no longer than a single day. Shakespeare only follows these twice, in *Comedy of Errors* and *The Tempest*, and even then the latter would offend further strict rules of unity of genre. In Shakespeare, subplots reflect upon the main action while geography can be limitless and time unrestrained. By fully exploiting his bare stage, Shakespearean action was set free. Attentive audiences would follow the actors' words to know where and when they now were, as scenes and plots intercut and interrelated in a manner not dissimilar to modern cinema.

The structure of Shakespeare's plays came from the way he set one scene off against another. Moods, situations and characters were contrasted and compared in the fluid and dynamic 'two hours' traffic of our stage'. This alacrity of staging allowed a concentration of powerful and far-reaching action. The settings for the CSF are ideal to exploit this to the maximum. Dave Rowan finds it exhilarating:

> When you do Shakespeare much more the way it would have been done when it was first performed, you don't have massive scene changes. As one person steps off the stage, you want another person to step on the stage. You get that complete flow of scenes, one thing going into another because between scenes you don't have a lighting change, you don't have music playing – something has got to keep happening on that stage, otherwise it is just a dead space. So, you are looking at ways to compensate and that creates an energy and you can use that to create an impetus. And, dependent on the next scene, you want to keep that space alive so you can change the pace and tempo of

a scene but you are much more thinking about the movement of actors and telling the story as opposed to being reliant on things like scenery changes or music or lighting – so you just get on with the story.

Daniel Simpson, picking up this theme from an actor's perspective, told me that

you can have instantaneous transitions – where a scene is finishing and the players are exiting the stage, another scene is beginning behind the audience as the players enter through the audience to the performance area; it is literally an instantaneous transition. It's marvellous, it keeps the life and the energy of the piece and it keeps the audience on their toes. It's a wonderful device; it's a joy in that sense.

This particular feature, rapid pace, is one way in which Shakespeare's plays are very suitable for cinematic productions. Due to the original absence of any delay between acts and scenes arising from the lack of scenic encumberments, scenes go by in a flash and their cheek-by-jowl enjambment works almost as rapidly as cuts from scene to scene at the movies. Jumping from Rome to Egypt or from the tavern with Hal with Falstaff to the palace with Hal and his father is all but instantaneous, with an obvious effect on the pace of the whole.

The CSF does, however, have an interval and this can extend beyond its allotted fifteen minutes if the audience is not expertly marshalled. This can be a tricky task if the toilet facilities are neither plentiful nor close by, or if non-experienced attendees, arriving with nothing to drink, cause a large queue at the mulled wine serving point. It would be very interesting to experience a production with no interval at all, as the settings are ideal for this. When I mentioned how much I would enjoy seeing this tried out, Daniel Simpson replied, 'You could do without an interval. People can go to the toilet when they have to.' I mentioned that the choice of an interval often tips the balance of the overall tenor of a play with this break being such an intrusion into the dynamics of acts and scenes otherwise unbroken by pauses. Daniel agreed and added that the interval often had to be shoe-horned in.

David Rowan, though, regretfully does not think it is feasible. He explained to me that, 'In our festival you need the interval, because of families and toilets and breaks and things like that. So, I understand that we have it but I'd love to run it all the way through.'

The decision of where to place this interval inevitably becomes a major editorial contribution to the overall experience. Rowan agreed that it could take some time to get this right and sometimes it was impossible to find the perfect place:

Setting the interval is quite interesting. Sometimes I will start the rehearsals and tell the actors I have not decided where the interval is. In an ideal world you're looking for a place that gives you a little bit of an upbeat ... something happens that carries the audience's energy and the play's energy over an interval. However, when you have got a cast of ten, usually what dictates it is that you come to a bit where the next actor on stage is doubling and there is no way they've got time to change. So often what sorts it out is pragmatism.

Different approaches are tried out for different plays and on different casts. 'Sometimes we will try in a couple of different places and we'll see. And sometimes we'll ask the actors.' Yet one play in particular is resistant to all attempts at placing it at a time that does not imbalance the play overall:

The one that is the most complicated is *A Midsummer Night's Dream*. It has that epic scene, act III, scene II, and in an ideal world you want the first half longer, it always feels better if the first half is longer than the second half. In *A Midsummer Night's Dream*, if you break before act III, scene II the big 'lovers in the forest' scene, then you end up with a really long second-half, but that scene is so epic, that if you break after that scene you end up with a ridiculously long first half and a very short second half. And when you get into act IV, a lot of that is people falling asleep and waking up, so it is not the most exciting part of the play. So, it always feels better for me to have act III, scene II in the second half, but you get a skewed play that feels slightly wrong. But those are the compromises you have to make.

Listening to his words made me crave for non-interval performances even more but it would not appear to be feasible. There are practical reasons for an interval, in both physical and psychological senses. As director Simon Bell explained, in a remark that reminds us that CSF props are carried on by 'attendant players' just as they were in Shakespeare's time:

we don't have stage hands, so there's always the technical issue of making sure props get on and off stage and then the interval is a gift because then I can come on and clear the stage. But also I think there's a psychology about it. In any theatre, the second-half audiences are very different because of the way that group psychology works ... they need to talk about the play to be reassured that they're not stupid or that they've got the play. And when they come back to it they're a much more relaxed audience. They've got the play right, they may have made up their mind, their opinions. They're more open too. They're not so wary, I think.

This interval is the only limiting factor on the productions which otherwise enjoy the same freedom from constraints that Shakespeare's company did when they were originally staged. I asked some of the CSF directors about how they are expected to imaginatively move hundreds of miles across country, or even to change countries and cross continents, by following only the language. How they felt, in other words, about managing this in an open space rather than achieving it through a change of background scenery. In their answers, the sense of the freedom we have been looking at was palpable.

Director David Salter remarked that 'working outside with the plays and the language' and not being 'distracted by choices you cannot make regarding the set', meant that 'the simplicity of what you are working towards was very fulfilling'. When I proposed that the less opportunity you have for modern staging, far less CGI, the more freedom and flexibility you seem to have and the less equipment the more choices and the more the language comes out, he replied, 'Yes, we have become so influenced by film, here it is an audio space, a language space, an imaginative space. And it is more so here than even in conventional theatre, it is so alive outside. The plays are always revealing more – and so much more so, outside.'

This almost bare stage, prepared with only the minimum embellishments necessary, is an absolute boon to any actor wishing to throw themselves into the experience. Andrew Stephen enthusiastically attested to this:

> You can actually take credit for it. At the end of the day you are standing on some grass; it's not special effects and hype, it's refreshingly free of all that stuff. It is just, 'Can you do it? Can you deliver the goods? Can you stand on that piece of bare grass and engage these good people who have just parted with their hard-earned cash?' And when it works, it is wonderful.

Props

As we have seen, although the Elizabethan stage was what we term 'bare' it was not as totally naked as Coleridge thought. Later scholastic investigation has ascertained that props were used more extensively in Shakespeare's time than previously believed. Nonetheless, this is clearly dependent on which venue the play is taking place in and would be dramatically reduced whenever the company were on tour.

Perhaps the phrase 'a generally bare stage with a minimum of props' would be most accurate both for the majority of productions in Shakespeare's time and at the CSF. One of a myriad of effective CSF prop examples would be a blue cloth held up at the beginning of *The Tempest* (2012) and *The Comedy of Errors* (2013), and in various earlier productions, to signify the ocean. It is effective, easy to replace and highly portable.

Minimal they may have been, but Shakespearean props are famous around the globe. If anyone hears 'dagger', they think *Macbeth*; similarly with skull/*Hamlet*, handkerchief/*Othello*, mirror/*Richard II* and so forth. Having so few props meant that those that were used were integrated thematically and symbolically into the play as a whole. For example, the dagger represents the shifting sands that reality is built upon in *Macbeth* and the turmoil and disintegration of the titular character's mind, while Desdemona's handkerchief is passed from person to person in a way that reflects exactly what Othello is tricked into believing has happened to her very body.

Some props are less character specific and common to most plays – items such as swords and crowns, and there was very often a need for blood. Records show that animal blood was used for this purpose, as it has been on stages ever since. David Crilly remembers that in the very first year of the CSF, in Oxford, in 1988 at Magdalen College, even animal blood was beyond his 'props department': 'that *Macbeth*, I remember we couldn't afford stage blood so used berries from the mulberry tree in the Deer Park, which were quite effective, but very difficult to get rid of'.

Elizabethan and Jacobean theatre were, like the real life that went on all around them, exceptionally gory. Gruesome executions were so common to theatregoers in the sixteenth century that it would not have been uncommon to 'catch' a slow execution, consisting of grotesque torture and disembowelling, on the way to the theatre. If you had done so in 1589 on the way to see George Peele's *The Battle of Alcazar*, you would have been previewing the play itself in which three characters are similarly dispatched. The directions for this production contained an instruction for the supply of three vials of blood along with sundry sheep organs.

The grisliest sight I have witnessed at the CSF was in 2012's *King Lear* when Gloucester's eyes were plucked out. This was on a much smaller scale than *The Battle of Alcazar*, but perhaps all the more effective for that. It certainly showed that a little bit of sticky goo can go a long way. It was such a superb example of minimal props and maximum effect that the horrific scene is still indelibly etched in my mind.

Two larger items that would always be useful were a bed and a grand seat of some kind to signify a throne. Nonetheless, this is a very far cry from being similar to the representational stage sets of standard modern theatre. Not long after the CSF in 2012, I saw Terry Johnson's play about Salvador Dalí meeting Sigmund Freud, *Hysteria: Or Fragments of an Analysis of an Obsessional*, at the Cambridge Arts Theatre. The setting was in Freud's room, in Hampstead 1938, and this was lovingly recreated and evoked by scenery and props. The play was a peculiar mixture of knockabout farce and deeply moving tragedy and effectively entertained while raising and investigating important and disturbing questions. However, despite the care and attention lavished on the scenery, I was not as involved as I had been when sitting in the gardens watching actors perform on only a patch of grass, nor did I ever believe I was looking at Freud in his London room. Whether the stage is representational or not, it is always an illusion. The upfront acknowledgement of this allows the dramatist incredible liberty and a rich vein of metatheatrical fun and import. It quickly becomes clear that creative imagination is what is important, rather than attempts at realism that convey nothing of the sort and instead can be distracting.

Fourteen-year-old Jade Rodrigo from Australia went to *Richard III* and noticed this lack of distraction keenly. She said, in reply to a survey question, that the play 'was great because being in the open meant that only limited props could be used, therefore making the play simple. I really liked how it was simple because the play itself is quite complicated, but because the presentation was simple we could focus on the characters more.'

Anachronistic props occur both in Shakespeare's original plays and in the CSF. A clock in Rome, spectacles in ancient Britain and a bookmark being used long before books were invented are among the more famous examples from Shakespeare's texts, though Cleopatra playing billiards probably tops them all.

Such things would not have concerned the bard in the slightest, for two reasons. Firstly, he did not mind introducing anachronisms in all sorts of other areas; cities, people, institutions are airily moved from their true historical timeframes to serve his dramatic vision. For instance, Hotspur and Hal face off, in all senses, to magnificent effect in *Henry IV Part One*. The duel where Hal defeats and kills the famous fighter, Hotspur, is key to the dramatic movement of the whole play. Shakespeare was not concerned with historical accuracy. It was crucial to his artistic vision that Hal 'took the honours' of a heroic character who was his contemporary and added these to the kingly skills he inherited from his father. When these attributes were combined with the common touch with which his roistering with Falstaff had endowed him, the sum of his parts became Henry V, 'the perfect King'.

So, Hotspur and Hal were brought together as rivals of a similar young age in a famous, era-defining duel. In reality, Hotspur was older than Hal's father and died at the age of thirty-nine. Hal would have been sixteen at that time and highly unlikely to beat Hotspur in a duel. The exact circumstances of Hotspur's death in the battle are not recorded, but his death lives on in folk memory as it occurs in these plays. Although Shakespeare was writing drama for entertainment as opposed to accurately chronicling history, the brilliance of his writing has led millions to 'know' English history via his plays which mix fiction and legend with fact.

The second reason is that Shakespeare was always writing drama for his own time. He addressed the concerns of those who came to see his plays at the time. Shakespeare's livelihood depended upon him successfully entertaining the audiences of his day. The breadth of Shakespeare's genius means he survives being merely topical. He rarely wrote for genres that were so time dependent that their plays have limited appeal to later generations, scholars aside. One thinks, in this regard, of the so-called 'city' plays. These were satirical pieces on contemporary London life but are only rarely performed now, even those by such luminaries as Jonson, Massinger, Marston and Middleton. *Measure for Measure* is the nearest thing to a London City comedy that Shakespeare wrote and even then critics are divided over how much of that play was written by Middleton rather than Shakespeare himself.

Due to the depth, range and power of his art we see Shakespeare as relevant to all ages, and nothing seems more obvious to us now than his old friend and rival Ben Jonson's claim that 'he was not of an *age*, but for all time'. Yet none of this future attention could be known to Shakespeare at the time he wrote. He may have expected some or all of his poetry to survive but, as we saw earlier, he never prepared any of his plays for posterity.

If Shakespeare was not overly concerned by the odd anachronism when writing and performing plays for his audiences, then it is questionable as to whether we should be, as long as they are in keeping with the tenor of the play and scene in which they appear. An excellent example of an out of date prop working perfectly on a twentieth-century stage was highlighted by Laurie Maguire and Emma Smith in their punchy *30 Great Myths about Shakespeare*. They referred to Snug revealing himself as the man behind the lion in Kenneth Branagh's *A Midsummer Night's Dream*. As the actor was delivering the line 'Then know that I as Snug the joiner am', he began distributing his business card. There was no feeling of breaking the spirit of the scene. On the contrary, it perfectly suited the text because Snug steps out of his lion role and back again in the play itself, too. It also simultaneously bonded the play with the modern audience watching it as business cards were particularly prevalent at that time. It matched the plot, as well as the character, as newlyweds are an ideal set of people to whom a joiner would advertise his services.

An analogous example that caused much hilarity at the CSF occurred in the same play, in one of Dave Rowan's productions. When the rest of the rude mechanicals lost Bottom, the actors came out from the stage area and started handing out photographs with Bottom's picture on it, while archly asking, 'Have you seen my bottom?' as they made their way through the audience. Again, this was something totally awry for the time being depicted, but again the audience loved it. It was fittingly silly and fully in the spirit of the scene. Far from spoiling the play, it enhanced it.

Nonetheless, out-of-time props that are introduced for their own effect and which have no good basis in the spirit, far less the text of the play, can be very jarring. Thankfully, the CSF rarely strays into this territory; the directors are very aware of the dangers of going too far. David Salter told me, 'You have to be true to the integrity of the piece. Each play, each production has its own integrity. There's a responsibility to the original play as well.'

There have been, nonetheless, some very controversial examples and while I bring a couple of these up as examples, I stress they are atypical of the normal productions. Simon Bell, having a strong artistic background and visual sense, is the most likely of the regular directors to supply the controversy in this area. Simon aims for his props always to evoke something special and integral to his production of the play. Additionally, I think it is fair to say that if they provoke as well as evoke, then he is even happier. Inevitably, in such circumstances, you do get the occasional clash between his vision and what the traditionalists want and expect.

Despite not being totally anti-experimentation myself, I think it is clear from this book that I lean heavily towards traditional, Elizabethan style productions of Shakespeare's plays. As such, I am in the 'faction' that is, I am pleased to report, overwhelmingly catered for at the CSF. However, this makes the infrequent use of a more modern prop all the more noteworthy. In other words, it tends to stick out like the proverbial thumb. One such instance was the use of a gramophone player in Bell's 2008 production of *Richard III* in Downing College gardens. The brothers Wellman were distinctly unimpressed: 'There was an old gramophone on-stage, with a hand winder, used by Richard to play records. We have never understood the purpose of that modern stage prop.'

My natural inclination causes me to side with them. Still, as Shakespeare himself was not averse to chronologically impossible references and, it seems likely, props, I am willing to hear the other point of view. Mr Bell was not slow to proffer it:

> For me, it's about Richard's very inability to hear music, which is why when 'my Richard' (Mike Eyres) played the gramophone, Richard's reaction to the music was quizzical. I believe he may even have tried (and failed) to dance to it at one point. However, it is that magnificent tree that actually had more of a say in to-gramophone or not-to-gramophone. The image of this camp-gothic figure like a great spindly vulture stooped in absurd puzzlement over a tinny gramophone under the skeletal branches of an enormous fir tree was too good to resist. It was *Gormenghast*, it was James Thurber's *Thirteen Clocks*, and it was very theatrical. Richard himself is a piece of theatre, and – like Cleopatra – his understanding of himself is performative.

I pushed Simon a bit further and queried whether, in the context of the rest of the setting, he felt it had been a successful prop. He had no doubt about it, and his reasons for thinking this way give you more than a suspicion that he enjoys playing the *enfant terrible* of the directorial stable:

> Yes, on two levels: it was thematically true to the character and text, and it disrupted a traditionalist reading of the performance. Anachronistic props that disrupt convention may work within a theatrical system maintained by the concept, depending on the play, whether that be the overt theatricality of Richard's character, or the farcical disruption of reality/convention in *Comedy of Errors*.

The tensions between David Crilly's vision of the festival and the innovative Bell, always pushing at the boundaries of what he can 'get away with', have proved fruitful and engaging over the years. The directors and the actors are working to a pre-set idea to ensure that it only appears that way, and boundaries and structures most certainly are followed. So, that use of the gramophone prop in *Richard III* was exceptional on a number of levels. Generally speaking such out-of-time props tend to be more prevalent in the comedies, especially the farces that have an air of 'whatever goes' about them. As for the audience, when your sides are splitting with laughter on a lawn in summer, you are not aware of anything other than the hilarious action in front of you.

This can lead to a sense of excess. In 2012's *The Taming of the Shrew*, Rory Thersby's Hortensio was determinedly wooing Helen Meadmore's Bianca. To aid him in his suit, he wore what Helen described as 'an enormous penis, a strap-on so that it stayed up'. You may already be thinking that this was going too far, but I have to point out that it was true to the bawdy nature of the scene and was the occasion of much genuine mirth. Helen continued,

> Of course he played with it, he brought it closer and closer to my face, every performance he tried harder to make me laugh. Fortunately I had this scroll I was reading that I could hide behind. The audience loved it when I had to lift it to cover my face because I was laughing so much that I was shaking. I kept having to put the scroll down and then up again and the audience loved it.

The reason this was successful was that it was well thought out in preparation and delivery. It stemmed directly from directorial planning arising straight from the text of the play. Rowan's thinking was clear:

> The idea with Hortensio and Gremio is that they are extremely unsuitable suitors for Bianca, Gremio is set out, he is 'the old pantaloon' but what's lovely

is that Hortensio can be played in totally different ways. Hortensio could be effete, or he could be a conceited, macho figure. With Rory's Hortensio, we used the idea that this guy could be slightly sleazy and very unfortunately, when he puts his leg up he's not aware that he's getting sort of 'friendly' and she, as a modest young girl, sees something she shouldn't, is actually quite funny.

Costumes

The Cambridge Shakespeare Festival website and annual programmes include variants on the following quote: 'No knee-bending to trendy revisionism but rather a tour de force of Elizabethan drama.' David Crilly told me, 'It's not a quote I direct at audiences, it's more an instruction to the directors and I have to keep repeating it, as it often falls on deaf ears.'

One can safely assume that those with auditory malfunctions do not include David Salter, who said to me, 'I hate contemporising Shakespeare ... what I can't stand is this idea that it has to be relevant and that it is only going to be relevant if we set it in a country which currently has an ongoing civil war ... ' However, the other two associate directors, Bell and Rowan, are more likely contenders for resisting the repeated instruction, albeit never to the deadening extent of those who impose a dreaded contemporary 'relevance' on proceedings.

Bell's visual imagination means that he conjures up productions that have their own symbolic coherence regardless of date, while Rowan has been known, very occasionally, to employ twentieth-century settings in his productions. Rules are for guidance, not strict laws that imprison artistic vision; there is a degree of give and take. Notwithstanding this, overall Crilly makes sure his festival stays true to its ethos and Elizabethan costume virtually always wins the day as it is just so very fitting for the texts and the venues. On the rare occasion non-Elizabethan dress has been allowed, it has been restricted to a maximum of one play per summer.

Dave Rowan, while happy to use modern settings and costumes elsewhere, admits that he views the CSF differently:

> I don't mind if it is 1920s, but I do think there are some venues where 1920s doesn't work. I have done an Athenian *A Midsummer Night's Dream* and an Elizabethan *A Midsummer Night's Dream* and I did a 1920s *A Midsummer Night's Dream* a long time ago. The least satisfying of them all was the 1920s one. Going back to the Elizabethan period helps you to differentiate between the characters, artist, and ultimately helps you to tell the story.
>
> At the CSF, people want to see something special and if you came in and everyone was in modern dress it would not feel special. We have these

beautiful sets and scenery so let's make it look and feel a little bit special. Yes, we don't have flying in scenery, we don't have lights, we don't have massive sound changes and we have only got a small cast – but having the costumes making it look 'nice and period' adds to making it feel like an event.

The vast majority of the audience concurs. Nearly everyone I interviewed about this strongly supported the employment of Elizabethan costumes. Indeed, many were surprised even to be asked the question. Nevertheless, it is an important debate that has long focused the minds of dramatists and their audiences and not as clear-cut a preference as one might first suppose. By investigating why this is so, we can even more fully appreciate the special qualities that the CSF credo of 'no knee-bending to trendy revisionism' brings to its productions.

Before that, it is worth noting that neither in Shakespeare's day nor at the CSF is one fully restricted to Elizabethan dress. The use of a toga in a Roman play, for example, has always been helpful. Nonetheless, costumes indicate a great deal to an attentive audience and consequently Cleopatra and all manner of other historical figures would have worn Elizabethan dress to convey as much latent meaning as possible for the audience of the day. Every costume revealed to them details of the wearer's social rank, status and wealth and, even more fundamentally, gender. In addition to this, there were and are many situational pointers in items such as riding boots, napkins, hoods, cloaks and sleeping attire.

As mentioned elsewhere, Shakespeare's plays, wherever they were notionally set, mostly reflect on the manners and mores of the London of his time. Everything about the structure, staging, language and focus is about the life around him and his live audience. *The Merchant of Venice* has little or nothing to do with Venice *per se*; no knowledge or interest in Venice is shown. Instead these themes in the play are all to do with the mercantilism in the rapidly expanding London. Linking that to a time when a similar thing happened in an exotic sounding location made sound dramatic and commercial sense, while it also steered clear of drawing a censor's eye to any direct contemporary references.

Even the History plays, which often reflected very closely on current events but had to be set in earlier periods for safety and censorship reasons, did not necessitate a change in this methodology. Or, rather, there was no felt need for a methodology. Servants and slaves from across the centuries are recognizably Elizabethan. Young ladies, especially in comedies, almost always find themselves in situations regarding virginity and marriage that are directly equivalent to those of Shakespeare's time. It was therefore doubly fitting that the clothes nearly everyone wore to perform these plays were contemporaneous.

The argument that would logically follow from this is that we should today produce our Shakespeare in contemporary clothing as that is what was done when they were first produced. Indeed, many very successful productions have taken this approach.

Judi Dench said, 'We did a modern *Measure for Measure* at Nottingham, and the "moated grange" was a nightclub, with Mariana sitting there after hours with a glass, and that proved to be a very helpful piece of storytelling.'[2]

Ian McKellen believes that

> modern dress is fine, because this isn't a pageant we're doing. These are recognisable characters and attitudes that we can share – where does he keep his money, does he sign cheques, use credit cards – instead of having some all-purpose purse full of money which he rattles and throws at the other actors. It's what we call naturalism or reality, but it seems to me to be what Hamlet was on to in his advice to the Players.[3]

However, it is not long before uncertainties and difficulties arise. The stories of Kate, Helena, Hero in *Taming of the Shrew*, *All's Well That Ends Well* and *Much Ado about Nothing* are three of the most striking examples of issues revolving around marriage that sit uncomfortably in any setting that is not patriarchal to a disturbing degree. The whole fascination with virginity that is prevalent in so many plays is not easy to portray convincingly in a modern setting, nor can the ending to *The Two Gentlemen of Verona* be carried off in a believable fashion.

McKellen continued,

> You can do *Much Ado* any period you like, but it has to be a time when it was easy for men to tell women what to do, and for women to be in a subservient role, and it has to be about a martial society. If these things aren't present, the play is distorted.[4]

So, although intellectually the idea of presenting the plays in modern dress to relate directly to the contemporary audience is consistent with what Shakespeare did, it often appears ill fitting. The attempt to appear on stage performing Shakespeare in modern dress draws so much attention to itself that it distracts from the play itself.

To pick one example before returning to our main topic, Rupert Goold's 2011 *The Merchant of Venice* for the RSC was set in contemporary Las Vegas. It featured, among other things, a TV prize show (to represent the casket scenes), an Elvis impersonator, casinos and showgirls. The aptness of the setting is clear as the reckless gambling, over-spending and impractical love stories of the play are perfectly mirrored in a Vegas setting. The end result of all this was predictably, though, fierce debate on the setting, not the play. Granted that this debate involves important points that Shakespeare's drama raises, but the focus was all on Goold not Shakespeare.

Modernising need not always take us into the here-and-now and, in fact, it never does at the CSF as Simon Bell explained:

> When we say modern-dress, it isn't really that. The nearest the festival would have got to that would be *The Comedy of Errors* over ten years ago, set in the '60s. So, the most modern era was the '60s. It looked lovely but I think that's the most modern we've got to. When we say, modern-dress, what we actually mean is evening wear. We had a *Twelfth Night* done in evening wear which looked very stylish. There was a lot of red and black and it was one of the best *Twelfth Night*s we've ever done. It was well directed and had a great elegance to it. It was antiquated in its own way. We'd never have anyone in jeans or in T-shirts or anything like that.

As much as I prefer the plays to be in Elizabethan costume, honesty compels me to report that I found Simon's 2014 production of *Merchant of Venice* a triumph despite the cast wearing unspecified Victorian Edwardian formal wear. Portia and Nerissa moving from elegant dresses to the clothes of male lawyers was especially effective and the apt, general ambience of businessmen was strongly conveyed.

One of the difficulties faced here is in achieving an equivalence of the amount of information that Elizabethan audience would take from the attire of their day – rank, wealth, social status, etc. A way round this is to set the play in an era and setting, usually military, where these things are easily communicated. This can be very successful and many famous productions have sprung from this approach.

The decadence of the 1920s, the depression of the 1930s and the rise of fascism and communism, the rock and roll 1950s and the swinging '60s all provide ready-made settings that have been exploited to greater or lesser degrees. Military and island scenarios of all times have clear attractions for the staging of particular plays. Again, however, such a setting has to be fully realised and to completely suit the original play. If it fails to do this, it appears as a compromise that reflects neither the costumes the plays were originally performed in nor the contemporary dress of the time. Consequently, as there seems no benefit in these situations of having set the play in such a locale, it comes across as mere attention seeking. Judi Dench recalls an awkward example of this tendency:

> I did Regan in an RSC *Lear*, and the designer set it in Czarist Russia, so the three daughters came on in white dresses and blue sashes and tiaras as if it was the state opening of parliament, and I found that very difficult to reconcile with the wild side of the play. I think in that world, you would

have to make Regan a kind of psychopath. The amalgam of the play and that period I found very difficult.[5]

Even the wonderful John Barton ran into difficulties. His 1976 *Much Ado about Nothing* was set in British India and thus addressed the military and gender problems that occur in relocating this play as detailed by Ian McKellen, above. His production was an acclaimed success. However, the odds against getting it exactly right are very high. Barton worried about the inherent problems of this approach:

I still don't know if I was right or wrong but I tried once setting *Othello* in the nineteenth century ... I wanted to define the social background. I tried to set Venice as a city in the Austrian Empire and Cyprus as an outpost of the Empire. I particularly wanted to clarify the different ranks of the soldiers, with Othello as General, Casio as Lieutenant Colonel and Iago as a Warrant Officer. I hoped thereby to make Othello himself a mythical, heightened figure who stood out from this real world of soldiers. So I was quite pleased with myself first, but in the end I felt that, with the best intentions, I had somewhat diminished him by putting him into a world too small for him. And that seems to be the great danger in modern-dress Shakespeare. It can reduce rather than resonate.[6]

Indeed it can and it usually does. There are a host of other losses, in addition to those already mentioned, in transferring from Elizabethan costumes to those of another era. These are due to practical and physical differences. Wearing and holding a sword, for example, is very different from holding a machine gun. The stance, movement and rhythm of the actor will be completely altered by such an exchange of weapon. This will alter how he speaks the text – text that was written with Elizabethan costumes in mind. Belting and buckling clothes play a major part in plays concerned with gender swapping. The gender differentials in clothing were extremely important in Elizabethan times and Shakespeare's text plays with these in words that are supposed to be matched by actions on stage. Even at very basic levels of action, something like doffing a cap is not the same as removing a fedora or bowler hat.

It is in the area of male and female costumes that most is lost. A vibrant subset of what is thrown out along with Elizabethan costumes is much of the pervasive bawdy subtext that runs throughout the plays. By keeping Elizabethan costumes, many of those allusions can be kept alive. Text that was designed to be spoken as the appropriate costumes were played with is no longer rendered meaningless. This is all lost on a set of *Much Ado about Nothing* that is set in later eras.

All of these problems, distractions and difficulties make one sigh with relief that the CSF has 'no trendy revisionism' as its motto. Graham Hall, who has included some CSF productions among the dozens of Shakespeare performances he has attended each year for some decades, made an interesting additional point about this subject to me: 'The more modern in dress you make the production the more the public expect props. Put the players in Elizabethan dress and the background and props are taken in a completely different light. This is where CSF can capitalise with the venues.' Perennial attendees Bill and Bob Wellman told me that

> through the years we have had many conversations with people in the streets of Cambridge and the CSF college garden audiences. All agree with us that what is most important is to hear what is being spoken and to have Shakespeare performed in period costumes. Visitors, especially Americans, expect Shakespeare plays in the historic university college gardens of Cambridge, to be performed in period costumes.

There is a twist to the quote of 'No knee-bending to trendy revisionism here, but rather a tour de force of Elizabethan tragedy'. Dave Rowan laughingly told me, 'For a number of reasons, the worst production I have done at the CSF was *Romeo and Juliet* many years ago and there was a review that said "no knee-bending to trendy revisionism here" and actually it was the least fulfilling production I have ever presided over and yet this quote about it has been carried on for years, and it didn't merit the quote whatsoever.'

Symbolic Theatre

Whether the props and costumes are correctly dated or not, all directors know that they will never be believed to be anything more than props and costumes. Even a real sword wielded by an actor in a college garden play is still a prop. Consequently, what the props symbolise becomes the important thing, which is just as it was in Shakespeare's day. This can be seen, firstly, even in the basic sense of signifying some extra information:

> Small handheld props and costumes also indicate location. A mirror and a hairbrush indicate a lady's (and sometimes a man's) chamber; a napkin from which one brushes imaginary crumbs indicates that the character has just finished dinner; spurred boots indicate a travel scene. Stage directions that require characters to enter 'as from bed,' 'as from hunting,' 'as in prison,' 'as in his study' use costumes and small props to set the scene: a nightgown

implies a bed, a hawk on a wrist implies an open field; gyves imply a cell; books on a table imply a backdrop of bookcases.[7]

However, there is also the much deeper symbolic sense, as Styan notes.

Richard II, act IV scene I is a scene in which Shakespeare seems to be experimenting with his properties as cues for poetry. Thus the King's business with the mirror:

> Give me that glass, and therein will I read ...
> No deeper wrinkles yet? Hath sorrow struck
> So many blows upon this face of mine,
> And made no deeper wounds ? O, flatt'ring glass,
> Like to my followers in prosperity,
> Thou dost beguile me! ...
> A brittle glory shineth in this face,
> As brittle as the glory is the face,
> For there it is, cracked in a hundred shivers.

Here he dashes the glass to the ground. This is an actor's piece, climactic with the rhetorical repetitions characteristic of Richard, and the property mirror is a first-rate aid to him. Yet for the sense, the property is especially apt: the speech is of self-scrutiny, and Shakespeare supplies a visible symbol for a self-conscious and over-sensitive man. Later, other sensitive men, like Cassius and Hamlet, speak also of the glass with which to 'see the inmost part', but for them Shakespeare is content with verbal imagery. For Richard he has made the feeling of the actor and the point of the speech theatrically objective.[8]

Simon Bell told me that with props you have to 'go symbolic'. In his then current *Hamlet* he used a spade that 'is not usable but has a face on it, part of the symbols/motifs' and 'the ghost is anything but a ghost, it is a part of theatre'. This particular ghost was made up to be overwhelmingly corporeal – an obese, rather than an ethereal, presence. Using props in this symbolic rather than realistic sense is, claims Bell, 'in a funny way, more real'. Again we return to the paradox of non-representational theatre portraying reality more fully than representational staging.

There are exceptions, as you would expect in a canon as rich and varied as Shakespeare's. He was, after all, forever experimenting with dramatic forms, and spectacle became more important as he aged. This was no doubt influenced by his company, now called the King's Men, after their new patron, James VI of Scotland, who succeeded Elizabeth and thus also became James I of England, moving into the indoor Blackfriars Theatre in winters from 1608 onwards. This is apparent not only in the last plays, the romance extravaganzas, but, most especially, in what was really the last play, *Henry VIII*.

Scholars dispute how much of this is in his own hand. While some claim it is all, or nearly all, Shakespeare's own work, most believe it was a collaboration with John Fletcher, who was soon to succeed Shakespeare as the leading playwright of the King's Men, contributing at least half of the play. Interesting though that debate is, it is not our concern here and the scene quoted below is, in any case, always attributed to Shakespeare himself.

This swansong was markedly divergent from the general Shakespearean model. It was a spectacle, and it has often been rolled out to celebrate royal occasions ever since. It consists to a large degree of representational processions and pageantry. The following stage directions are an eye-opener to those of us long accustomed to seeing so many plain 'Enter X' directions over the preceding years. Clearly, staging this following scene would test the ingenuity even of those ever-inventive CSF directors:

Act II scene IV.

> Trumpets, sennet, and cornets. Enter two Vergers with short silver wands; next them, two SCRIBES, in the habit of doctors; after them the ARCHBISHOP OF CANTERBURY alone; after him, the BISHOPS OF LINCOLN, ELY, ROCHESTER, and ST ASAPH: next them, with some small distance, follows a Gentleman bearing the purse, with the great seal, and a cardinal's hat: then two Priests, bearing each a silver cross: then a GENTLEMAN-USHER bare-headed, accompanied with a Sergeant-At-Arms, bearing a silver mace: then two Gentlemen bearing two great silver pillars: after them, side by side, the two CARDINALS; two Noblemen with the sword and mace. The KING takes place under the cloth of state. The two CARDINALS sit under him as judges. The QUEEN takes place some distance from the King. The Bishops place themselves on each side the court, in manner of a consistory: below them, the Scribes. The Lords sit next the Bishops. The rest of the attendants stand in convenient order about the stage.[9]

This is very much the opposite of 'less is more'. Although *Henry VIII* has its own strengths, it is not considered to be on a par with Shakespeare's many masterpieces, all of which were built upon the opposite principle. The fact that Shakespeare could produce such intricate and demanding stage directions but nearly always chose not to is revealing in itself. *Henry VIII*, in so many ways, fits the old saying of 'the exception that proves the rule'.

David Crilly, however, tells me that he would not baulk form putting *Henry VIII* on at the CSF and could devise a production that would work on its own terms, within the 'bare stage, few props' parameters. So impressed have I been by the CSF's stagings of other late plays that I am sure his confidence in them making a success of it is not misplaced (*The Winter's Tale* and *The Tempest* have both been performed on more than one occasion, while the rarely seen *Cymbeline* and *Pericles* had inspired debuts in 2013 and 2014 respectively). I very much look forward to finding out and, as the CSF are by now approaching ever closer to having covered the entire canon, have reasonable hope that I will do so shortly.

In the meantime, it may be salutary to remind ourselves of how far theatre had strayed from such authentic Shakespearean staging. From the Restoration to a peak in Victorian and early twentieth-century years, productions went about as far away from putting on a Shakespeare play in an appropriate manner as one could imagine. The language was treated as a near irrelevance to the spectacular scenic shows that would have been anathema to Shakespeare, who poked merciless fun at attempts at representational scenery via Quince and company in *A Midsummer Night's Dream*.

The extent to which theatrical productions moved away from Shakespeare's original dramatic vision can be gleaned from this heartfelt appeal to cease and desist from the excesses that had been reached by 1907. The following quote is from a near solitary voice in the wilderness at the time:

> In the most influential circles of the theatrical profession it has become a commonplace to assert that Shakespearean drama cannot be successfully produced, cannot be rendered tolerable to any substantial section of the playgoing public, without a plethora of scenic spectacle and gorgeous costume, much of which the student regards as superfluous and inappropriate. An accepted tradition of the modern stage ordains that every revival of a Shakespearean play at a leading theatre shall base some part of its claim to public favour on its spectacular magnificence ... Pictorial tableaux, even though they suggest topics without relevance to the development of the plot, have at times to be interpolated in order to keep the attention of the audience sufficiently alive. One deduction to be drawn from this position of affairs is irrefutable. The pleasure which recent Shakespearean revivals offer the spectator reaches him mainly through the eye. That is the manager's avowed intention. Yet no one would seriously deny that the Shakespearean drama appeals, both primarily and ultimately, to the head and to the heart. Whoever seeks, therefore, by the production of Shakespearean drama chiefly to please the spectator's eye shows scant respect both for the dramatist and for the spectator.[10]

One of the most effective recent demonstrations of how magnificently the CSF returns us from this wayward path and back into the illuminating and welcoming arms of Elizabethan staging was the very real, face-to-face, drama of *King Lear* as staged on a plot of land in central Cambridge. Particularly effective in this regard was the wonderfully disturbing, disturbingly wonderful scene with Lear and the Fool out in the storm. Simon Bell's symbolic approach was unerringly effective. He describes the rationale behind his staging of this scene:

> Here, you work on the level of the symbolic. For example, the storm scene in *Lear* takes place in daylight at the CSF. What I did, was I had Lear pulling the Fool about really violently. The violence of the language and the violence of the action created the storm – this makes it more Elizabethan. You are left with just the power of theatre to convey the storm scene. What were the alternatives? The audience would have giggled if we'd have had thunder sheets hidden in the bushes, because all you would then have had would have been the image of someone in the bushes bashing a piece of metal.

An additional effect in this chilling production was the Fool, still with the rope around him, crouched not far from Lear and wailing with a keening noise that never seemed to end, echoing and re-echoing round the garden. This drove you to distraction as it accurately reflected the turmoil of madness in Lear's mind.

4

Venues

Within the Temple-hall we were too loud;
The garden here is more convenient.

Henry VI Part One, act II scene IV

Venues, Exits and Entrances, Audience, Lighting, Simultaneous Staging, Animals

Venues: The College Gardens

Cambridge University colleges' private gardens impart a magical atmosphere that has important influences on directors, actors and audiences. You feel transported into another time and place where the Elizabethan dress and music fit perfectly into cultivated gardens bounded by impressive, traditional architecture. Professor William Steen wrote to me emphasising these attractions: 'The idea of watching Shakespeare in a centre of culture and learning as in a Cambridge college garden among wonderful trees and extensive heritage is fascinating for me. To have a picnic on a fine evening at the same time is a unique experience. I look forward to it each year.'

Shakespeare's plays were written to be performed under an open sky with an audience partly seated and partly not, so this environment suits them perfectly. In addition, there is the added bonus of impressionistically transporting us into the past before the productions even begin. The resonance behind L. P. Hartley's poetically charged opening line of *The Go Between*, 'The past is a foreign country: they do things differently there', is physically enacted as you turn off a city road and make your way through the college buildings and gardens to the stage area.

Additionally, as mentioned previously when talking about the 'bare stage', the natural scenery aids in the production of many scenes. Massive trees are a godsend and can be utilised for many purposes, from castles or ship rigging to providing cover for a conveniently located 'tiring house' as the Elizabethans called the actors' changing room. Clumps of trees are natural forests, while natural hollows, trees and shrubs can provide cover or even just be handy to gesture to at appropriate moments. The actor playing Gonzalo in *The Tempest*, for another example from the large store of these sprinkled throughout Shakespeare's work, can point around himself as he exclaims, 'How lush and lusty the grass looks! How green!' (Act II, scene I).

To be simultaneously both larger than life and confidentially close is essential for the Shakespearean actor to convey his part fully. The settings at the CSF support the actors' achievements in triumphantly carrying off this challenging feat. Two girls, from the Cambridge Programme Summer School at Churchill College, were part of a large crowd that witnessed *Richard III* in the most expansive of all CSF settings in St John's College gardens. Fourteen-year-old Chelsea Bodimeade from Australia had been sitting on the grass at the front and reported in my survey that 'Being in the college garden was close to the action and cosy'. Meanwhile sixteen-year-old Jasmine Lam from China, from a more remote spot, commented, 'It's a very nice environment, with the natural sunlight and then night sky. It's also amazing how loudly the actors can project their voices.'

If the actors mumble, only the front row can hear them. On the other hand, if they concentrate only on projecting their voice to the back rows, they end up shouting or declaiming like a bombastic caricature of the late nineteenth-century delivery style. The latter is a particularly enticing trap as outdoor audiences are more boisterous and mobile than the quiet, neatly arranged and subdued indoor ones. The actors are acutely aware of their situation. Daniel Simpson advised me that

> when you're playing outdoors you have to be aware not only of the audience, but of the climatic conditions and aeroplanes. The wind in the trees is an absolute killer. And the fact is that your job in those circumstances is to look after the people in row Z rather than row A because they've paid their money too and they deserve to be as absorbed as the people in the front row. So you have to really project and make sure that the people at the back are getting it too. It can be a challenge just for your voice to reach that far. When they're sold out, these things, the audience are literally miles away. I remember with *Love's Labour's Lost* at Downing, which was a surprise hit in 2010, the audience just grew and grew through the course of the run. There's an entrance road as you come in and then you turn left and then there's those trees and you go through there and there's the audience space and then the performance bit. Well, the audience were virtually at those trees. That's a long way from the stage and if

it's wet or windy, you've got to really, really project and make sure that you're communicating, even the nuances, effectively to the back row. To an actor it can feel dishonest, and I mentioned earlier about trying to communicate the nuances, but actually that's slight bullshit. The reality is that in looking after row Z, there's a kind of physical effort there and an unnaturalness because that's not how people speak obviously. You're are acting rather than being, if you see what I mean. As soon as you stand on a stage and declaim to row Z through the wind, it feels as an actor like you're acting rather than being. It's unnatural. But it's stagecraft; there's no point in being there at all if they're not going to hear you. So, it's trying to balance the stage craft of being heard and understood at the back, with keeping the truth of the emotion and the experiences of that character in that moment, and it is a difficult balance. I'm not going to lie to you. I often feel that it's forced and it feels unnatural and dishonest.

Hamlet felt much the same, when he gave his advice to the players:

> ... O, there be
> players that I have seen play, and heard others
> praise, and that highly, not to speak it profanely,
> that, neither having the accent of Christians nor
> the gait of Christian, pagan, nor man, have so
> strutted and bellowed that I have thought some of
> nature's journeymen had made men and not made them
> well, they imitated humanity so abominably.
>
> *Hamlet,* act III scene II

It is a perennial problem, whatever the stage setting, for the Shakespearean actor. In large auditoriums an actor is faced by an audience stretching away into the darkness and the temptation is to fill the cavernous gloom with overblown gestures and vocals. The Globe in its time could be so packed that the intimacy we so associate with it was not always available to all. Whatever the setting, in other words, the same challenge is often present. Shakespeare, though, is characteristically helpful to the actors in his text. There are many instances of this, such as Desdemona helpfully letting us all know, in *Othello*, act V scene II, what only those with a good view of Othello can see: 'Alas, why gnaw you so your nether lip?' An outstanding example occurs in *Henry VIII*. Cardinal Wolsey has portrayed distress at the realisation that he is doomed, and this would have been visible to everyone in the indoor Blackfriar's Theatre audience and to those at the front and the middle of the Globe. However, it would not be clear to those at the back of the Globe. Similarly at St John's at the CSF, it would be apparent to many, but not all, of one of the large crowds that venue customarily attracts. Consequently, Shakespeare has another character tell us what he would have us all see, were that possible:

> NORFOLK: My lord, we have
> Stood here observing him: some strange commotion
> Is in his brain: he bites his lip, and starts;
> Stops on a sudden, looks upon the ground,
> Then lays his finger on his temple, straight
> Springs out into fast gait; then stops again,
> Strikes his breast hard, and anon he casts
> His eye against the moon: in most strange postures
> We have seen him set himself.
>
> *Henry VIII,* act III scene II

So, I told Daniel that he should not worry about it 'feeling unnatural and dishonest' as, after all, being dishonest is part of the point of actors. We joked about the Greek name for actors being hypocrites. It brought to mind those famous lines in *Richard III*:

> BUCKINGHAM: Tut, I can counterfeit the deep tragedian,
> Speak and look back, and pry on every side,
> Tremble and start at wagging of a straw.
> Intending deep suspicion, ghastly looks
> Are at my service, like enforced smiles;
> And both are ready in their offices,
> At any time, to grace my stratagems.
>
> *Richard III,* act III scene V

Still, the issue clearly troubled Daniel. Keith Chanter, who began playing at the festival in 2012 (Antonio in *The Tempest* and a particularly marvellous Gloucester in *King Lear*) also talked to me at length about similar concerns:

> I think one of the main priorities, if not the main priority, when you're performing in the open air is that everybody gets to hear you. Obviously that's a bit of a worry in the theatre but not a major worry, particularly in a small theatre. But in the open air, with four or five hundred people, it plays on your mind all the time: 'Can the people at the back hear what I'm saying?'

Keith, if I may be so bold, may have over-thought this question because he went on to be overly and unjustly critical of himself. He continued,

For me a lot of the subtleties go out of the performance. It's much more declamatory. It's probably more like the Victorian style of acting. You have to project. The strange thing is obviously you have got some people who are right by your feet. So in a way you feel that you're letting them down because if you're acting for them then obviously you don't need to project, but you have to think about the people at the back. So in a funny sort of way you're forgetting about the people by your feet, you're not acting for those because you're projecting too far away. It's difficult, it's tricky.

Keith's concern here, while understandable, is not reflective of how he comes across at the CSF. He, like all the actors, conveys much through facial and bodily gesture to those 'right by your feet'. Perhaps it is more subconscious on Keith's part than is usual, or perhaps his concern stems from the roles in which he tends to be cast. Keith carries himself with a certain gravitas that lends itself to roles as statesman or patricians with important statements to declaim. Whatever the reason, I can allay his concern. I witnessed his performance of Gloucester, in *King Lear* at King's in 2012, on two different days and from two different vantage points. I heard him clearly both from the front of the audience one afternoon and near the back of a large crowd on a late August night, and I did not at all feel forgotten when at the front.

It is clearly a good thing that the directors and actors are aware of the perennial problem of balancing bombast and close familiarity as this ensures that they are always striving to keep on top of it. Keith and all the CSF actors are to be commended for the manner in which they project their voices without shouting, for the way in which they engage people both close by and relatively further away and for their continual remembrance that outdoors necessitates a constantly clear enunciation of all lines.

Venues vary from year to year and, given that each college has spacious and numerous gardens, the location can also vary within a given college. At Downing, for example, the CSF productions began in a perfect space, complete with a huge central tree as backdrop. After a couple of years the College decided that this was too close to their main hall as the performances could interfere with formal occasions staged there. That was their reasoning, though the CSF audience of a matinee production of *Much Ado about Nothing* that had to constantly compete with a steel band playing at a wedding ceremony would have probably presumed the CSF moved due to the disruption that it had to endure that afternoon. The following overview is an alphabetical list of the locations most used in recent years.

Girton College gardens provide the only out-of-town venue, lying, as they do, just over a mile north of the city centre. This can be a good thing in regards to intrusive noise, though that benefit is partly counterbalanced by the busy Huntingdon Road that runs along one side of the College.

The plays take place in the splendid courtyard, which affords intimacy amid the imposing and expansive college grounds. A cluster of some half-dozen trees in the centre of the staging area can represent anything from a garden to an orchard, to a wood or forest without any need for alteration. They have also been used as a cave and places from which to eavesdrop or hide. Strung with lanterns, their natural canopy has been utilised to bewitching effect in late-August evening performances.

The courtyard has a distinct echo effect, which adds to the actors' challenge in projecting their voices without over-projecting. It also has more pleasing effects such us allowing Elizabethan string music to reverberate softly around, enveloping the whole area and adding a unique ambience.

There is also a noticeable, if much slighter, echo effect at *Homerton College*, arising from the layout of the College buildings. Debuting as a CSF venue in 2013, Homerton's lovely, extensive and enclosed gardens seemed almost to have been deliberately designed to host such an event. The original buildings of the old Cavendish College are tastefully incorporated into more modern extensions, creating an attractive and spacious milieu. The college also very kindly allowed complete access to its private bar, toilet and car-parking facilities making the whole setting seem like an extravagantly laid-on, purpose-built environment for the performances of 2013's *A Midsummer Night's Dream*. A year later, for *The Taming of the Shrew*, the spot within the grounds had been changed. Although the new setting was still very good, it fell short of that seemingly custom-made setting of the previous summer.

The awe-inspiring chapel of *King's College* is probably the most iconic of all Cambridge sights. The college's original Fellows' Garden dated back to 1690, but today's version is an outstanding example of the Victorian garden style, providing a peaceful haven from the outside world and featuring both mature English and samples of uncommon trees. This special area is one that not even the students at Kings have access to, far less the general public. Generously, however, the college allows the CSF to stage performances there and this creates a terrific combination of a rarely seen and romantic setting.

Robinson College was opened in 1979 but its stunning, landscaped gardens which, like its architecture, merge pre-existing and modern structures, are as evocative of the past as any other setting. As at King's, the CSF attendee has the pleasure of moving through a mixture of wilder and more formal garden areas that are breathtaking in their beauty and home to many mature trees.

Robinson provides the CSF with a purpose-built amphitheatre, named in honour of renowned stage designer Maria Björnson. This features dimmable lights, a tiny frontage, and a facing, slight terrace. Consequently, there is a notable contrast between Robinson and all the other venues. There is a much more limited area in front of the stage but it does have a very nice buttress to lean back on, for those who get in early and take up this prized position.

There is also a dressing room, behind one of the hedges that surround the site, where the cast can change and where costumes and props can be stored. The college have also benevolently provided an exclusive entrance, built into the brick wall on Adams Road, to allow direct access to the theatre from outside the college. This was an important addition, as the general public used to have to walk past rubbish bins, with their accompanying aromas, before arriving at the idyllic setting.

St John's College provides a large grass area that arcs around a fabulous, grand old tree. There is a pavilion to the extreme left of this area but this is only seldom used as it cannot easily accommodate comfortable viewing for the large crowds that regularly flock to St John's. St John's is the venue most likely to host the CSF's summer blockbuster as far as attendances go, despite having the inconvenience of portaloos as the only toileting facilities and the trickiest sound challenges of all the locations. Due to the expansive spread of the audience, wide to both sides and deep directly in front, actors have a difficult task to pitch their voices properly, especially as they also must take into account the dangers of traffic or pedestrian noise from the busy road behind the audience or the wind whipping through the trees as it snatches the actors' voices away. Over the years the cast have devised ways to overcome all these problems as well as is humanly possible and the site has witnessed many a triumphant staging; it continues to draw the largest attendances, year after year.

When I discussed this with director Simon Bell he said, 'Robinson attracts things like *Merchant of Venice*, and *Measure for Measure*. So you get an audience there who want to go and see *Merchant of Venice* and *Measure for Measure*, whereas the bigger sellers will play in St John's.'

This struck me as a classic 'chicken and egg' situation. Does St John's (Trinity and King's come into a similar category) attract larger audiences because the most popular plays are staged there or are favourites selected to be performed there because it is already known that they will attract the most people? Simon laughed at this follow-up question and said, 'One day we should do a test festival and just put tiny plays like *Pericles* in St John's and see how big the audience is.'

As at King's, the Fellows' Garden at *Trinity College* is normally inaccessible to college members and closed to the public on all but National Garden Day. It is a delightful environment, with a wooden gazebo, sundial and herb garden. The plays take place in an atmosheric enclave affording unique exits and entrances around the stage area, including one long walkway through the audience to the front of the players. This parade, as Simon Bell describes it, is perfect for regal entrances.

I arrived early to this venue for *Hamlet* in 2013, as I wanted to pick my spot carefully. I drank in the views and ambience as the huge attendance began to build up behind me and found my eye repeatedly drawn to the imposing tower of the University Library. This 157-foot colossus, designed by Sir Giles Gilbert Scott in his iconic style, inevitably dominates much of the Cambridge skyline. Sitting in the Fellows' Garden at Trinity, it was right in front of me looming in the background over the area that would soon be the stage.

My mind was taken back to when I was standing, in the library, tenderly turning over the pages of *Hamlet* in the precious first folio on the table in front of me. It was somehow very moving to think that the play I was reading then, from a 1623 publication, was soon to begin in the shadow of that tower.

These varied venues obviously afford individual opportunities and challenges to the directors when planning their productions and blocking their stage spaces. I was talking to Daniel Simpson about the differences for an actor when facing an audience at Robinson College, where he can see all of them at all times, and at St John's where this is not possible. I asked him how the actors cope with such differences, albeit that I had postulated the two extremes of CSF audience layout. He replied,

> It starts with the director's awareness of the issues for a particular space. A good director will block the play with the space absolutely in mind and understand completely sight lines, auditory issues, all the rest of it, and block the play accordingly. But the fact is there has to be compromise with the space, like St John's in particular.

This topic came up again when I was quizzing Simon Bell on whether any of Shakespeare's plays seemed to be resistant to outdoor staging. He commented,

> Although I don't think any Shakespeare play is unstageable outdoors – after all, they were written to be so – there are however certainly more 'indoor' shows. I'm doing *Merchant of Venice* this year, and its urban tone means it's best at Robinson. When we suit plays to venues, the outdoors/indoors thing isn't really an issue, it's much more the suitability of the grounds. For example, the enormous tree of Downing is spot-on for the whimsy of *The Winter's Tale*, or the gothic of *Richard III* or *Macbeth*. The variable entrances available at Robinson cry out for *Comedy of Errors*, whilst the sculpted lawns of Trinity or King's best suit *Love's Labour's Lost* or *Much Ado about Nothing*. This isn't of course set in stone – when you're doing *King Lear* on those same sculpted lawns, and you have to face staging the storm scene in the summer sun on a balmy evening, then a director's theatrical imagination is vital.

I was interviewing David Salter at a window overlooking Robinson College's theatre and mentioned how ideal it was for that year's *The Comedy of Errors* but that you could not have the same production at St John's. He agreed,

> No, you couldn't. That's part of the job as well. You're using what you can in the space. When I was at King's the first time with *The Comedy of Errors* there were these two huts and we just used them. In fact, the gardeners, I don't know why, had cut a hole in the back door of one and we had it as an exit and entrance. It's terrific making those moments and I've always wanted to use the pavilion at St John's, but the problem with the pavilion is, in that arrangement, it's so far off. So, I had Richard in the tree instead [*Richard III*, 2013]. I had him originally in the pavilion and I thought the tree's better and some light relief and it puts him more centre stage.

I have often wished to see the pavilion used more but his point was sound. There simply were too many in attendance to have made that viable and, in any case, the tree worked brilliantly. This was especially so in act III scene vii when Richard is pretending to be a pious religious man, who is reluctantly dragged away from his study of holy books only by the pleading of those who beg him to become their king. Andrew Stephen carried off the affected saintliness from amid the giant tree, allowing the audience to simultaneously follow the effect his words were having while letting us in on the joke that it was all a charade. The audience reaction when his head popped out of the tree was one of spontaneous glee and recognition. The magnetic attraction of this character, even though we all know he is repellent, was obvious and irresistible to one and all.

All of the various settings in the different college gardens offer intriguing challenges and opportunities for innovative 'exit and entrance' movement strategies. Actors can surprise the audience by sitting among them and entering the stage space from there, or by suddenly appearing from behind a hedge, tree or other natural or architectural feature. If it is an apparently insurmountably long entrance, they can attract audience attention by a variety of noises such as buckling on armour or loudly beginning a speech and thus their entrance path becomes a temporary part of the stage area. On other occasions the gardens provide perfect exit and entrance pathways by their very design. Exits and entrances at the CSF come in all shapes and sizes.

There are, however, two distinct, main groupings of them: the compact and the spacious (though in certain venues both can be present simultaneously). In those with compact entrances and exits, the actors are, as Daniel Simpson expressed it, 'never dropping the ball; as one exit is made another entrance is happening'. These rapid, on-and-off routines, especially at compact venues such as Robinson College, nicely keep the audience off balance during comic romps. They also help make possible the speedy, two to two-and-a-half-hour passage of the plays, akin to the timings back when the plays were first staged in the sixteenth and seventeenth centuries.

In wider spaces, different approaches are necessary. The 2014 production of *A Midsummer Night's Dream* utilised the wide grass spaces facing and around the audience for a variety of effects. The opening of the play, with the young love quadrangle, the parents and the Duke and his captive bride-to-be were all spaced out in a way that reflected their social and psychological positions and the distances between them as the tug-of-war between Demetrius and Lysander over Hermia was enacted. At the end the characters all stood, again spaced cleverly and effectively, to take turns in intoning lines from the epilogue. In between these instances, there were many other fine uses of the expansive space throughout the play. Set scenes such as Oberon overhearing the lovers, and the lovers running about were well handled, and there was a deft moment where Titania and Oberon exited arguing only to enter seconds later as Hippolyta and Theseus. Unsurprisingly, given the detail paid to spatial logistics throughout this production, there was inventive use of the broad expanse in the area of exits and entrances.

One extremely effective example of how to use long entrances, while still maintaining a fast flowing production, occurred during one of those scenes where the play seems to demand as much running about as an episode of *Doctor Who*. At one point Demetrius ran very, very far from the audience into the distance. You naturally craned around to see where he was heading. As you did so, you espied Puck was crossing him running in the opposite direction towards the stage, conveying the magical flower to Oberon.

Long entrances that need to be made in a more stately manner, on the other hand, clearly have to be managed differently. Tessa Hatts explained this to me while talking about 2013's production of *Hamlet* in The Fellows' Garden at Trinity:

> You have to have two cues, one is when you leave the tree that you're hiding behind usually, and then the other when you get on stage. You have to judge the time. It's like our cue to start walking after the graveyard scene. We're watching and when Rory [Hamlet] hands the skull back to the gravedigger – that's our cue to start walking with the trolley.

I mentioned to Tessa that timing things like this must be tricky and take up quite a bit of rehearsal time. She surprised me by answering,

> You just have to try to time it; we only really get the one day in the venues. I think at St John's they're lucky, because they were allowed to rehearse there too, so they actually would have been able to practice it, but at Trinity, we

were only allowed to go there on the Sunday which was the technical and the dress rehearsal. So, we didn't get much practice at how long it took us.

I then presumed that she must have been relying on her memory of playing there in previous years. I had failed, though, to take into account that the precise location in each college's gardens can vary from year to year. Tessa replied,

No, because I've never used that particular space, but it wasn't too bad. Of course, if you mis-time it, you just have to start speaking from wherever you are, presuming that the audience can hear you. If in doubt and you're a bit late, just start talking, and then at least there isn't a silence and a blank stage for ages.

A lot depends on the particular stage and audience area allocated, obviously, but there are many other possibilities and combinations. The CSF settings, with no stage barriers, afford what Daniel Simpson calls the 'luxury of more options'. Often players who are anticipating an entrance will arrive through the audience and attach themselves to groups of spectators, sitting among them waiting for the cue. This is always well received and further cements the close kinship between cast and audience. It is another way of destroying any false barriers and again brings the special chemistry of the Elizabethan stagings back into play.

The Audience

With the solitary exception of Robinson College, the venues have large areas in front, between the performance area and the rows of seats, marked out by string for picnicking. Most regular attendees who aim for these spots bring their own rugs and/or seating. Some people stand at the sides, or lie in the summer sun at the back. Some bring their own portable seating of all imaginable kinds from walk-stools and garden chairs, to deck chairs and folding stools. Rows of plastic seats are provided, stretching out behind the picnicking areas. These are not fixed and so are eminently moveable until the crowd builds up and force of numbers makes this more troublesome. Overall, this mixture of standing, lying and sitting has many parallels with the audiences at the Globe in Shakespeare's time when the groundlings massed in front of the stage with seated areas rearing up behind and around them.

The groundlings were at liberty to move around and if they had a poor or obstructed view they would shift their position to try to obtain the best view possible. Similarly, at the CSF, moving around is part of the experience; it is fun to try out different vantage points. Another similarity, generally speaking, is that of the age-old adage of 'first come, first served'. In both these sixteenth and twenty-first-century settings, the first to arrive gain the reward of taking up the prime positions.

Again, as in Shakespeare's day, the attendance numbers are not known in advance of performance by either cast or audience. You may be in a relatively sparse crowd with lots of room to spread out or, alternatively, you may be more closely packed together if larger numbers turn up.

Unsurprisingly, this variability can have noticeable effects on audience responses. The same scene performed in front of a scattered handful will generate a different dynamic from when it is staged before hundreds, crammed shoulder to shoulder in a tight pack. Audiences with more room are naturally more likely to move around, lounge and lay out more expansive picnic spreads.

In another parallel with Elizabethan times, the CSF audiences consist of all society, a mix of classes, ages, genders, international travellers and people from all sorts of varied educational backgrounds. I have sat beside or amid ageing intellectuals, children, Cambridge students, non-native speakers, curiosity seekers, people that come every year, business people, school pupils, families, lovers, academics, serious picnicking crowds more intent on their victuals, and serious Shakespeare Festival goers intent on every word and action. I have been surrounded by an animated hen night on one side and a birthday celebration on the other. I have sat alongside business parties where seriously expensive wine and champagne flowed all evening long.

Although there are many parallels between then and now, a list of differences would also be lengthy. Drunkenness and brawling would have been more in evidence in Elizabethan times, though on nowhere near the scale as once thought. That view was akin to basing an impression on attending football matches in the later twentieth century based only on tabloid coverage of hooligan occurrences in stadiums. Most crucially, Shakespeare's original audiences would far outstrip us in their ability to follow the play aurally and would have knowledge of subjects like rhetoric, fencing, manners and customs that are now lost to us.

On our side we carry an understanding of Shakespeare shaped by centuries of study. These are plays we have probably learnt at school, if not also later. Even without study, we have heard so much about them that we usually know what is going to happen. No one nowadays, you suspect, goes to *King Lear* thinking that Cordelia will survive and inherit Lear's kingdom. We, as modern spectators, all have our own, often highly detailed, idea of what a play is about before we see it.

Even for the same person, there is a vast difference in seeing *A Midsummer Night's Dream* at the festival for the eighth year in a row, or seeing *Cymbeline* or *Pericles* there for the very first time. Additionally, each audience comprises of its own distinct elements. An eight-year-old schoolboy going to *A Midsummer*

Night's Dream will not have the same expectations or the same experience as a seventy-eight-year-old retired literature don from the university. They will usually be seated close to each other, though, and be intermingled with all the other individuals that coalesce for a few hours into a garden community being presented with a Shakespeare play.

Children of all ages are very much a part of this community. Thoughtful parents, with infants who may need to be walked or pushed in carry cots in an attempt to quieten them when they begin to cry, tend to hang out at the perimeters for obvious reasons. Sadly, this seems to be an ever decreasing percentage of parents. On the other hand, festival founder Mr Crilly is always willing to provide recompense for anyone whose enjoyment of a play is ruined by disruptive behaviour. Lively kids with lots of energy are best placed near open areas to run about in and can bring a special quality to the events. As audience member Ute Heinze told me, 'I like them running around, it's a good idea. They make it lively, they're not disturbing, they are part of the play.' David Crilly would be pleased to hear such comments as he has always seen the festival as being for the whole of the Cambridge community and views children's attendance as an essential part of this. Yet again this has parallels with the theatre of the Elizabethan age where family parties are recorded as going to watch the latest plays.

Business groupings on a company night out tend to come early and commandeer a suitable picnicking area. James Stephen, who was in charge of a company's sponsorship of the CSF, brought such groupings each year, as well as families and children. When I mentioned how impressive the range of attendees was, he enthusiastically picked up on my theme:

> It's fantastic. I thought it was wonderful when I first went to a performance. As you say, the huge cross-section: whether it's students, domestic students, international students, tourists. There's a really good contingent of, I think, the retired and semi-retired who come along with their cool boxes and their picnics, which is lovely. But there are also very young people as well. So, this year, I'll be taking my children who are nine and eleven. And I know that they'll love it. My son is very theatrical.

I remarked that he must have struck some good business deals over the champagne on certain evenings and added that I thought it must be an ideal place for such gatherings. James agreed:

> Exactly! And they're not feeling academically and/or socially intimidated by the environment. And it's absolutely fine to go to a performance, whatever age you are and whatever level of knowledge you have, and take from it what

you want. And the point is that you can enjoy it on whatever level you want, and all people want you to do is come and enjoy it.

Once again, David Crilly would be beaming with pleasure to hear this. One of his core instructions to his directors is that the play must be open and understandable to everyone, whatever their level of knowledge.

Lighting

In Shakespeare's time, his plays were performed outdoors. At the Globe, the usual starting time, as far as we can ascertain, was two o'clock in the afternoon. In the last stage of Shakespeare's career he would also have had the use of the indoor Blackfriars Theatre which, although allowing minimal control over lighting, was generally brightly lit by torches and candles, with the audience and stage both simultaneously bathed in light.

The recently opened Wanamaker Theatre in London gives a taste of what Blackfriars must have been like. I witnessed a candlelit performance of John Webster's *The Duchess of Malfi* where the lighting effects were intriguingly altered by lowering or raising rings of candles and where some of the many horrors were usefully set in the very dark back of the stage. At one point all shutters were closed for a total night-time scene.

Indoor theatre only became a regular option for Shakespeare at the end of his career and even then the late romances would have been performed outdoors at the Globe as well as indoors at Blackfriars. Furthermore, one of the plays often cited as most demonstrating the difference that the indoor theatre made to Shakespeare's art is *Pericles*. There are fundamental problems with this claim. By all available evidence, *Pericles* pre-dates the move to indoor theatres. Additionally, its title page states (I have modernised the spelling and characters, but kept the original capitalisation), 'As it has been diverse and sundry times acted by his Majesty's Servants at the Globe on Bank-side.' Thus, intriguing though this whole development can be in theory, it has shaky foundations, and, even were it to have been the case, it would have been very far from the norm. The norm was daylight, and this singularly affects the way the plays were written and constructed.

Once seen with stage and audience fully lit, you realise this was how they were designed, and this is how they are meant to be. Experiencing this at the CSF has been so revelatory to me that I now have difficulty fully enjoying plays in more usual theatrical settings. I feel too distanced and uninvolved; I am a mere spectator rather than part of an audience.

Despite the daylight settings in which they were performed, all of Shakespeare's plays, regardless of genre, are peppered with night-time scenes.

Consequently, the plays' texts are full of references to night in order to constantly remind the spectators to imagine darkness. This was not viewed as a problem, either by the dramatist or his audience. Indeed, despite being performed in real or artificial light, many of Shakespeare's plays take place mostly, or have key scenes set, at night-time. You just need to start thinking of night and bedtime scenes and *A Midsummer Night's Dream, Macbeth, Othello, Henry V*, and *Romeo and Juliet* spring to mind. Unsurprisingly, then, the plays are pullulating with time markers to alert us to when the action is taking place. A few examples, from the multitude, will suffice to make the point:

> INNOGEN: What hour is it?
> LADY: Almost midnight, madam.
> INNOGEN: I have read three hours then mine eyes are weak;
> Fold down the leaf where I have left. To bed:
> Take not away the taper, leave it burning;
> And if thou canst awake by four o'th'clock,
> I prithee call me. Sleep hath seized me wholly.
>
> *Cymbeline,* act II scene II

Orleans constantly refers to the night in *Henry V* while Hal himself is using the cover of its darkness. 'Will it never be morning?' Orleans plaintively asks at one point. 'Morning is coming' is a frequent refrain in Shakespeare plays. It alerts the audience that night is turning to dawn, even as they watch in broad daylight. Such alerts appear frequently throughout the plays. Puck announces, in *A Midsummer Night's Dream*, 'Fairy king, attend, and mark/I do hear the morning lark'. Richard, in *Henry VI Part Three*, declaims, 'See how the morning opes her golden gates', while in the same scene from *Cymbeline* just quoted, we also have,

> CLOTEN: Winning will put any man into courage. If I could get this foolish
> Innogen, I should have gold enough. It's almost morning, is't not?
> First Lord: Day, my lord.

Hamlet opens with the nightwatch in wintery darkness. Horatio draws the opening scene to a close with lines including the memorable,

> But, look, the morn, in russet mantle clad,
> Walks o'er the dew of yon high eastward hill:
> Break we our watch up; and by my advice,
> Let us impart what we have seen tonight.

Antony and Cleopatra is particularly replete in such combinations of night and morning imagery and audience imagination prompters. Time markers are especially crucial in this fast-paced, multi-scene, location changing extravaganza:

> CAPTAIN: The morn is fair. Good morrow, general.
> ALL: Good morrow, general.
> MARK ANTONY: 'tis well blown, lads:
> This morning, like the spirit of a youth
> That means to be of note, begins betimes.
> So, so. Come, give me that. This way. Well said.
> Fare thee well, dame.
>
> *Antony and Cleopatra,* act IV scene IV

Shakespeare, as he does in many plays, even the most tragic of all, puts in self-referential jokes which deliberately highlight that the audience is being asked to imagine total darkness despite being in full sunlight:

> For I spake to you for your comfort; did desire you
> To burn this night with torches
>
> *Antony and Cleopatra,* act IV scene IV

Such instances are found throughout the plays. They range from hundreds of small remarks made merely to orientate the audience, to some of the most famous scenes in the canon. Perhaps the most celebrated of these is the unforgettable opening to act II, scene v of *Romeo and Juliet.* There the emotions of the young lovers become entwined with the reality of night becoming day, whether they wish to accept it or not:

> JULIET: Wilt thou be gone? it is not yet near day:
> It was the nightingale, and not the lark,
> That pierced the fearful hollow of thine ear;
> Nightly she sings on yon pomegranate-tree.
> Believe me, love, it was the nightingale.
> ROMEO: It was the lark, the herald of the morn,
> No nightingale. Look, love, what envious streaks
> Do lace the severing clouds in yonder east:
> Night's candles are burnt out, and jocund day
> Stands tiptoe on the misty mountain tops.
> I must be gone and live, or stay and die.
> JULIET: Yond light is not day-light, I know it, I:
> It is some meteor that the sun exhaled,

To be to thee this night a torch-bearer,
And light thee on thy way to Mantua.
Therefore stay yet, thou need'st not to be gone.
ROMEO: Let me be taen, let me be put to death,
I am content, so thou wilt have it so.
I'll say yon grey is not the morning's eye,
'Tis but the pale reflex of Cynthia's brow;
Nor that is not the lark whose notes do beat
The vaulty heaven so high above our heads.
I have more care to stay than will to go:
Come, death, and welcome! Juliet wills it so.
How is't, my soul? Let's talk, it is not day.
JULIET: It is, it is, hie hence, be gone, away!

We have already seen how props such as torches and candles were used to indicate night-time or darkness. Nightdress conveyed the same message, and the point can be underscored by actors walking cautiously and feeling their way as though they were groping in the dark. We are alerted to the 'fact' we are witnessing a night scene in many different ways.

Consequently, the CSF audience, much like that of Shakespeare's own time, becomes accustomed to, and adept at, imagining they are witnessing a scene cloaked in gloom even when the sun is shining overhead. Shakespeare made very effective use of this imagined darkness. There is much play to be had, and thought provoking commentary to be made, from having actors pretending to be in the dark while performing to an audience who can see them perfectly clearly. Indeed, so many important dramatic effects were achieved via this route that the same techniques were used at the indoor theatre. Man-made lighting was utilised to ensure that the scenes that worked so well outside at the Globe in the summer could still be effective inside Blackfriars. To this end the indoor theatre was lit as fully as was possible at the time. So much so, that the necessity of trimming all the candles that they used to achieve this, is thought to be the origin of breaks between acts in the plays.

This was due to another of those paradoxes that arise out of authentic Elizabethan staging. Namely, that night-time scenes in Shakespeare actually are far more effective when viewed in daylight. This is not as surprising as it may first appear when we recall that he wrote them specifically for daytime performances. Shakespeare's plays are structured and patterned around light and dark imagery and scenes all predicated on the fact he is presenting night-time in daylight. Illusion and reality are doubly intertwined and set off against each other by this feature of Elizabethan staging. The audience is left believing that the current state of light or darkness is whatever the actor is currently telling them it is. Shakespeare, as was his wont, pushes his audience's imagination and tests their ability to keep the conjuring of balls of illusion and reality spinning in the air with the consummate skill of a master juggler.

Performing in daylight gives the actor a direct communication with the audience that is completely different from the darkness he looks out to in a standard theatre. This forms one of the main planks of the feelings of closeness whose virtues I have been extolling. As Andrew Stephen stated to me, 'The fact that the audience are in broad daylight when the show opens is important. It would be different if you were on the stage, the Theatre Royal or whatever, and the lights go down. You get a sense of the audience there but it is not the same, you can't see the whites of their eyes, as it were.'

For the audience in such settings, there is nowhere to hide and maintain anonymity, the actors can see you and direct lines straight at you. This in turn makes you more readily respond to them. When you are in that audience you are affected strongly by the way the people around you react to both the actor and to your own responses. This chain reaction creates a dynamic atmosphere and a feeling of sharing in the event. Spontaneous applause erupts naturally and is such a refreshing contrast to the dutiful clapping, reserved for the curtain calls of darkened auditoriums. Yet again, the CSF is recreating a facet of live performances from Shakespeare's own age. The poet and playwright John Marston reported that individual lines in *Romeo and Juliet* were applauded in this manner in 1598.

Over and above all of this, there are also some clear practical benefits to this shared daylight. A number of cast members told me how beneficial it was in allowing them to accurately gauge the make-up and mood of their audience, especially just before the plays begin. Moreover, playing in the open air means it is both easy and natural for actors to point at audience members while speaking. This can be useful at all kinds of times, especially in comedies or comic scenes. For example, when the text refers to a lawyer, a soldier, an old man, a young woman, well, the list goes on and on: bald men, portly men, aged men, almost anyone, in fact; the actor can indicate a member of the audience as being the person, or representative of the person, that he is speaking about.

I saw a lovely use of this in 2014 when a young girl sitting near me in the front row was skilfully included into *A Midsummer Night's Dream* without altering the spirit of the play in the slightest. On the contrary, it was enhanced by this momentary and textually appropriate inclusion. It was hard to tell who enjoyed this fleeting exchange most – the actor, the girl, the rest of the audience or the child's parents.

Simultaneous Staging

A key element of the CSF performances is what is known as simultaneous staging. So important is this concept of multiple actions occurring at the same time at the festival that it crops up at various points in this book. Simultaneous staging occurs in diverse ways at the CSF: action is taking place both on stage, and other cast members are in, or interacting with, the audience, when we have action behind the hedges or in highly visible off-stage areas, or when multiple actions are unfolding in a college garden at the same time. The key to the prevalence and efficacy of simultaneous staging lies in the fact that the performances take place, almost wholly, in natural light.

As we have just observed, this lack of separation in lighting between audience and stage has a profound bearing on how the plays are performed and received. As a spectator you can, as in normal daily life, look wherever you please at any given moment. You do not need to look only at the actor currently in a centre stage spotlight, nor do you need to look only at the character who happens to be the one speaking at that moment. The open, daylit stage space gives a tremendous amount of empowerment and control to each audience member. This makes each play a very individual experience as none of us will follow exactly the same action at precisely the same time. We will all experience slightly different plays despite always being engaged in everything that is going on, and doing so as part of an audience community with which we are continually interacting.

As a result, the CSF, like the Elizabethan theatre, is perfectly designed to exploit the many benefits of simultaneous staging. Everywhere is equally lit, be that stage, audience space or off-stage spaces to the side of where the main action unfolds. This, by its very nature, encourages the audience to pay attention to varied action and compare and contrast them. For the director it allows them to subtly modify one piece of action by counterpointing it with another. Cinema does something similar with split screens, though that is still more limited than the unobstructed range of the human eye, as well as being prescriptive as to what content is available.

Shakespeare wrote scenes that kept his actors moving about in various groupings on stage. Dominant centres of attention would be created then dissolved, and another would appear elsewhere. CSF directors must do likewise. 2013's *Richard III* was performed in the wide arc of St John's. Andrew Stephen gave a powerful performance as Richard. Andrew is a charismatic presence to begin with and Richard is a mesmeric character who is constantly the centre of attention in the play.

The popularity of, and layout at, St John's mean that a large audience is widely spread out and consequently not everyone can see the actors 'up close and personal'. As the CSF is built on the audience being in that very position, the actors move around and continually engage the crowd to compensate for any sense of distancing. Andrew Stephen was forever walking around, constantly making facial gestures, even in the brief periods where he was not at the centre of the story. As the play progressed I realised I was always aware of him, even out of the extreme corner of my eye when he was at the far end of the garden from me. It was almost impossible to take your eyes off him, which absolutely suited the play.

This did present David Salter a problem as director of this *Richard III*, however. There were times when it was essential to his production that the audience forgot about all the possibilities provided by simultaneous staging and instead paid close attention to a main piece of action or speech that did not involve the central character. Salter expertly choreographed the action to ensure we all did so. I remember once when Margaret was about to launch into a tirade that I knew was important to follow. Despite knowing this, I was still consciously more aware of Andrew as Richard off to my right where he was prowling on the outskirts of the audience. In the centre of the garden, the cast began to move in a pattern, catching one's attention. As they neared Margaret's position, they created a circle around her. You could not help but wonder what was happening at that point of the stage area. Your eyes were, albeit a touch reluctantly, dragged away from Richard and focused on Margaret when she began to speak. I mentioned how effective I thought this had been to Andrew Stephen and he replied,

> David Salter is extremely good at that, and they were very carefully blocked, those scenes. There is a degree of flexibility in them but very much there was this idea that most of those characters are not the best of friends, most of them have got issues with each other. But when somebody like Margaret was thrown into the mix, how does that make people behave – and to what extent? And Richard manipulates that scene whereby he sides with the others. He speaks as if representing them against Margaret, and therefore gets himself a little bit of leeway within that group. And, before Margaret gets there, he's obviously having a dig at Elizabeth and she's threatened to go and tell the King about what he's up to. With all those little dynamics about it's like shoals of fish when a shark comes and they suddenly clump together, or they disperse. And it was very carefully thought out, and I was very impressed with that because I thought a lesser director could have left that scene a lot more static with people in a sort of senate situation, and just having a conversation.

Such visual groupings make you concentrate your eyes and, consequently, ears on where the director wishes and where Shakespeare intended.

Although it sometimes needs to be constrained in this manner, the power of simultaneous staging is apparent in every CSF production. It is, though, perhaps most starkly seen in *Hamlet*. For this most famous of plays, the cast are faced with an audience already very familiar with seeing it in conventional theatre and in television and cinematic productions. Stereotypically we imagine Hamlet alone under a spotlight or speaking to a camera in close-up. You do not see anyone else or what they are doing. This is not always so at the CSF, nor was it in Shakespeare's time. The possibility of staging soliloquies this way is always available but it is not the only possibility. In Simon Bell's 2013 *Hamlet*, when the prince was delivering perhaps the most famous speech ever written, each audience member had choices. You could concentrate only on his mediation on the question of 'to be or not to be', or you could listen to and watch that while also being aware of Ophelia and/ or the unfolding plot of Claudius and Polonius. The symbolic crosses, which appeared throughout the play, were also in evidence and subtly coloured your response to the musings of the central character.

Similar benefits of concurrent action were exploited to superb effect throughout that performance of *Hamlet*. Many things were going on at one single point in time, which aided greatly in managing to stage the play's long action in less than two and a half hours. Most memorably, it allowed us to witness the psychological destruction of Ophelia as other action unfolded. It is possible, to a limited extent, to replicate this indoors in artificially lit theatres. However, outside performances entirely lend themselves to it due to the even spread of light and the way the eye is allowed to roam freely. When you are in a theatre the main action always has the brightest light and your eyes are drawn to it. The action is shaped by the stage you are looking at – a rectangular box reminiscent of nothing so much as a giant TV set with 3-D enhancements. Whereas, at the CSF with everybody both on and off-stage in the same, uniform light, watching multiple things simultaneously is completely natural.

Consequently, in this production of *Hamlet*, Ophelia was absolutely riveting. I loved the way she wistfully played with Hamlet's hair as *The Mousetrap* was being performed. She used small but tellingly tender gestures that spoke eloquently of genuine love. From seeing them I could feel the love and intimate relationship the couple had enjoyed before we ever get to meet them. I was swept by an apprehension of their pain and loss caused by the knowledge they could now never have the future they had planned for together. And yet, all the while, I was also watching the play wherein Hamlet was aiming 'to catch the conscience of a king' and studying Claudius closely for his reactions as he looked on the play within the play we were all witnessing in the grounds of Trinity College.

I would have been most unlikely to have seen or felt all these things, all at the same time in a regular theatre. In the overall production this might seem a small thing, but it affected everything for me, and I can only presume anyone else who was looking at that 'sideshow' action at that moment. My experience of the whole play was changed. If you did not catch that particular moment, there were many other intuitive touches which led to a cohesive web of imagery and symbolism that lit the relationships of the characters from within carefully crafted, multi-action scenes. Ophelia's relationship with Hamlet, her involvement in the whole story of the play in fact, was thrillingly clear that night. It is something that is so often swamped by other developments that it can be easily, if criminally, overlooked. That represented just one thread to the tapestry of relationships in the play; similar explorations were made of all the dynamics circling around the famous Danish court. They were all always in front of you, always in your mind, inter-weaving and circling back to Hamlet and his ongoing dilemma.

This resurrection of a staple of Elizabethan staging is evident throughout the festival and all the directors are keenly aware of its power and of the concomitant need to manage it carefully. Again, it is an aspect of outdoor staging that offers huge benefits, not least in helping to convey the full action of the play in a limited time span, but brings with it some directorial challenges. David Crilly explained:

> There's a depth of feel, it's a more naturalistic thing if there are other things happening on the stage as well. You have to strike a balance, obviously you don't want to mix focus and be confusing but it means you can see different things happening at the same time and as long as it is something that the audience can take in, in its totality, then it works. But if they are choosing whether to watch this action or that action, then you have a problem.

While Simon Bell noted that

> I think you direct instinctually and you know that because you're directing outdoors there is no centre point of light. You have to be very careful when you're blocking, where you put the actors, because you know that the audience are wondering who's speaking. You have to set levels of physical action sometimes and you have to say to an actor, 'you're doing too much because I need the audience to be looking in this direction'.

I have been writing about the CSF performances taking place in daylight, yet this is not the full story. The CSF Saturday charity performances take place in the afternoon and share the same two o'clock starting time as Shakespeare's company's performances at the Globe. However, the weekday and Saturday night shows begin at seven-thirty in the evening against a background of steadily dimming light, especially in the last weeks. There is a marked contrast in the amount of sunlight between the opening and closing weeks of the festival. In the opening week the sun sets at approximately twenty past nine, and by the close it is around an hour earlier. The changeover from the first to the second set of four plays occurs when sunset is almost exactly at nine o'clock.

The sky darkens as night approaches to a variable degree depending on both the dates of performances and the prevailing weather conditions. This gathering gloom has been an effective enhancement to plays where darkness, either actual or spiritual, increases as the play progresses. There are so many plays that end in the darkness of death, be they history plays like *Henry VI III*, *Richard II* and *III* or tragedies such as *Hamlet* and *Lear*. Plays such as *Romeo and Juliet*, *Othello* and *Macbeth*, in particular, with their gathering foreboding and fatal endings, are perfectly suited to the gradual dimming of the light.

In Shakespeare's time, although the performances were always in the afternoon, the roof of the partially covered Globe may have also brought about encroaching murkiness as the sun passed behind the coverings, especially on days of inclement weather. The effect would have been analogous to much of a CSF season. The very end of the festival, the third week of August, sees plays end in actual darkness. Crucially, though, the 'stage' and audience remain equally lit via portable lighting racks. This is the CSF equivalent of the artificial lighting conditions of the Blackfriars Theatre, where, again, both stage and spectating areas were customarily brightly and steadily illuminated.

It is known, also, that a few experiments with changeable lighting were made at the Blackfriars. For example, torch light was refracted through glass vials containing coloured liquid to create a haunting atmosphere. The short period of darkness in the plays in the second half of the CSF similarly affords directors the chance to experiment with creating special lighting effects. Simon Bell recalls one of his favourite implementations of these from *Romeo and Juliet* 2011:

> The bit where Romeo comes in at the end and looks at what he thinks is a dead Juliet, is actually not about Romeo at all. It is a big mistake to think so. Even though he's the one talking for ages, it's all about Juliet. So we set up the system as night fell that meant she was actually lit. It's one of my favourite effects. We set up this gauze tent on the podium on the stage. She's lying there and if you extend the light behind the podium the light bounces inside the white gauze and makes it glow. It's a most fantastic effect; it's a suffused light that you wouldn't get of a direct light source. And this beautiful white tent which was glowing with Juliet's wonder, it just *bathed* the audience.
>
> We didn't light Romeo at all. He had a nice silhouette. I turned the lights off, and under the stars, everything looked lovely and I got Tom [Tom

Synnott-Bell was playing Romeo that year] to walk behind the audience. I just said, 'you've just got to be a voice'. I instructed him to walk behind the audience and he was being their voice and they had no option but to look at how wonderful Juliet was. That atmosphere, you'd have to be outside for that. You can't ask an actor to go to the back of the stalls, it just becomes somebody at the back talking.

As in so many things, Robinson College is a partial exception to the general rule at the CSF. It is the only venue that has a dimmable lighting system. At the other venues, portable lighting is employed via banks of arc lights on moveable stands that have only the two settings – on or off.

In previous years at the CSF, lights on scaffolding were employed, which were very convenient as they could double for rigging on a ship where appropriate. However, these involved quite a bit of setting up and once they were put in position that was them set for the duration. The tripods, on the other hand, can be moved, albeit with a bit of effort and a great deal of patience in refocusing them. The light from them is regrettably stark and so can throw up some extreme and distracting shadows. On the plus side, they are more flexible than the scaffolding even though extremely careful planning is still necessary before they are put into action. A similar degree of planning is also required to manage the changing amount of sunlight as summer progresses. I asked Simon Bell if this was an issue and he responded,

> You have to take the changing sunlight and the potential need for these lights into account. So I was wondering, looking ahead to summer 2014, if I could have something in *Pericles*. And it did occur to me that I could not as it won't be really fully dark even by the climax. But then I'm doing *Merchant of Venice* later, in the second half, and I can have a lovely effect at the end with lanterns and fairy lights. So, yes, that is certainly an issue, but it can also be a blessing. When I used that tent, that glowing tent effect and that light in *Othello* and *Romeo and Juliet*, they were both in the second half which is the only time that it would work. We did that when it was fully dark.

Animals

A major factor in garden performances is that it is inevitable that 'extras' will appear who are neither trained nor predictable. The space is shared with the birds, insects and animals that normally inhabit such gardens. These are discussed at various points throughout this book, especially in the section on 'when things go wrong' in chapter five. There we will consider the downside of their unplanned intrusion, but there are sometimes benefits to be gained from creatures suddenly appearing. They can have the benefit of inspiring the actors to most apt and memorable improvisation.

An example of this occurred in a 2008 performance of *Othello* when a grasshopper landed on Othello. As Othello was about to leave the stage clear for one of Iago's soliloquies, Iago (Sean McGrath) leant across and took the grasshopper up onto his finger. He then proceeded to address the speech beginning 'And what's he then that says I play the villain? /When this advice is free I give and honest' to the grasshopper on his finger. As luck would have it, the grasshopper stayed there all the way until Iago ended by saying,

> So will I turn her virtue into pitch,
> And out of her own goodness make the net
> That shall enmesh them all.
>
> *Othello,* act II scene III

At which point Sean gently blew the grasshopper off his finger to tumultuous applause from a bewitched audience. If the actor is aware enough of the situation and can exploit the presence of a live creature it creates a powerful, seemingly magical, impression.

In 2013, a beautiful cat appeared with even more appropriate timing in *Richard III*, directed by David Salter. 'It's a blue cat, a stunning cat', he told me, during that run. 'And thankfully it knew its timing.' Andrew Stephen, playing Richard, picks up the story: 'There's this extraordinary cat in St John's. It looks like a Burmese but it's a sort of silvery, sort of lavender colour with a little diamanté collar, but it just owns the gardens and wanders about.'

It did more than wander one night, when Richard was supposed to make a long entrance, in act IV, scene IV, with much noise and buckling on of armour, before being interrupted. Andrew relived the incident as he recalled what happened next:

When Margaret's just walked off and I am supposed to come on, clanking in my armour, from the dark of the far stage, I can see the cat was on stage just walking around their legs as they were doing a scene. I come out there ready to do my line. As I am coming out of the darkness, the cat just walks towards me, blocking my path. So instead of saying my line as normal, I bent down and addressed my line to the cat, 'who intercepts me in my expedition to ...', and stroked the cat and carried on. It was very naughty, but it got a round of applause and I don't even know how many of the audience knew that it was the actual line that I was supposed to say and how many thought I was just ad-libbing the line, but it was the line and it was just perfect. Everybody can see the cat, I can't pretend it's not there because, at my peril, they'll just be giggling and watching it while I'm transfixed. So I have to sort of acknowledge it and then just get on with the scene. And it seemed the best thing to do at the time. It seemed to work because the cat had got its credit.

5

History and Practicalities

More than history can pattern, though devised
And play'd to take spectators
                                    The Winter's Tale, act II scene II

History, Practicalities, When Things Go Wrong

History

Founder David Crilly takes us back to how it all began:

> I was doing my DPhil at Magdalen College in Oxford, in music, and a friend of mine at Queen's College was doing a production of *The Taming of the Shrew* and asked me if I would be the musical director. I was to provide incidental music between scenes, John Dowland lute songs, together with some Elizabethan pastiche of my own. It was a strange time, since I was working as a public convenience attendant, a toilet cleaner to you and me, during the summer to help pay for my research. So, I'd go straight from work, sometimes still in my overalls, to open the show in the beauty of an Oxford garden, still smelling of bleach and disinfectant. I would need to go along to rehearsals to see where it would be appropriate to put in a musical interlude, see how long that would need to be, so I composed twenty-five seconds of pseudo John Dowland lute music for that. Up until that point I had no drama background and so I didn't really know anything about it.

When David went to the rehearsal it did not make any sense to him. His friend appeared disturbingly ego driven in the director's role and very discourteous in his dealings with everyone. David was upset at what he witnessed and reckoned that there was no reason things had to be like that:

I thought the guy was offhand and arrogant, the production was a complete ego-fest – on stage and off – and although I got on with the people outside of that environment I just couldn't stand the posturing that went on during rehearsals. All that angst for so little reward! I thought this is not the way it should be and that I could do a better job myself. So, I thought I would just give it a go. I thought that the only qualification that you needed to be a theatre director was to tell people that you were! I thought I'd start with *Macbeth* [laughing], something easy, lightweight, having never directed anything before in my life. So, I put an advert in the paper saying 'actors needed for a production of *Macbeth*, please apply to the artistic director'. Well, the applications came in, auditions happened, no one ever asked me if I'd done anything else before or if I was any good. They just assumed that I was experienced. Before that, I hadn't thought about directing something. I hadn't thought about the plays or anything like that.

I sounded out David as to why he had taken on the challenge of *Macbeth* as his first production and he told me that when he started to read *Macbeth*, he was

… just completely bowled over. I used to spend days just reading it back to back. I'd go through it and as soon as I'd finished the last line, I'd just go back to the start and go through it again. It's still the same now. Every time I encounter a play I see something else in it. There's always something that I've missed earlier on, and there's always something new to find in it. It's just endless. I just got owned by the majesty of it all to begin with, and imagining what it would look like. And because my encounter with Shakespeare had been in an Oxford garden, I started to visualise it in those terms. But I've never been able to just read a play, if you know what I mean. I always have images in my mind of how it would *look*.

The production, in Magdalen College Deer Park, was a success despite 1988 recording the wettest summer then on record. It rained every day of the three weeks the play was on. On the other hand, an unexpected boost to the production came from a strange source. At precisely the right time for advertising purposes, there were reports of supernatural occurrences in Magdalen College. A number of students had fled their rooms in the night, claiming to be plagued by visions and ghostly visitations. Newspapers pounced on this as a story as, it was sensationally claimed, the students reported this without knowing that building work on the side of the college nearest the river had uncovered a medieval hospital with accompanying graveyard. This grisly discovery of a burial site that predated the founding of Magdalen in 1458 was tailor-made for the tabloid press. The connection with *Macbeth* added to the irresistible nature of such a story for an easily deluded and excitable readership. As a result, the festival's large advertising hoarding on the corner of the college was featured in every photograph that accompanied the papers' lurid coverage of this 'story'.

After this initial boost, the festival went from strength to strength. In 1989 it was extended from three to five weeks for *Romeo and Juliet* at New College which, despite its name, was founded in 1379. Trepidation was understandably in the air at this bold move, especially as their first year had been a rain festival as much as a Shakespeare one. David remembers going to the ticket office on opening night and 'in contrast to 1988, 1989 was a lovely summer. I returned and the cast asked nervously if we'd sold any tickets. I told them that not only were we sold out for the opening night, but the show was sold out for the next two weeks!'

1990 saw a different kind of expansion, this time to two shows. These were *A Midsummer Night's Dream* (at New College) and *Hamlet* (in Magdalen College Deer Park). Running two plays proved a success and therefore 1991 saw *The Taming of the Shrew* and *Othello* in the same venues.

1992 brought further growth. That year featured two productions: *Macbeth* and *Romeo and Juliet* at New College plus an indoor *Hamlet* at the Oxford Union Debating Chamber. 1993 replicated the same format with *Much Ado about Nothing* and *A Midsummer Night's Dream* at New College and *The Merchant of Venice* in the Debating Chamber.

The festival had flourished and established itself quickly at Oxford, but there was a problem – David and Jan had moved:

That first production of *Macbeth* was the year my daughter was born. I was a poor student and Jan Burns, who's the executive producer of the company, had been working, but now she couldn't work anymore. So, although I had to finish my DPhil, we needed an income. I looked around for a job and the first job I saw was a lecturer in music at Cambridge. I applied for it and got it and moved across. So for the first two years in the summer I would go back to Oxford and carry on doing the productions there.

As he was running plays simultaneously at Magdalen College and New College in Oxford, it inevitably struck David that as he was at another very similar university, also with lots of college gardens, that he might as well put them on in Cambridge as well. As a result, for the next couple of years the festival was run at both universities at the same time. Early in the Oxford years Dave Rowan had appeared as an actor, as one of a cast of ten in New College in *The*

Taming of the Shrew. The two Davids, Crilly and Rowan, hit it off immediately and their creative Shakespearean partnership has continued ever since. For his first couple of years Rowan was there solely as an actor but then when Crilly had been called away on a couple of emergencies, Rowan had stepped in to keep the direction going.

Crilly recalls, 'David Rowan had directed *Hamlet* in 1992 and done a great job, so that was the start of his shift away from acting into directing for us (though he's been on stage, to cover for sick or injured actors, almost continually since then).'

At the same time as the festival was expanding, David Crilly was needed full time in Cambridge. So, Dave Rowan stayed in Oxford and oversaw it, combining his acting roles with directing. Like Crilly with *Macbeth*, Rowan jumped in at the deep end, and he laughed as he informed me that

> my previous experience was only in youth theatre and helping out Dave Crilly and suddenly I was directing *Hamlet*! 'Cos, you know, if you are going to direct your first Shakespeare you may as well make it *Hamlet*. That was an inside venue, the Oxford University Debating Chamber. We had two outside venues too. It was big in Oxford, a bit like it is in Cambridge. We had three companies doing plays, but for the last two years we just did one show that I presided over. I was overseeing it for Dave, a lot of managing actors and things. It was fun, both directing and acting.

It may have been fun running the festival at both universities, but it was becoming impractical and was placing an unsustainable drain on resources. Rowan continued, 'Then David decided just to have it in Cambridge, even though New College, Oxford did very well every year. David was living in Cambridge, it was less stress, more manageable in Cambridge. It was good to have less driving between the two!' In addition, the environment in Oxford had changed, too. The success of the festival had led others to try and duplicate the Oxford Shakespeare Festival's success, and not all of the competition was scrupulous in how it went about its business. In any case this environment inevitably had an effect on the plays that could viably be staged. David Crilly recalls that time:

> A couple of other companies sprung up doing the same thing at the same time and an absurd situation developed where the director of each company would ring the others to find out who would be doing *A Midsummer Night's Dream*, or *Romeo and Juliet*, or *Macbeth* – the idea of doing *Pericles* or *Richard II* would have been unthinkable in that environment. In trying to establish the Company as something viable, we were having to rely on doing

the favourites each year. The problem got worse as more companies jumped on the bandwagon, so the move to Cambridge was well-timed.

Looking back now, relocating the festival to Cambridge seems an inevitable journey and a smooth ride, but it could have all been very different. Uncertainty and risk were very much in evidence back at the beginning. In Oxford David Crilly was on 'home territory'. He got into Magdalen quite smoothly as it was his *alma mater*. It was true he now lectured at Cambridge but his background was Oxford and to this day he very much sees himself as an Oxford man. Even in Oxford where David was, as he put it, 'part of the gang', the situation was hazardous, so one can easily imagine the increased danger of pitfalls in Cambridge colleges.

The 1991 production of *Othello* in Magdalen College Deer Park sadly proved to be the last one at David's old college. David explains,

> Our Othello blacked up for the role – that wasn't as bad as it sounds – but one night we forgot to clean the shower after the show and we received complaints from the domestic staff. It shows how precarious our foothold with the colleges actually is, since when we applied again the following year the domestic bursar couldn't remember quite what the problem was, but remembered that he'd had a complaint from somewhere.

That vague memory was enough to refuse to allow any future performance. The following year, the only way the organisers could be sure of the co-operation of the warden in keeping *Hamlet* running at the Oxford Union Debating Chamber 'was to keep her supplied with gin and cigarettes for the three weeks of our stay'.

It is easy to imagine the resistance David met with when he first started approaching the colleges in Cambridge. He would go to a college and say, 'we'd like to take over your gardens for three weeks. Is that okay?' Unsurprisingly, the answer was in the negative. A period of very patient and painstaking negotiation was required. David managed to persuade the bursars and the Masters of Colleges to contact their counterparts in Oxford for reassurance that the festival was run responsibly and nothing was damaged in the staging of the plays in the gardens. As we will see elsewhere, this has not been 100 per cent the case but it has nearly been so, and it is certainly true that all efforts are made to make it so.

Eventually David overcame the misgivings of one college and once the CSF had its foot in the door, it had a point of reference. They now could demonstrate, as well as declare, their conscientiousness in preserving the environment of their garden stage space and surroundings. The CSF have spent a lot of time honing what they do to make sure that they do not impact negatively on the grounds. The seats for the customers are rolled along the grounds gently to ensure no damage is done to the lawns and care is taken not to leave any visible alteration to the grass, flowers, trees or any other vegetation. The first college was the key, after that the CSF were able to contact other Cambridge colleges with the confidence of having a local reference that would report that it was fine to allow them to stage plays in the gardens. Slowly but surely, the CSF gained the trust of the colleges. David Crilly fondly remembers the change from fragile beginnings to established presence:

> In time it became 'the Shakespeare Festival and we could say, 'so your delegates will be able to see this cultural event on their doorstep'. And I think it started to permeate into the mindsets that actually, we're a good thing to have and we're an asset to the college rather than a nuisance. And that we are something that they can include in their literature.

I was intrigued to note that there is still a Shakespeare festival running in Oxford called the Oxford Shakespeare Company and asked David Crilly what the connections were between that and the festival he had begun there and then later moved to Cambridge. He replied,

> We were the first company to present a Shakespeare Festival in Oxford, though some student and amateur groups did short runs of plays from time to time. Sarah Davey, who had played Kate in *The Taming of the* Shrew, the nurse in *Romeo and Juliet* and Desdemona in *Othello* for the festival, decided to set up her own company called Bold and Saucy Theatre Company to present plays at Wadham College.

Crilly decided to incorporate her production into the Oxford Shakespeare Festival and share publicity for the event. This worked well but came to a close with the relocation to Cambridge. David finished off by saying that

> Sarah got married and has children now, and although she's still active in theatre – mainly teaching, last I heard – she handed over the company to someone else. They changed the name to the Oxford Shakespeare. Until just a few months ago I still held the rights to the Oxford Shakespeare Festival as a limited company – but I've now relinquished that as I don't plan to return to Oxford any time soon.

Practicalities

Each year the CSF endeavours to produce eight plays over a period of six weeks, plus an extra week to give one or two plays an extended run. Four plays start in the second week of July and run for three weeks. Then the other four begin in the first week of August. Each play also has one Saturday matinee charity performance. The official Facebook page proudly announced, after the last performance in 2013, 'The Cambridge Shakespeare Festival 2013 ended last night. Eight productions, six venues, 182 performances and approximately 455 hours of stage time.' These productions attracted over 20,000 attendees.

As you can imagine, there are many practicalities to consider in running such an enterprise as this and, as ever in life, most of these revolve around finance. It is never the easiest of areas and becomes even more of a minefield given David Crilly's attitude, which is, to his great credit, one of art first and money a very distant secondary consideration.

I learnt that this was his approach many years before I ever thought of writing this book. I was very enthused by my first visit to the CSF and so the next year I booked various tickets soon after they were announced. My enthusiasm had, alas, made me forget my busy and volatile summer schedule and I had not yet discovered the flexible season ticket options. As it transpired I could not go to three out of the first four productions on the dates I had booked. I contacted David and he said, 'Oh, don't worry, just go when you can or go to other plays in the second half of the season. It'll be fine, just give my name where they sell tickets and say I said it was OK.'

I had not realised that when I called him it was on his private phone. I learned that was the case, years later, when interviewing Jan Burns. Jan has been executive producer of CSF since 1996 and manages the financial and practical sides of the festival, in addition to being the company's literary advisor on text editing. She told me, 'We put some personal mobile numbers in the information so we can't go out for a meal or a break without members of the public ringing us. And they ring and they say, "We want to come tonight but we're not sure if it's going to rain." And they want a bit of reassurance and you tell them that it's going to go on.'

If they are uncomfortable with the weather forecast, or have a clash of appointments like I did, they get good news. Jan continued,

> I think we have a policy that is good and it's quite unique: if you have a ticket for tonight and it rains you can use that for any other night, any other show, so it's fully transferable. Now most theatre companies can't operate like that and my accountant will probably be saying that we shouldn't, that we're shooting ourselves in the foot.

The festival comes before bullet-ridden toes in David's mind, and he eschews booking fees or additional credit card charges. This admirable attitude also affects his approach to scheduling in two major ways. Firstly, the question of which plays go on at which venues: 'I like to think that scheduling isn't too tied up with finance, though to a certain extent it must be. I accept that some productions will fail financially, but as long as we have a balance I'm happy to live with that in order to have a vibrant and varied programme.' David added , 'I expect *Richard II* and *Pericles* to die financially in 2014, for example.' In this he was more or less correct – the latter did slightly better than expected though the former attracted far fewer than even he had feared.

There is also the matter of the total number of plays. It is nearly always eight plays per season but there were just six in 2009, for example. I asked David about this and he responded, 'Yes, just six shows in a season!' He pointed out, forcefully, if with a laugh, that organisations with many more resources and months of rehearsal time still fell far short of such a number. David carried on:

> It has never been something as fixed as any kind of policy on my part and is much more to do with how I'm feeling at the time of planning the festival. That sounds quite fickle, doesn't it? Well it probably is! It's also to do with the programme I'd like to do, combined with the likely availability of the venues I want. The thing to remember is that, although we have to run the festival as a business, I never think of it in those terms and just think about what I'd like to do and cut the cloth accordingly.

The purchase and upkeep of costumes presents both financial and practical challenges. Bob and Bill Wellman noted this in their marvellous report to me of their years following the CSF:

> David Crilly and Jan realise the importance of maintaining their large wardrobe of period costumes and props. It is a colossal job each year getting garments cleaned, repaired and ready for each play and to fit each actor. Every year forty or more actors need costumes to appear in eight plays. Many of the actors play several parts in one play and so will need more than one costume. We admire David Crilly and Jan for managing this mammoth task for twenty-six years. We know they search the country for sales of theatrical costumes and are sometimes lucky to find an opera company selling ideal garments and props.

Jan let me know about one such source: 'We buy a lot of costumes from the RSC when they have sales on. We go to Stratford and queue up nearly all night. At the moment we have someone in *Richard III* wearing a breastplate from there – we recycle them! But, a lot of people who buy from the RSC don't want them for theatre companies, they want them because they've got names and things inside. It's frustrating, especially because people buy them for their own personal reasons and then they turn up on eBay because they're making a profit on these things.

The precious costumes can, as the Wellmans observed, be found in a variety of places. Sometimes they are discovered through personal ads. The following tale appeared in the *Independent on Sunday* online edition:

> David Grilly [*sic*], fifty-one, and Jan Burns, forty-five, from the Cambridge Shakespeare Festival drove through the night from Liverpool to be here at 5.30 a.m., so they could scoop up cheap costumes and props for this summer's festival. They are clutching six enormous bin bags of costumes and wait nervously for the total to be totted up on a calculator. Unlike the 'celebrity' items, the only limit to what you buy is how much you can carry. Propping up a bag of doublets and breeches, Ms Burns' hands shake as she gets out her credit card to settle the final tally of more than £700.

Once obtained there is the matter of wardrobe upkeep. Some costumes are involved in fight scenes, others clothe bodies dragged along, or thrown to, the ground. A tight fit on one actor may be problematic the following year when a bulkier actor is playing the same role. Matching and mending, therefore, are essential CSF skills. Jan says, 'Oh, I can sew. I've always been able to sew and I've always been interested in that sort of thing.'

The acting fraternity have to chip in here too; in the section on bawdy in the following chapter, you will read the visiting Erin Weinberg marvel at actor Charlotte Ellen sewing a codpiece together at seven o'clock in the morning for that day's show. Tessa Hatts tells a good story regarding the gender split in relative enthusiasm for this necessary chore:

> The CSF uses all my skills! I'm very good at making props out of nothing, for a very low budget. I'm good with scissors, paper, glue, string, that sort of thing. And I'm quite good at sewing, which is highly necessary. The hem's always the wrong length, and not just mine, but other people's. We try to encourage people to do their own sewing, but some things are just a bit trickier. If it's a hem or a straight line, just the seam has come undone, I start it off and tell them what you do… and then how to go over and over in the same spot until it's done. And the men are really good, they often say, 'Wow, I've learned something new, thank you.' They really are thrilled, they now know how to do it, and don't have to rely on some girlfriend. But the girls are always a bit grumpy about it, they think they're being made to sew because they're girls, but they're not, they're being made to sew because everybody at the Cambridge Shakespeare Festival has to help when costumes need to be altered.

Costumes and their upkeep once obtained were of similar significance in Shakespeare's day. The costumes were the most valuable of an acting company's assets and among the most difficult to replace as they were cripplingly expensive. Henslowe's aforementioned inventory from the end of the sixteenth century lists high payments on luxurious clothing and accessories such as cloaks, doublets, velvet breeches, lace and cloth along with details of their design and ornamentation.

Companies back then were helped out from a surprising source. Thomas Platter, a visitor from Basle, noted, in his diary of 1599, that 'it is the English usage for eminent lords or knights at their decease to bequeath and leave almost the best of their clothes to their serving men, which it is unseemly for the latter to wear, so that they offer them then for sale for a small sum to the actors'. The CSF has an enthusiastic supporter and regular attendee from Cambridge, Margaret Steen, who is a modern equivalent, though without charge in her case, in her donations of dresses, material for costumes (such as curtains) and even items of furniture.

It has been claimed that acting companies in Shakespeare's day spent more on their costumes than they did even on the theatre buildings in which they performed. While they take a huge chunk of the CSF's expenditure, they are secondary to the major financial burden of the festival – that of paying for accommodation in Cambridge at the height of summer for all the actors, directors and other bodies needed to run all their rehearsals and performances through summer.

The cost of this accommodation has changed out of all proportion in relation to inflation since the CSF began. Putting everyone up in or near the city centre, for approximately two months at the height of the Cambridge tourist season, is obviously a heavy burden. It was not always so, though, as Jan Burns remembers:

> If I go back ten years, we got college accommodation at student rates and the colleges were happy. But then they cottoned onto the fact that there's a big tourist industry out there and summer schools from abroad, so they can charge what the hell they like. So, it's not far off small hotel prices now. So my biggest battle now by far is the accommodation for forty people for two months in the centre.

In addition to the competition from those summer schools, there is also the even more price-raising presence of big-spending business corporations who book conventions and conferences at the colleges throughout the summer. As if this was not more than enough pressure on accommodation, the CSF also coincides with a number of graduation ceremonies which further the demand and subsequently raise the cost of accommodation in the period.

The actors are currently housed together in Robinson College accommodation, away from the rest of the college, conveniently near the custom-built amphitheatre there.

The CSF was recently supported by a four-figure sponsorship deal with the law firm Penningtons. This developed from a previous sponsorship arrangement. Near the end of the first decade of the new millennium, a legal firm called Charles Russell opened an office in Cambridge. James Stephen, now of recent sponsors Penningtons, recalls it well: 'We were a new name in town and as part of that, what we looked to do was to hook up with a local event in the usual commercial way of commercial organisations to support something we thought was really a great local event, but would also increase our profile, as a new local law firm.'

As a result, Charles Russell co-sponsored the CSF with John Lewis. James remembers it as being both a success in terms of 'getting the brand name out there' and an enjoyable experience. Charles Russell then decided to close their Cambridge offices and asked the staff to relocate to, or at least work in, London. No one in their Cambridge office was keen to do so and the entire office instead joined Penningtons.

James picks up the story again at that juncture:

We had had a thoroughly good experience with David in sponsoring the festival, and, of course, it's a wonderful event. So, we, as Penningtons, wanted to do it again and for exactly the same reason, because Penningtons as a brand was a new brand in the market. And, therefore, we agreed with David to do a two-year sponsorship, covering 2012 and 2013.

There is no doubt that James views the sponsorship as having been a big success:

We will do a number of hosted events where we'll do an informal, fun picnic and drinks before the performance. And then we'd also offer clients and contacts tickets if they'd like to go on their own with their families. So, that's a very nice thing to be able to do. It's not just the business people you deal with. It's really nice to be able to say, look, would you like to take the children to this? So, that's a lovely, lovely thing. And we recognise some people would prefer to just go on their own, but they would really appreciate us giving them that opportunity. Other people really enjoy coming along to a sort of picnic-type event and the company of everyone else who goes along.

You want to support the local community. And it ticks the box that we need it to tick from a business perspective, but it also gives us the extra benefit of supporting the ability of people locally to enjoy the festival. You, of course, want to get your name out there. But it's one of those lovely, unusual and slightly Cambridge-y things almost, in the way that it's done. It's a wonderful thing to take guests to, and clients and contacts as a thank you for their loyalty or just as a way of chatting further with them. And we had great feedback from taking them. It's lovely to support something that benefits the wider community. Of course it benefits us, otherwise we wouldn't be doing it commercially. But it's a nice opportunity to do both.

Printing the programmes is another task to be managed. There are currently two programmes, each covering one half of the festival. They provide a synopsis of each play and interesting information about each college venue. They also contain biographies and photographs of each actor. Originally there was a single festival programme, containing information on the whole event but David Crilly was concerned that as the festival progressed the information in that programme was becoming more and more redundant. Thinking that audience members would rather have a programme only for each individual play, he changed to that format in 2008. It was a change that lasted only one year because, as he explains,

> How wrong I was! I was overwhelmed by comments from people who attend more than one production who wanted a return to 'the Festival Programme'. Apparently there are lots of people who keep them as souvenirs and have quite a collection. That still left me with the problem of selling programmes with half the information out of date.

David's son, Josh, proposed a compromise solution that has been in use ever since, with programmes being divided into parts one and two. Programmes can be bought from the tables where cloak-room style tickets are bought, or pre-paid ones collected, at a table across the entrance to the garden space to be used for each performance.

Author and Cambridge resident Ali Smith gives us a fictional insight into working at the festival and helping out with practical duties in her Booker-listed new novel *How to be both*:

> H worked last year at the Shakespeare Festival in the summer as a ticket-seller and cleaner-upper for £10 a night ... She was selling and tearing tickets for *As You Like It* at St John's. She was doing a double shift and for the evening showing the audience was unexpectedly huge, there were nearly three hundred people – about seventy was usually more like it. So I was ripping tickets like mad, she says, and doing my eleven and fifteen times tables, fifteen was full price and eleven was concession and we started with almost no change, two five-pound notes, one single pound coin and a handful of pennies, which meant that for a bit I could only really sell tickets to people who had the right money. And it was a really cold evening so the people queuing were cold as well as furious, I know exactly how cold it was because I had no jacket.

The festival organisers are well aware that it can get cold even in summer in the UK. As they cannot heat the gardens, they do the next best thing by offering a way of heating the people themselves. This they achieve via big urns of mulled wine that is served every interval. Ali Smith describes this from the perspective of the person on the other side of the perennial queue for the hot beverage:

After the tickets I had to serve two hundred and seventy five people polystyrene cups of mulled wine from the urn and they all wanted it because it was so cold, and there was only me, and the urn would only work if you tipped it, which was quite hard because it was heavy and really hard to hold a cup to without it just emptying out all over the cup and my hand. And I'd seen *As You Like It* one-and-a-half times that day already; I'd seen the last half in the morning and the whole run-through in the afternoon and wanted to go home but I couldn't because my next job was to hold the torch after the second half to show people where to walk in the dark and how to get to the exit. So I spent a lot of the second half trying to keep warm next to the urn, actually with my arm round the urn a lot of it, and trying to read though it was nearly dark and I wasn't allowed to use the torch because it would distract from the performers.

Still, I am sure everyone else was happy that night and it should be pointed out that actors and directors are usually the ones who 'muck in' and carry out these necessary chores. They all help wherever they can, from selling tickets and programmes, dispensing the mulled wine, clearing away the rubbish and the chairs to cleaning toilets. It is not unusual to be guided out of a garden by a torch held by a Juliet or Cleopatra or to find the artistic director fighting with a blocked drain or malfunctioning set of lights.

When Things Go Wrong

This book has been unashamedly celebratory in honour of all the wonderful things the CSF has brought to its audiences, but it would not be possible that every production of every play would be a success. Live theatre, by its very nature, runs the risk of not always being successful. Good productions can have a bad night, many things can go wrong and this is especially so in such a changeable environment. More rarely, whole productions can be 'off' for one reason or another: inappropriate directors can be hired, a 'bad apple' somehow can get through the cast audition system and upset the whole community. So, I have not loved every single performance I have seen. Additionally, such things are, in any case, very subjective and are affected by one's own personal mood and life at the time of attending.

Notwithstanding this, as ever with Shakespeare productions, even in such cases, there is always something learnt, always something to take away as a good memory. In addition to that, all regular CSF goers have a special fondness for when certain things go wrong, as these times remain fresh in our minds and are usually the first thing we tell our fellow regular attendees when we next see them. The 'all being in it together' ethos engenders a spirit in the core audience of never leaving as long as the play is going on, no matter what happens or however wet it becomes.

Weather and Insects

That bane of outdoor events in the UK, rain, is not usually as troublesome as you might first suppose. Generally speaking the plays just continue and the enchanted spectators stay watching them. So seldom are shows cancelled that I am always really surprised to hear one has been called off. I have been to one show where the rain was torrential and this spectacular deluge did drive all but a handful of us away by the end, but even then the cast soldiered on to the saturated conclusion.

Perhaps the festival handles precipitation so well due to its drenched debut year of 1988. David Crilly remembers,

> It rained every day of the three weeks. One night our audience insisted we go ahead despite the sodden conditions. When we said it was too dangerous to do the fight scenes they just asked us to cut them from the show, the thinking being that it was silly to cancel a two-hour performance because of a two-minute fight scene.

Cast member Helen Meadmore surprised me by telling me a performance had to be abandoned due to a downpour, but it turned out this was indirectly due to the rain, not the rainfall per se:

> First of all, any sword fights or anything like that, you have to be extra careful when the ground is wet. Second of all, if people are rolling around so much on the floor, you have to be very, very wary of the costumes, and because they can just get ruined in a minute, but the third thing is that, however much water there is on the stage, even if we are willing and able to carry on, we may have to stop. Last year with *The Taming of the Shrew*, there was only one performance that we stopped. It was in the second half. Not because of the opening scene of the second half was all people throwing around and jumping around, and of course they kept slipping, but it was the fact that the audience, who didn't have a tree or anything to hide under like they did at *Comedy of*

Errors this year [2013], all put up their umbrellas, but they couldn't then hear anything because the noise of the rain hitting the umbrellas was so loud.

There are things to comfort yourself with in the rain; it gets rid of any annoying summer midges. You can imagine that it was the same for Shakespeare attendees back when he was on stage himself. There is a long-standing tradition of downpours causing problems. Even the famous Shakespeare Jubilee in Stratford-upon-Avon, 1769, organised by the renowned actor and theatre manager David Garrick, had to cancel its long-planned pageant of Shakespeare characters due to a downpour.

Continuous rainfall obviously has a bad financial impact, as Jan Crilly (*née* Burns) told me in 2013: 'The last two years have been good but before that we had several wet summers on the trot and it was financially a disaster and we were on the point of wondering how much more of it we could take.'

It may surprise you more to hear that sunshine can also cause problems. My wife Pia and I spent *Richard II* moving carefully ahead of a blinding sun as it inched its rays along the rows of seats before we could seek full sanctuary from it, further back, at the interval. Those on stage were affected too. Elena Clements recalled, 'That was the most sun I have ever had in my eyes and I don't say anything in that scene and the reviewer wrote that I looked bored! I tell you what, it's because I couldn't see. I couldn't believe the light that was in my eyes. There were some moments where I thought, "I've got to get down from this tower because I'm going to get blinded!"'

In the chapter on venues, we looked at unexpected encounters with animals, though a more pressing problem is the sudden appearance of certain insects. If you are playing the part of a character who is supposed to be asleep on the ground and you feel a bug scurrying up your leg, it is bad enough, but if you are supposed to be dead or drugged into unconsciousness it can be much worse. Helen Meadmore encountered this problem when playing Titania:

> Fair enough, she's asleep, she's not dead, so she can actually move if need be, but oh my goodness me. I've learned how to control it now and cover myself with my dress, but the number of times I've had bugs crawling on me. I just want to just go 'aaargh' ... and you have to find a time when somebody walks on from the other side and the audience members look over there and I just quickly go down and brush them off.

Worse still are the bugs that sting or bite. Helen made the mistake of supplementing her dress with flowers, thereby attracting bees. 'It's not so bad if you've got a costume that covers you but with my Titania costume I've got my arms bare, my legs bare and also, although most of the flowers I have around me are fake ones, occasionally if I find a nice flower that's just fallen or whatever I'll put it around me and there have been times when I thought, "Oh God, that's probably the wrong thing to do."' I asked Tessa Hatts if she had encountered this problem and she replied,

> Yes, Romeo was stung by a wasp last year as he lay dead and he had to just lie there and be stung. And for myself, one time this thing bit me. I didn't know what it was, but it was on my face. I was ready for a wasp; I thought 'this could be a wasp be ready to be in pain and not move.' I didn't feel a sting and I didn't think it had bitten me but then there was a bump. Still, it was gone by the next morning so it wasn't something nasty.

Missing Actors, Lines and Even Trousers

With casts being so small, and many actors already playing two or more roles, the prospect of a cast member being injured, falling ill or otherwise becoming disbarred from appearing is an alarming one. It is also bound to happen sometimes. The first occurrence was way back in 1990 for *Hamlet* in Magdalen College Deer Park. David Crilly can still recall it vividly:

> This was the *Hamlet* when our Claudius had some kind of breakdown after the opening night. We didn't find out until forty minutes before we were due on the following evening. He'd gone back to London, with his costume, and so I made my acting debut. I tried going on with the book but made so many mistakes that I abandoned it and carried on without for the remaining three weeks of performances.

He added, laughingly, 'It was a triumph, as you can imagine.' The lead in *Othello* was similarly afflicted some years later while *Cymbeline* and *Pericles* in 2013 and 2014, respectively, lost actors to broken bones.

I asked what on Earth they did in these situations and it transpires that there are two main ways of saving the day. Firstly, there is the ever-adaptable Dave Rowan who is, not at all reluctantly, often taken from directorial duties to fill in on stage. Most commonly, and even more non-reluctantly it seems, in female roles. Jan explained, 'We laugh because every year Dave Rowan gets to do someone. He's excellent at learning lines quickly and he would rather go on than have it cancelled, and in fact I think he misses performing, especially if it involves a dress and a wig. He'll throw himself into it. And it's great for us, so he's the main back up.'

I asked what happened if he was unavailable. Jan told me that 'we have actors and actresses that have done previous years and for whatever reason can't do it, but they love to come back and they love to see the shows'. This very handily means that there are many occasions when actors are, in effect, available and on hand in Cambridge. Jan continued, 'We've got a core of actors and actresses that we can ring up and say, well, look, we know you couldn't do the whole festival but are you free for … could you step in? And they love that as well.'

Actors can also forget where they are or what they are supposed to say. Daniel Simpson recollected a crazy moment from a performance of *Antony and Cleopatra* where an actor walked on to the stage, forgot his lines, and then thought, for some reason, 'Oh, God I shouldn't be here, I am not in this bit.' Worrying that he was spoiling the scene, our forgetful thespian looked for a way out. With assumed nonchalance, he sauntered over to, and past, Daniel. As he passed, he tapped Daniel on the shoulder, saying 'Thank God I remembered that I am not in this scene.' He then scampered off, happily content at having, in his mind, saved the situation. 'But you are!' whispered Daniel, urgently. However it was too late, he was left waiting in a state of perplexed anxiety one can only imagine as he watched the fast-receding head of his dialogue partner disappear into the distance.

Less dramatically, but more commonly, actors will freeze or forget their next line. There is no safety net at the CSF, as there are no helpful prompters in attendance. Daniel advised me, 'I've learned one trick and that is not to stop. If you stop the audience normally will pick that up – if you're in the middle of a sentence and you stop. The trick is to keep going even if it's gobbledegook, it's Shakespearian gobbledegook, so it's very special.' Tessa Hatts advised me that the trick is to say 'quick, couch me awhile and mark it', which 'apparently is a phrase that actors use in Shakespeare if they get stuck. They say that and walk offstage and look at their lines and then come back on again.'

Some things are harder to ad-lib, though, and Rory Thesby remembers one such time when a co-actor had forgotten to put on his trousers!

I was on the stage in *The Taming of the Shrew* about ten years ago when a lad called Thomas came on wearing his cloak. Then he took his cloak off because he was revealing his real identity, he was travelling in disguise, and he said, 'I'm Vincentio', or whatever it is, then looked down and he was just wearing tights, he said, 'and I've forgotten my trousers'. So, we had to carry on doing this scene with him wearing his top and just a pair of tights, and an enormous pair of modern boxer shorts showing through the tights.

Corpsing and Horseplay

Having read how much fun there is at the CSF, you will not be surprised that laughter abounds and can slip out at inappropriate times onstage. Actors call this corpsing and fight hard to restrain themselves from succumbing to it. One time *A Midsummer Night's Dream* was moved indoors to escape a torrential downpour. This proved relatively successful but the audience were packed in, pressed right up to the action. Helen Meadmore picks up the story:

> Titania was lying on top of Bottom, falling asleep … and Bottom has an ass's head and as I moved the head around, we were so close to the front of the audience that this poor dog who was literally as close as I am to you, started to growl. And Eddie, who makes me laugh anyway, he hasn't got the smallest of tummies, let's put it that way, and he laughed and his tummy started jiggling. And of course then that made me giggle and I just couldn't stop laughing.

Not all such laughter happens unintentionally, a few long-term cast members are known for attempts to force their colleagues to corpse to see how they cope. Sometimes this can threaten to get out of hand. Robin Owen recalls, 'Harry Winterbottom is a funny guy, he's one of those actors who likes to sometimes play around and sometimes it's to play little pranks on people to try and make you giggle when you shouldn't be giggling.' Harry had been trying all through a week of *Richard II* to get Robin to corpse during a scene of high tension when two characters are spoiling for a fight and throwing their gauntlets to the ground.

> He was trying to make me laugh, he kept trying to do it. Come the last night he tries to make me laugh and he's saying his lines and he's purposely not looking at me, doing funny things with his eyes, the audience couldn't really see but I could see. So, I didn't look at him because I knew this was coming and I thought, right, I'm going to give him his comeuppance here. I usually have to go head to head with him, there's no contact but this time I gave him a little shove, and when I did he actually went all the way over and I was thinking, 'Oh no!'. He got up, he was fine and we played on but I was thinking, have I done too much? I didn't push him to make him fall over, I just wanted to give him a little shove. But we carried on and it was just one of those things where I felt in a way I'd given him his comeuppance and a lot of the members of the cast afterwards were high-fiving me.

Despite Harry taking it all in good spirits and just getting on with things, Robin is rather regretful about this incident, admitting that 'it's one of the most unprofessional things I've ever done in my life, to push another actor over on stage, but maybe it taught him a lesson about trying to make people laugh on stage'.

My final example of on-stage mishap is a less light-hearted one and so very out of character for the festival. It was drama of a different kind one wet night in Cambridge. Daniel Simpson had the proverbial baptism of fire one evening in his first year. The omens were not good to begin with.

As you say, you can be very, very close to the audience, especially when it's full, and people are sitting in front of the seats. Sometimes it's so busy that you'll actually lose exits and entrances and that happened that night. And so we had a load of French students in, closer than I am to you to the performance space, and we had in our cast a very funny, very angry, very strong-willed actor who was known to have a bit of a short fuse, a bit of a temper.

The weather had been beautiful up until that night but on this packed occasion the actors were rained upon, much to the anger of the central character in our story. Meanwhile, one French student was kindly explaining what was happening on stage to his friends who were asking him questions. Daniel could see that this was what was happening but the actor with his back to the students could only hear a steady stream of French from right behind him and presumably thought it was bored French boys just chattering. Daniel continued,

Our two characters were conversing, and I remember looking out and thinking, well, this guy is not happy. The rain was pouring down, it was flowing off his face; the actor, rather than the character, had a face like thunder. This fellow actor of mine was getting angrier and angrier. I could see it in his eyes because I was talking to him so closely I could see the rain dripping off his nose and his face was just darkening and darkening.

Then suddenly he turned to this French kid and just shouted, 'Will you shut the fuck up?' Right on the stage, he screamed at this kid. I've never heard of such a thing: and I was absolutely stunned. And so were they, he's a very big, strong guy, and I think they were shocked and probably slightly terrified of this guy. I wasn't long out of drama school at this point, it was the summer after I graduated, and I couldn't believe it.

What surprised Daniel almost as much was the way this incident polarised opinion within the festival. When they got off stage Daniel discovered that quite a lot of people thought the actor who had lost his temper had actually done the right thing: 'I was horrified. I would quite happily stop a play and tell people to turn a phone off; I would take a phone off someone, actually. But I understood that this had a different slant on it and I was horrified, frankly.' Thankfully, something like this is very much the exception to the rule.

Competition

The CSF exists in a competitive environment because Cambridge is full of theatres and the college grounds host student productions. The latter bring an unfortunate side effect of many people presupposing that the CSF productions are amateur. Time and again at shows I have heard people say a variant on 'Surely these guys cannot really be amateurs, they are so good.' It is inevitable as such productions are so common in Cambridge. I asked David Crilly if this perception causes him problems, and he replied,

> It's something that irritates me quite a bit, to be honest, though I realise why it's like that. Cambridge residents are familiar with all the theatre events happening at the colleges all year – especially the summer term productions, which are almost all Shakespeare and in the college gardens. As we perform in the colleges it's natural to think that students are involved, though I hope the biographies in the programme show that not to be the case. I'm not sure how to tackle it – a note on the publicity saying 'by the way, we're all professional' smacks of protesting too much.

Even more seriously, the *Globe on Tour* brings the Globe players every summer to exploit the venues, customer base and tradition so painstakingly built up by the CSF. I am tremendously fond of visiting the Globe and I think it is a very good thing that they tour for those who do not live near the capital. It seems a shame, however, that they have to muscle in on the success of the CSF in locations only 60 miles from the Globe itself. Again, audiences turn up at the colleges to see a Shakespeare play and do not necessarily pay attention to which company is putting on the show. In this case the easiest way to tell is if you have to pay a booking fee and credit card extra and find that your ticket is immovable from one performance to another. The Globe brand is, needless to say, a huge draw and there must be many who only go to one or two outdoor shows a year and are thereby lost to the CSF.

Some competition has gone much further and descended into truly disturbing depths. It has on occasion threatened to change the path the CSF was on, if not its very existence. Crilly describes with passion how the waters in Oxford became muddied with a latecomer entering in around 1994 in lookalike productions, but staffed by totally inexperienced and desperate wannabes playing for virtually nothing and with no proper rehearsals or direction. They even followed the CSF to Cambridge and again tried to cash in on the CSF's success by putting on rival performances at the same time. Confused attendees would find themselves watching an outdoor *A Midsummer Night's Dream* in Cambridge on the advertised date but it would not be by the CSF nor feature professional actors.

The CSF eventually saw off this challenge by simply continuing to produce professional performances that garnered enough good feeling to outweigh the damage being wrought by others. Undoubtedly, though, takings and reputation were tarnished for a time, as anyone going to the shambolic alternate performances and thinking it was the CSF was unlikely to revisit the festival. David Crilly had to make clear to a steady stream of complainants that what they had witnessed was nothing to do with the CSF.

2014: Attempt to Close the Festival Down

As I have been writing this book, the CSF faced one of its greatest challenges of all. This unexpected threat came from David Crilly's employers or, more precisely, Gerald Pillay, the vice-chancellor of Liverpool Hope University where David was lecturing until the end of November 2014.

Pillay visited a performance at Trinity in Cambridge, much to David's delight. This delight soon turned to despair when it became clear that Pillay's plans were to relocate the whole festival and rename it The Liverpool Hope University Shakespeare Festival. Unsuspecting of this at the time, David led the company to perform a preview run of first-half Cambridge shows one week in Liverpool. 'It was great, we did matinees full of school kids and the evening shows all went really well.'

Things soon turned sour: 'Then he suddenly said, "Well of course, we're your employer, you shouldn't really be doing the Cambridge Shakespeare Festival, it should be the Liverpool Hope Shakespeare Festival, so you can stop doing all that now and just bring it all up here."' Pillay not only planned to close Cambridge and move everything to Liverpool but he was also going to relegate David, after over twenty years of running the event, to being a bit-part player whose advice may be called upon if any questions arose.

Unsurprisingly, Crilly indicated that he would not be supporting this idea but the vice-chancellor was already entranced by his own dream and the kudos that it would bring and spent, according to David, 'an absolute fortune creating what he described as an Elizabethan garden'. Sadly this was at a time of cutbacks and redundancies.

There were other unsavoury aspects to this somewhat half-baked plan, yet it rumbled on and David soon found himself ruthlessly outflanked. Life became more and more troublesome for him at the university he had only moved to a year and a half earlier. It was decided that any proposed work outside the university could only be undertaken with written permission. A sensible proposal for those involved in developing drugs for medical research or other scientific research where university labs, time and expertise has contributed to the academic's knowledge. It did not seem to David that this could be applied to his Shakespeare work on the festival in his annual leave as it had no connection to his work as a music lecturer. However, this new document was targeted specifically at Crilly, with an eye to forcing him to relinquish the Cambridge Festival to the university. They made their position abundantly clear to him:

What they were implying was that I was not being responsible in my obligations as an academic because I'm too involved in this. Well, the thing is the festival started before I became an academic so it's been the backdrop throughout my whole academic career, which has never been a problem; and it certainly wasn't a problem when I was doing shows for him, then it didn't get in the way. But because now I won't do shows for him, now it's a problem. And they've said that I have to apply for permission to do the festival. Which I stupidly did and then they came back and said that they did not give me permission to do the festival.

The university was holding a gun to its lecturer's head. The choice they gave him was a stark one: either alternative would have ended the CSF. He was either to agree to move the festival to Liverpool Hope University and relinquish control over it or he would be forbidden to continue running it in his own time. David did the only thing he could to preserve the festival; he resigned.

Evidently then, there have been many challenges off the stage as well as, occasionally, on it. The strength of the acting and audience communities that we are going to examine in the next chapter are the key to the continuing ability of the festival to overcome these. The staff have fought long and hard to keep going in the face of any adversity and to ensure standards always remain as high as possible. As for the audience, we are not only forgiving of any individual hiccups at a performance, but rather we positively revel in them. Dave Rowan reminisced about one such occasion:

We had a situation in Trinity College where the generator they provided, along with a lovely space, packed in. As I was trying to get it started, I said to the audience, 'There are some lamp posts at the other end of the College. We can move there. Then a voice said in a German accent, 'Can't we stay here? It's so romantic in the dark.' So the audience shone some torches and I had some lanterns and we kept going. They had the opportunity to move and they stayed. We had about twenty minutes of this and although everyone was happy I was working hard to get the lights back on because I knew that the batteries for the lanterns would not last.

The lights came back on with about twenty-five minutes of the play left and they were greeted with sighs and groans! The audience had loved it and were disappointed that the problem had been solved. However, they did not know, as I did, that the lanterns would not last.

They love the experience. One of the things the open air can do is take people out of that theatrical setting. So it's a different experience, and if you get it right, you involve the audience in a very unique experience. And that's why I love doing it.

1, 2. The proximity of the actors to the audience is a key component of the CSF experience.

3. The sleeping Titania is close, not only to the audience, but also to crawling insects.

4. A wide expanse of grass in sunlight affords wonderful opportunities for simultaneous staging.

5, 6. Sea journeys and shipwrecks are depicted in a myriad of ways, the audience imagination being the key component in them all.

7. Actors interacting with audience members is a special thrill of the festival.

8, 9. The bawdy bard: Jamie Alan Osborn strutting his stuff as Thurio in 2013's *The Two Gentlemen of Verona*.

10, 11. Doubling is often a necessity. Helen Meadmore as Hippolyta/Titania and Finnigan Morris as Theseus/Oberon.

12, 13. Gareth Llewelyn doubles as Gardener and Bush in *Richard II*.

14, 15. Director David Rowan in his 'super-sub' role, learning his lines as he goes and saving the day in two roles and genders.

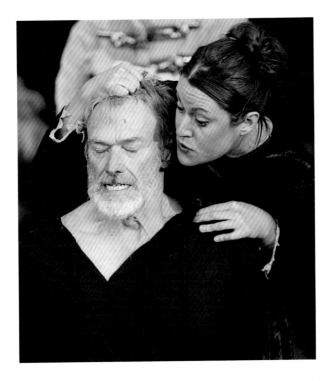

16–19. 'A little bit of goo goes a long way': The blinding of Gloucester (Keith Chanter) in 2012's *King Lear* by Regan (Helen Meadmore) and Cornwall (Daniel Jennings).

20. The curious paradox of night scenes being better in daylight: a lantern lets the audience know it is dark.

21. Staging the *King Lear* storm scene in sunlight.

22. 'For the rain it raineth every day'. Trinity College Fellows' Garden in 2012, which was the year with the highest Cambridge rainfall on record.

23. An audience gathers in St John's College garden.

24–27. Trees are a boon and perfect places from which to eavesdrop.

28, 29. The same props are used repeatedly: a castle tower for Richard II is also used as a balcony for Juliet.

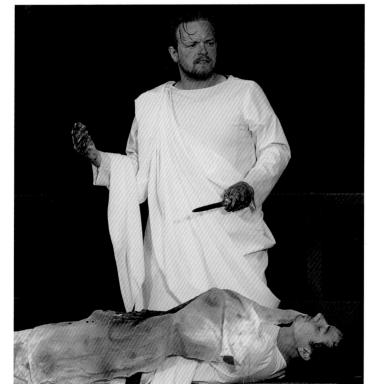

30. Animal blood
is much easier
to clean than
mulberry juice.

31. Sword-fighting
scenes are
performed
thrillingly close
to the audiences
at the CSF.

32. Encore! Encore!

6

Communities

shall set them in present action.
So, sir, heartily well met, and most glad of your company
Coriolanus, act IV, scene III

Actor, Director and Audience Communities/Bawdy

This chapter takes a look at the actor, director and audience communities that surround the CSF and how the tricky matter of Shakespeare's all pervasive bawdy element is dealt with in these contexts. Appropriately enough we begin by looking at the actors' introduction to the festival experience.

Audition and Induction

The audition and induction period for new actors is a crucial part of the running of the festival. David Crilly told me that, 'We start the audition process in March, we need about forty-five actors all together and we always get well over 1,000 applications.' I was amazed at the number of applicants, thinking of all the work this must entail, and asked how many of the applications were genuine. David said that

> about 99 per cent of those who apply are genuine, and by that I mean experienced actors who have attended a three-year actors' course at one of the major drama schools. We get the occasional nutter, of course. Someone once sent an application written in pen on a torn-off page from a jotter, accompanied by a photocopy of his bus pass! Occasionally some 'colourful' characters have made it past our screening process and made it to audition, and in one or two extreme instances have even managed to get into the festival, though not for long!

As well as performing speeches in the way one would expect, the actors are put through an extremely testing improvisation sequence. They are asked to pick a number and whatever number they choose describes their task, which is to perform a speech under the most ludicrous of conditions. Elena Clements remembered, 'I had to do two contrasting Shakespeare speeches and then take part in the workshop-y talk at the beginning, and then you go in and see people individually. For my day it was just Simon Bell and Jan who were there.'

Simon Bell told Elena to pick a number between one and twenty-five. Elena's lucky number is eight and so she chose that, which surprised Simon because, as he said, 'people don't normally go for the single figures'. I asked if she had drawn something like performing Lady Macbeth while giving birth. 'No,' she replied, 'I had to be Lady Macbeth while giving an autopsy and then realising halfway through that the person's alive; that was my pick of the pack!'

That nice twist of the presumed corpse turning out to be a live person gives you an idea of the Machiavellian minds behind these auditions. Another example would be Jamie Alan Osborn's experience. His twist was that the inebriated doctor in a theatre (a nice pun, there, too), whom he had to play while delivering a speech from Prince Hal, discovers halfway through that he has botched the operation. Tessa Hatts recollected a similar experience:

> I didn't mind doing my pieces but then we had this communal thing, where you have to do improvisation with people and I'd sussed that what they were looking for are actors who can work with other actors. So, I thought, 'Don't hog the thing, try to work with them as you are doing the improvisation.'

When I mentioned that the improvisation part of the process sounded like torture to me, she agreed that it was just that. 'Oh, yes, I hated all that stuff – do your audition speech again as badly as you can, or like a dwarf or something. I told the others not to choose number six because it was awful.'

Even a festival cornerstone, and star turn in role after role such as Tessa has turned out to be, does not easily pass the rigorous screening process. Tessa remembers it clearly:

> I did the audition but they didn't offer me anything. Someone else, who had done the previous year, had already been chosen for the things that I was actually ideal for – Maria and Biondello. So, I didn't get an offer. But about ten days before the festival started I got a phone call, 'Would you like to be Maria and Biondello?' 'Yes!' And it turned out that the person who had agreed to do the festival had then dropped out. They were the sort of parts that I would get, because I did Maria at my audition.

Not only had Tessa given what she thought was a good audition, but she had also been warmly recognised and created quite an impression due to her TV work in *Wizadora* and *Let's Pretend*, and yet still she was only immediately accepted into the fold due to someone else dropping out. The selection process is obviously a very rigorous one and there are good reasons why this should be so, over and above the high number of qualified applicants, to do with the community spirit of the CSF acting troupes.

Community Spirit

The community aspect of the festival is not an easy thing to build, or maintain, as one bad apple can upset the whole cart. Less dramatically but almost as importantly, even talented and responsible actors may find themselves antipathetic to the working practices of the festival. If even one actor does not buy into the ethos, the whole play will suffer quite severely. Andrew Stephen stressed to me that

> there isn't such a hierarchy here that there perhaps might be in other star-led establishments where the star comes out of a big dressing room and everybody parts the way. Where you're still made very aware of who are the top names, who are the top turns. They'll say, 'You're not going to move on my line, are you, *dahhling*?' All that sort of thing.

I mentioned to more than one of the actors how such behaviour would destroy the festival's team spirit and recounted horror stories I had heard in the past of such celebrity misbehaviour elsewhere, such as clearing a whole floor of people before they would use the toilet. To my astonishment I was told that there are places where this still goes on. Without going anywhere near those extremes, even one person behaving in such a fashion to almost any degree would tear a hole in the ethos surrounding each CSF performance.

In addition, it is not just someone behaving badly that can upset the apple cart; it is quite possible, even likely, that a highly skilled Shakespearean actor would find themselves totally unsuited to the particular environment of the CSF. Actors, after all, are accustomed to exits and entrances being in the same place each performance, to playing indoors with no concern for changing weather and constant lighting, and to the audience usually being the same size and always in the same place in relation to the stage.

As actor Gareth Llewelyn observed, 'You might have a brilliant actor but if that actor isn't particularly open, and easy to work with and to get on with, then that could sway the selectors against you. You're living in close proximity to everyone and it is a real company atmosphere; I think they very much look for that.' Co-cast member Elena Clements picked up on Gareth's thoughts:

> Yes, it's not necessarily that they're going to cause trouble or they're not going to get on with us. But I definitely know that there were people in the audition room with me that were put off by the fact that you'd have to get in a wet costume and that you wouldn't have any help, that there's no stage manager. People would be put off by the level of self-reliance needed.

The day of the audition also contains an 'induction' segment. Robin Maurice Owen emphasised the importance of this:

> I think that they are very honest with us, as actors, on that day. It was about an hour's talk that Simon gave and he tells you all the things, the truth about the festival. That you'll be performing when it rains, you might be performing the next day when your costume's still sodden, that the money's not great, and you have to look after your own stuff and all these things. They're just so honest with you that those people that we said might be a bad egg, would probably be put off by those things.

This is not surprising, and there are all the other factors too, like repairing your own costumes, the fact there is no prompter, that you have to play many parts and if somebody goes sick you may, at very short notice, have to play an extra part. With the best will in the world, and without meaning this at all disparagingly, many actors might not want to put their reputation on the line at the CSF. Or it might simply not be what they want to do. As Gareth further commented, with commendable understatement, 'You need to know, obviously, because if you arrived and you weren't expecting that – then you might be a bit put out.'

Thérèse Robinson's first year was 2014, and like Tessa Hatts before her, Thérèse was helped by a late call-off by a regular actor and landed the roles of Hippolyta/Titania and Olivia. An actor from a previous CSF engagement had pulled out when there was only a week to go before the festival started.

> I was very lucky, I got two major roles in my first year which was great, but I only had a week to get ready and I was moving house, but I was incredibly lucky with the roles. I was emailed by Casting Call Pro. They sent a really long e-mail listing all the disadvantages, and letting you know what you were letting yourself in for. But it excited me far more than put me off. I think they were trying to work out who would be right for the festival. So, then I had my audition.

Thérèse's audition was in a similar vein to those mentioned above. She remembered,

> Simon Bell asked me to do part of my speech as though I were selling kitchenware in an alluring manner while aroused. It was a mixture of brainwork with as much sex in it as possible, so that was interesting. Then we had to do some improvisations. In one we did the 'Zoo Keeper's Wedding' and I decided to jump to the floor and become a monkey.

That willingness to throw herself into the spirit of the day must have been very attractive to the selection committee.

The talk at the end of the auditioning and induction process is also a decisive part in choosing between the many qualified applicants. Elena is convinced it was that part of the whole day that clinched her place in 2014: 'I think what swayed me coming here, for them, was probably the conversation afterwards and they could tell that I was enthusiastic.'

The CSF selectors are obviously very adept at spotting the right characters among the applicants. Regardless of acting ability, they will be looking for the traits so eloquently summed up to me by Jamie Alan Osborn:

> I was trained to go with the idea that the best thing you can get out of leaving a company is to be thought of as a good company member. That regardless of performances, notices, regardless of how the audiences have been or how many people have turned up, if you are regarded as being a good member of the company, if you are good to work with and people like you and get on with you and you've been valuable to be around, then that's the best you can do. And if someone doesn't want to come punting, doesn't want to socialise and shuts themselves away, then they are ostracising themselves.

Once the casts are assembled they knit together remarkably speedily; their comradeship is evident to everyone. Bob Wellman remarked, 'What is so nice about the CSF is that I think the majority of actors here all seem to get on very well with each other and there's a nice social atmosphere.' His twin, Bill, added that, 'It makes a difference when you've a vast number of actors together for such a long time. Where else does that happen but here? It doesn't, does it?'

It certainly lends the whole summer of shows a very pleasant and inspirational community feel. Naturally, as in all walks of life, you get rivalries and, given the intense and enclosed circumstances in which they work, there are bound to be occasional blow ups. Notwithstanding this, I have always noticed that there is a tremendous overall camaraderie. The cast members from other shows get the chance on Saturdays of seeing the charity matinee of one of the other plays.

They attend in great numbers, despite this being one of their few breaks in a gruelling schedule of plays and rehearsals, and are very supportive of their performing colleagues.

Daniel Simpson agreed with my observations: 'Oh yes, honestly, I can't believe that some of my closest friends in the world now, I've only known since 2010; my first year at the festival I made some of the closest friends that I now have, and not just one or two, half a dozen people that I see more regularly than anybody else.'

I asked him if he thought these would be long-standing friendships, and if he envisaged them still being as strong as they currently were in ten years' time. He answered, unhesitatingly,

> Yes, these are absolutely friendships for life. As actors we come into something new and then say goodbye to it so frequently, and you leave with the good intention of staying in touch, but it's actually very rare that you genuinely forge proper strong, unshakeable friendships in reality through performing a piece. But with Cambridge, because of its unique nature, the way that you live together for so long, and just have that luxury of living and breathing Shakespeare for a few months in the summer, it forges really strong friendships, and I literally have friends that I see every single week.

Osborn also has no doubts as to the value of the social aspect:

> The CSF feels more like rep that I have done before, because you are reliant on each other a lot more than when you are turning up and doing a show in a town and then going away. You are living together, you are rehearsing another play with other people in the same overall group, you are performing in the evening and then there's all the socialising together. The social aspect almost carries the whole experience through.

These friendships begin with the actors socialising together, and so quickly are the bonds that Daniel speaks about forged, that within a few weeks the casts that are all working long days together choose to spend their free time together too. Helen Meadmore recollected 'It's nice in the second half when the first play is finished, you do have the days free to go off. The thing is that that's when you almost always go and do things together; you go out to lunch or to do whatever, together.'

I thought that this was marvellous. Here were lots of people thrown together, living and working side by side for weeks and then, when given the chance of getting away from each other, instead they just wanted to spend even more time together. I asked Helen to backtrack and tell me how it all started:

'The first night, obviously we all get here and then it's an open bar for ages. Then there's a massive buffet and that's the first time when everybody gets to know each other.' How quickly people do so can depend on the mixture of newcomers and old hands. Sometimes the balance can be slightly askew. As Helen recalled, 'It was my first year, last year, and I remember there was a huge proportion of people who had done the festival before. I did find that the people who had done it before kept themselves in various groups.' Usually, however, it is perfectly aligned. She continued, 'And this year there's only been about five, maybe like five or six people who have done it before, and of course that includes Tessa and Rory and Alex who have been here many years. They know where to go and what to do but we all can suggest things too.'

Even as a newcomer, Helen threw herself into the process of getting to know everyone. It is this spirit that the selection process is so good at identifying in applicants.

> Right away I said, 'Right, let's do this thing and then let's go here.' Then the next night someone else will, and it was a great way for people to really get to know each other. And then also to get to know the areas around Cambridge. We've all organised big parties or walks for whoever wants to come. And last year, on the first weekend of the second part, I held a massive curry day. I cooked curry for about forty-five people. And I did it again for about thirty-five to forty this year. I had a huge pot for the meat one, and then another one for the veggie one.

Events like this are important because for actors that are not in the same cast or sharing a house would not get to know each other very well.

Years afterwards, as Daniel Simpson has confidently predicted about himself, the fellowship thus instilled at the festival is a light that still burns brightly and attracts actors from previous years back again, like moths to a flame. Andrew Stephen informed me,

> Actors from other years, they always support the festival and people do come back and watch, they make the effort, they travel some distance in many cases, to come and see them. If they're not doing it because they can't afford it or due to circumstances like they have a child or something, they always go a bit misty-eyed and wish they were here because it's a completely different experience. We were punting the other day and a chap, not young, put it on Facebook that 'this is one of the best days of my life, this punting with the cast'. Whereas there are other things that you do that will pay the rent and give you work with somebody on the telly or whatever, with this there are moments that you will always remember. And there is a golden glow about it. It's incredibly

hard work, though. It's harder work than most other jobs, particularly that middle period and particularly if you are rehearsing a big play in the second half. If you are rehearsing nine to four on something heavy like *Richard III*, it's exhausting. But you get an enormous sense of satisfaction.

Relationships

Living and working in such an intense atmosphere and at such close quarters for weeks on end inevitably results in intimate relationships, as well as deep friendships, being formed. In addition to the many lifelong friendships that have been made, the festival can also boast the creation of seven marriages, five children and an unknown number of long term co-habitees. As time has passed, there have been some inevitable break-ups, including one divorce and, alas, at least five actors from previous CSF summers have since passed away.

The first marriage from within the festival was of a couple playing Macbeth (Craig Garbutt) and Lady Macbeth (Heidi Gjertsen). You would be forgiven for guessing that they were tempting fate and also provide us with our only CSF divorce statistic. They married a year or so after meeting at the festival, and David Crilly recalls that, 'I was best man and Heidi wore a blood-red wedding dress! And their daughter Grace Millie was born a couple of years later.' Jan Crilly told me that Grace 'has just been accepted at RADA but her first role was as Young Macduff in the festival'. Grace, as I type this, is currently playing a part in Alter Ego's *Chelsea's Choice*, a play about internet grooming which is directed by Sean McGrath, another actor with a CSF background and who directed 2014's festival performance of *As You Like It*. You could say, then, that Grace's life – as well as her acting career – arose from the CSF experience.

The Crilly's own progeny were not allowed to escape entering into the spirit of things. Their son, Josh, has made a few appearances in the festival among which the most notable were probably his portrayals of 'Young Macduff' and what his father describes as 'a quite chilling non-speaking role in *King Lear*. When asked to "Bring in the traitor, Gloucester" – he brought Gloucester in by the hand, stood facing the audience and witnessed the blinding!' It was by then almost superfluous for David to add that the director had been Simon Bell.

However, it was their daughter, Lauren, who first appeared on the festival stage. As David recalled, 'She was two and we were potty-training her. During the interval of an *Othello* matinee in Magdalen Deer Park, she wandered into the middle of the stage, pulled down her knickers and peed, receiving rapturous applause from the 200 or so in the audience!'

Such friendships, relationships and family stories forge ties that strengthen on-stage collaboration. Naturally, such collaborative partnerships are evident in all theatres where the cast perform together over a time, but the set-up of the CSF that I have just been describing lends extra depth and intricacies to this. It has an unmistakable influence that is immediately evident to everyone present.

Andrew Stephen, when talking about this process in general, described a specific example of it for me:

> I think that in the short period of rehearsal things can often be missed that are discovered in the performance, just as a kind of on-stage relationship. The relationship between Don John and Borachio in *Much Ado about Nothing* [2013] grew greatly in the playing of it. Don John is a particularly inept villain, he relies entirely on Borachio. He wants to be so bad and he is not very good at it. So, he's got this manservant who is not particularly evil but he's got some mischievous ideas, and Don John entirely depends on that, and so that sort of interdependence definitely grew. At the beginning I had this idea of how I wanted to do Don John, almost in spite of how Tim [Timothy Weston] did Borachio, but it evolved, and there was so much more communication.
>
> The audience picks up on this. They see and they recognise the little intricacies and the give and take of human relationships between the actors, and that is why it's so important that actors do work with and use each other and don't just play their part in spite of everyone else, because surprisingly that can happen a lot. You've got a lot of star performers that just kind of use the other actors as props or as scenery, disregarding them, but what you do has so much more depth and intimacy if it's based on these relationships. And I think it is easier for it to happen here; I certainly find it so. In most instances the more satisfying parts do develop these rapports that make it worth more.

Andrew talks about work there, and stressed how strenuous that work is in his previous quote. I mentioned to some of my interviewees that I was astonished they managed to socialise as much as they were claiming because, especially at the beginning, I felt it must just be a treadmill of rehearsal, practice, perform, rehearsal, practice, perform etc. Helen Meadmore replied,

> Yes, that first two weeks is intense. You'll maybe start at nine o'clock and then some rehearsals won't finish until nine o'clock at night. But as it's only the director that is there the entire time, you do get a bit of time to go off and learn your lines. And then once you've really got that nailed then you can really focus in on the second play in which you're appearing. And those lines should already be quite well learnt by that point, anyway. But then, it's just so liberating to rehearse one play and then go off and perform another one. And I just love that. I love doing this, because not only are you in two plays, but then you get to watch six others.

This mixture of hard work and enjoyment is so ingrained that the two things become inseparable. I was asking Helen how strange it felt for those actors left in the so-called ghost week, when only one play is still going on and the other casts have departed. I speculated that there was a big farewell party and she laughingly picked up my train of thought,

> We have a massive, *massive* farewell party, but then some people stay. I did, in fact, last year. What happened was that my friend Fleur, who played Kate, said, 'I've got this problem, I did tell them in the audition that I can't do that final week and I just don't know what to do because I really want to do this festival. I know this is the most bizarre question and I wouldn't expect you to say yes, but any chance you'd want to swap second roles?' And I said, 'I'm sorry, I'm not giving up Regan at all but, how about this – why don't you suggest to them that we do our parts, but then in that final week, I just take over your roles in *As You Like It* because my *King Lear* will be finished by then?' She asked them and they thought it was a great idea, so that's what we did. So then I ended up doing three plays, which was amazing, and it was four very great roles.

I expressed my astonishment, as I so often had to during these talks, as to how she managed to accomplish this, given all that I already knew that she had packed into the summer on and off-stage. Helen explained,

> Well, on that Saturday, it was that massive farewell party and I didn't get to bed till about seven in the morning. Then waking up at around three in the afternoon and hearing all these people packing and going off was just great. I was so happy because I could think of nothing worse right then! To be just lying on the lawn outside instead and not packing and getting up and going was very nice.

That was all well and good, I replied, but you had a whole new part to learn. Helen dismissed this, airily, as having been no real imposition:

> It was easy. I'd been learning it. I'd been learning it as I went along. What I did was – I watched them. I went to a few of their rehearsals and all I did was film Fleur and film her scenes and so I literally learnt it from my phone, learnt the moves from my phone and then I went through it all myself, and then we only had two rehearsals with everybody before I went on and did it.

The actors clearly work exceptionally well together but I wondered how they got on with the directors. Unsurprisingly, given the obvious good feeling and warm ambience the plays regularly exude, they all reported that this was generally very easy-going, smooth and productive. The exceptions to this were so far and few between that they were clearly remembered as something remarkable. Tessa Hatts agreed that negotiating points of view with directors went 'mostly quite well'. But she continued by saying, 'There was one who just wouldn't listen to me. I was Feste and I wanted that bit about living by the church:

> CLOWN: No, sir, I live by the church.
> VIOLA: Art thou a churchman?
> CLOWN: No such matter, sir: I do live by the church; for
> I do live at my house, and my house doth stand by the church.
>
> *Twelfth Night*, act III scene I

'I wanted that in, but he had taken it out and he wouldn't put it back in, he wouldn't even discuss it. I wasn't happy working for him. He is a lovely geezer, a lovely actor, but he just wouldn't have it. But Simon Bell and Dave Rowan, who I've mostly worked with, are very good. As long as I can give a good reason why I want it back in.'

Jamie Alan Osborn also found Dave Rowan very good to work with as they combined their creative talents to create the extraordinary portrayal of Thurio in 2013's *Two Gentlemen of Verona*. In fact, there was a litany of praise for the partnerships over the years, the disputes were very few in number and, in any case, were often moot. Tessa went on to make a point that other actors (and directors, albeit in more resigned tones), also stressed to me, 'Of course, in the end you can always threaten them, "You can't stop me Simon. How are you going to stop me? I'm going to say it anyway!" Of course, I rarely do.'

If one ill-fitting actor can cause the problems we have already seen, then imagine the chaos that would be caused by a 'wrong sort' of director. It is rare, but it has, perhaps inevitably, happened a few times over the decades. Daniel Simpson told me that

> you work as a company, under the direction of the director, and for the sake of the company, especially with something like the Cambridge Shakespeare Festival, the last thing you'd want to do is undermine him, because in doing so you could undermine the whole company. A good director will be co-operative and open to ideas and suggestions and will trust his actors to bring something to the table. And conversely, a bad director is incredibly prescriptive, which wouldn't work here. I've never had this experience, but it has happened to us, with certain guest directors, and it's a disaster because what they're saying is that they don't trust you as a performer, in a way. A director should never be overly prescriptive. They should have their concept,

obviously, and their interpretation and their scenes and ideas for the vision for the piece, and you should do your best to serve that vision.

The long-standing directors form a community of their own, too. Dave Rowan, David Salter and Simon Bell pay close attention to what each other does and are constantly learning from each other's strengths. It is probably no coincidence that David Crilly has gathered three directors who have disparate approaches but who all are perfectly attuned to the festival ethos. As Rowan explained to me,

> The nice thing about it is, myself, David and Simon, we all have a different perspective. Simon's very visual and very creative in a different way. David really thinks about the history and the heart of his plays very much. I think of the nuts and the bolts of the performance maybe a bit more than other people because I think a play's a little bit mathematical. It is about setting things up and I look at the structure of the play much more than I think the others do. So, it's nice that we're all essentially doing the same thing – which is stripping away the furniture, making something happen on stage which is vital and interesting – but we all come at it from slightly different ways and use a slightly different language.

A Shakespeare play is created by individuals, be it the writer who creates the text, the actor currently portraying a Viola or a Hamlet or the director trying to bring his vision of the writer's text to life. Yet, at the same time, it is a totally collaborative artistic creation that we eventually witness, and, in the case of the CSF, in which we feel as though we are participating. Every part of the whole is completely reliant on the other parts. The close acting community of the CSF exemplifies this collaboration at its organic best. Andrew Stephen enthused,

> It's all the better for it, because having a stage full of believable characters just helps production infinitely. You don't want that sort of situation where everyone else is just a cipher and it is all only about the main character. It's so important that, in something like *Richard III*, you get what the other characters are all about: who they are, and why they're there and what their very specific personal relationship is to each other, and to him. So, in terms of specifically the festival, I think there's a great spirit about the festival.

Audience Community

This spirit radiates out from the grass stages and the acting community and into the audience. For those who only ever come once or twice to the festival it is a temporary feeling associated with the only performance(s) that they see. For more frequent attendees, it is an all-enveloping feeling that permeates each summer.

It is difficult to generalise too much about the festival audience because it is both varied and variable. In many ways the range of gender, wealth, age, education and social status in the audiences is a perfect match for that of Shakespeare's characters. It is very different from elsewhere. I went to a Saturday matinee performance of *Richard II* by the RSC at Stratford and, with the exception of my companion and a handful of teenage girls swooning for and shrieking at (during the closing applause) David Tennant, I was the youngest there. I was fifty-five at the time. It is very different at the CSF, as Andrew Stephen describes:

> Sometimes when you are in a play that's touring, you know that what you're going to get, at the matinee, is ladies of a certain age, the blue rinse brigade, but that's your audience. But here you'll get children, you'll get academics, you'll get block bookings and sixty Italian thirteen-year-olds who have no desire to be here at all, but they're perhaps just being kept out of trouble for two hours.

Non-native speakers make up a surprising number of attendees at the CSF. It is not just morose teenagers sent along by the omnipresent city language schools but people drawn from all walks of life from all over the world. Their level of understanding English similarly covers the full range, from beginner to bilingual. Everyone can still enjoy the plays and it is worth remembering that much of what we know of Elizabethan playgoing comes from the enthusiastic reports of performances by foreign travellers, some with little or no English at all.

The majority of the non-native speakers are not residents of Cambridge and they come and go as their studies, work and other life commitments take them. Yet, I know a number that return from Europe as many summers as they can to catch a few performances, and there must be many more who do this than those who happen to be personal acquaintances of mine.

There is a more permanent community of regular audience members and local Cambridge devotees of the Festival that have their own special relationship with the annual jamboree. The sharing of the same physical space in natural conditions, open to the elements, plus the interplay and interaction between the actors and the audience creates a community for each performance. Additionally, an even stronger bond develops when you attend more or all of the plays over the six-week run each summer.

This again is analogous to what happened in Shakespeare's time. Back then, the theatres of London and their audiences formed two tight communities that were constantly overlapping. So it is for me as a Cambridge resident who regularly attends shows. I have met friends from other parts of my life there that I had hitherto not known were Shakespeare aficionados. You make new friends, too, as you get to know those beside you at a play or you are drawn to features that have become familiar from many a performance. I found myself, by chance, sitting beside two long-term CSF supporters, William and Margaret Steen, at a performance of *Twelfth Night* at the Cambridge Arts Theatre only last week. Our conversation immediately fell into what we had next seen at the CSF after we had last met there.

Many regulars travel from further afield than Cambridge and they also share in this special relationship. Indeed, they often become temporary Cambridge residents for a few weeks. You can get to feel that you know the actors, too. Bill and Bob Wellman, from Waterlooville, wrote in a letter to me that 'We're biased towards the CSF because you get to know certain actors. We wouldn't like as much to go to a strange theatre and see a strange cast. We look forward to seeing actors we know in new roles, like Rory as Hamlet and Tessa as Polonia in 2013.'

On the last day of the 2014 festival, I was at the afternoon performance of *The Taming of the Shrew* and while at the lavatory in the interval, turned around to find myself facing actor Tino Orsini resplendent in full costume as Baptista Minola. We exchanged a few words about the play, how it was going, and he let me know what a good vibe they were getting from the audience as they performed. The Saturday prior to that, I was in the same Sainsbury queue as Pericles, which is how I will always think of Max Sterne after his splendid portrayal of the Prince of Tyre. I confess I sometimes find these meetings rather odd and especially so when I see some of the younger actors, who have just performed something very profound, doing something silly in the city centre like any other young people. Sometimes these mental pictures can be difficult to reconcile, but these chance meetings do show how nicely intertwined the communities of actors and audience can be.

This togetherness further strengthens the feeling that we are all part of the festival. Cancellations are extremely rare at the festival but when they do occur, they are felt as an almost personal blow to cast and regular audience members alike. Andrew Stephen told me, 'I bumped into Catherine, who is playing Elizabeth in *Richard III*, when we were in Sainsbury's just now and she said that we've just got five performances left. I replied by asking her how terrible it would be if we lost one at the drop of a hat.' The idea that one of them might suddenly be postponed and then there would only actually be four left was upsetting to Andrew. He continued,

I don't want that, I want every one of them to be vital and important. I don't want that feeling you can get if you are on a long tour, that a cancellation means you now have the night to yourself. You don't get that here. I feel robbed if we ever have to cancel any of these. I want to be doing the show and I want to feel that I've earned it.

Andrew lives in Cambridge permanently so he has an added bonus:

And the actual opportunity to perform in your own community is relatively rare for actors, you tend to go elsewhere and ply your trade. To be able to do it at home, to just go down the road and do it for people that you are going to see in the street is wonderful. And I've been in some bookshops and some old chap, that I don't know personally, will come and say, 'Hello Mr Stephen, I did enjoy your …' and you think 'I don't know you, but how marvellous to be appreciated.'

There are very special ways in which the communities interact. There are communal events and individual experiences that say much about the CSF's spirit. The actors get to hear about all manner of uplifting stories as well as satisfied feedback. Tessa said, 'Dave Crilly is very good about, eventually, forwarding the emails, because he gets emails from happy punters.' Sometimes these e-mails contain something even more magical. In 2013 for example, Tessa found out that there was

a family who've got an autistic son. They'd been desperately trying to find activities that he would enjoy, that the whole family could join in with, and coming to these plays was it. He had the scripts and stuff, he was just beside himself with joy, and they've come to see everything, and it's really transformed them as a family. And so they wrote to David Crilly and thanked him, saying, 'Thank you so much for your plays and what it's done for us.'

For many the festival plays provide an ideal location for a communal celebration: a birthday party, a farewell party, a reunion, an office night out. All of this adds to the feeling of geniality and of a community pulling together. Having a closely-knit group as the core of your audience undoubtedly adds to the communal feel of each play as well as the festival as a whole. It is not fanciful to suggest a similar experience was felt at the Globe, and the other theatres, all those years ago among the regular attendees. Crilly has always envisioned his festival as being part of the Cambridge community and serving it. He is right in this and it inspires many of us in Cambridge, and from further afield, to reciprocate and become part of his community and lend our support to it.

Bawdy

We have already noted, in chapter three, the explosive fun that both audience and cast had with Hortensio's 'enormous strap-on penis' in *The Taming of the Shrew* (2012). Shakespeare's plays are absolutely riddled with bawdy action, lewd jokes and sexual puns. Whole books have been dedicated to this field, as well as specialised glossaries focusing solely on this area.

The claim, first raised in the Restoration, that lewd innuendo was merely a regrettable addition that the high-minded, saintly Shakespeare was enforced to include to entertain the rabble has long been disproved. Instead, it is now recognised that such imagery is used by every facet of the writer's imagination. It is there in delicate fantasy as well as in the vulgarity of an obscenity-ridden farce. From the most sophisticated to the most blunt, it permeates all. It underpins, intertwines and supports other imagery in the wondrous web of language that binds each play together. In the plays themselves the high born indulge in it just as readily as the low born. Nor is it confined only to the comedies; it is never far away in any history play or tragedy either. In Shakespeare's time this was unremarkable, and the plays of his contemporary dramatists are similarly packed with sexual puns and coarse interchanges. It is only the witless Sir Andrew Aguecheek who needs such things as 'this is my lady's hand these be her very C's, her U's and her T's and thus makes she her great P's' explained to him. Aguecheek is held up as a figure for everyone else, both on and off the stage, to mock for his non-comprehension of a literally spelled out innuendo.

While bawdiness runs throughout Shakespeare's work in all genres, it is certainly true that the comedies and farces are particularly full of opportunities for the physical enactment of lewd humour, and they still provoke laughter time after time in performance at the CSF. This is yet another instance where reading the plays simply does not convey the full meaning of the text, which was written for, and no doubt tweaked by, an ensemble for the express purpose of performance in front of an appreciative audience.

Here is an extract from a blog by a visitor to the festival from America. Avowedly primarily a lover of Shakespeare on the page, Erin Weinberg was captivated by the sheer physicality of the CSF performances. Among other astute observations, she commented on 2013's *The Comedy of Errors* that

> the funniest use of physical comedy goes to Doctor Pinch and his codpiece. I'll be honest, I thought Charlotte [1] was crazy when I found her up at seven am, sewing together primary-coloured felt; it looked more like a child's toy than a body part! Let me tell you, though, it got laughs! The actor playing Pinch thrust his hips to the beat of a bongo, infusing the ridiculous character

with sexuality, while bringing up one of the play's central questions: who's the crazy one? Who is the doctor, and who is the patient, or is Shakespeare teaching us to blur the line between caregivers and genuine quacks? As much as I'd love to get this production on DVD so I can relive the moment that Pinch made his way into the audience, it's impossible to relive that sense of pee-your-pants laughter I felt as the actor shook his money-maker![2]

As someone else who was once attracted mainly to Shakespeare on the page, I cannot concur heartily enough with this assessment. Nick Saunter's Dr Pinch was so outlandishly over the top in action and costume that were you to read a description of him or see him in a picture, you would think to yourself that they had gone too far. Were you to see him in action running into and through the audience, though, you too would have been in fits of uncontrollable laughter. It was all encompassing, and no one of any age, gender or social class was immune. Howls of glee filled the air.

There are many who would deny such pleasures to the public, however. Over the centuries a determined campaign was waged to strip Shakespeare of all connection to real life and turn his work into a sin-free expression of saintly virtue. The very verb 'bowdlerise' is derived from the names of Thomas Bowdler and his sister, Henrietta Marie, who produced *The Family Shakspeare* in 1807. This declared itself to have 'omitted words and expressions which cannot be expressed in the family'. One wonders how such families were ever conceived in the first place.

The book was edited by his sister but her name was kept out of things as this would be an admission that a female actually understood what the excised passages meant and this would never do. Bowdler's introduction continued, with breathtaking arrogance, 'My great objects in this undertaking are to remove from Shakespeare some defects which diminish their value.' Alas, it was a popular undertaking, and this censored version of the plays went through eleven editions by 1850 and has had a lasting effect on how Shakespeare's work has been subsequently regarded.

All plays that are rewritten to any degree in this manner lose a great deal of their author's creative accomplishments. The way a couple banter by punning on crude matters is how they flirt and we learn much of their inner being and their relationships from this. There is, in addition, a whole sub-genre of bawdy insults that provide another layer of meaning to many a Shakespearean play, and communicate many nuances of his characters' inter-relationships. These have often been pruned injudiciously for no reason other than a false sense of propriety.

We are left with opposing demands on producers and directors. Polite society, as it likes to think of itself, shuns the coarse bawdy that is endemic in Shakespeare's work, while the intimacy and immediacy of the CSF brings out a sense of liberating fun in boisterous vulgarity. As we have seen when looking at audience demographics, the CSF is family oriented and David Crilly is as protective of the CSF's reputation as a mother bear is of her cub. Yet at the same time he knows that Shakespeare without its earthy element is not Shakespeare at all, but instead a censored rewrite according to the specifications of a portion of a society alien to that of the Bard. I asked him how he dealt with this conundrum and he told me, 'I'm always very enthusiastic about the bawdy elements of Shakespeare – they're there for a reason and I grab any opportunity to dispel the myth that Shakespeare is dull, cerebral and removed from everyday life. I'm happy to give the directors a lot of rope in that regard.'

Appreciating this is all very well, but Dave Crilly still has to sometimes rein in directorial excess due to the all inclusive, family-friendly nature of the festival. Despite his innate understanding of the nature of the plays he has had to draw the line to keep modern sensibilities satisfied at times.

The problem arises due to changes in society at large from when the plays were written. It is noteworthy that differing sensibilities between the genders does not seem to have been an issue in sixteenth-century England. It is true that women were unlikely to go to the theatres on their own, but this was primarily for safety reasons: Unattended females were presumed to be prostitutes looking for clients. Women did attend the plays, though, and in numbers so large that they astonished visitors from Europe. It seems that they matched their male counterparts not only in attendance at the plays but in appreciation of, and expertise in, bawdy exchanges. It is noteworthy that they usually come out on top in such exchanges in the plays themselves, too.

We also need to bear in mind that certain facets of life and death that were openly discussed in the sixteenth century are shied away from now. We live in an era in which for many people, in the countries where Shakespeare is most often performed, life is almost incomparably softer than it was in the society from which the plays were born. Topics that would have been openly discussed then are played down or avoided altogether in the societies of what is currently called 'the developed world'. Mutilation, torture, putrefying disease, rotting carcasses – human and otherwise – starvations, plague and so forth were regularly witnessed in the sixteenth century.

It was no time for the squeamish, and in the city of London there were no hiding places. The very river that the Globe stood beside, surrounded by brothels and bear-baiting, was an open sewer. A visit to the theatre could be combined with witnessing the ritual torture, mutilation and slow execution of someone deemed guilty, rightly or wrongly, of a crime. If you crossed the stinking river via the Tower to get to the south side, you would have passed severed heads on sticks. The plays of the time reflected this; all of human nature from the most sublime to the most disturbing and degraded was reflected on the stages of the day. Such a combination was familiar from the Mystery Plays, like those performed in nearby Coventry, which intertwined toilet humour into their recreations of the key Bible stories, when Shakespeare was a child.

Where to draw the line in reflecting accurately what is in the plays has been a problem for directors and producers ever since those days. What is considered acceptably bawdy in one society, or part of the same society, will horrify another. I asked David how he resolved such issues and he answered that, in addition to making the tone of the play clear in publicity material,

> the guide is if something is likely to offend. I'm very happy for people to think the humour is in bad taste Shakespeare is full of knob gags, even if some people prefer to resist that reality. The other thing, too, is a consideration of the play in question. If people, seeing the nature of our publicity for *A Midsummer Night's Dream*, turn up with their kids dressed up as fairies, then they can have a reasonable expectation of the production. Anyone coming to see *Titus Andronicus* in 2015 will deserve everything they get!

The directors are aware of the twin pull of certain elements of audience expectation and the undeniable content of the plays and how managing these can be a difficult balancing act. Of the 'giant penis' scene in *Taming of the Shrew*, director Dave Rowan said, wonderingly, 'It was interesting actually because we didn't have any complaints. You could expect parents with small children to complain but actually none did. I don't know why that was not booed.'

The answer lies, I believe, in a combination of the nature of the play and in the overall ambience of the festival where almost anything goes as long as it is within the spirit of the play. The intimacy and community feelings bring out the fun element in what is, when all is said and done, the most natural areas of human existence. Notwithstanding this, limits are sometimes needed when the make-up of the audience is taken into account. Hopefully this is achieved without going to the extent of rewriting Shakespeare completely to suit the overly prudish. I returned to the theme, later, with Dave Rowan and he told me that

> it has to be centred in the play, it must have context, it's not just put in. Dave Crilly does talk to us, certainly, about the nature of that. There have been situations, in Hamlet's relationship with Ophelia for example, where a director might envisage that Hamlet could try to potentially rape her. Things like that, like simulated sex for example, all those things – you have to be careful how you use them with a family audience. And that is really down to Crilly because he is the artistic director. He will set some boundaries for us [considered pause] but then part of the director's role is to test those boundaries!

7

Comparisons and Conclusion

therefore never flout at me, for what I have said
against it: for man is a giddy thing, and this is my
conclusion.
Much Ado about Nothing, act V scene IV

Other Theatres, Audio, Visual, Live Transmissions and Virtual Spectating

Much of what I have written about the CSF applies equally to other open-air productions. Clearly, individual venues will bring out particular differences, but the basic principles will be the same. I trust the reader can apply the general values I have written about to their experiences of any outdoor production, especially those utilising mainly Elizabethan period costumes and minimal props.

Throughout this book I have been highlighting the contrasts between the experience of seeing a play at the CSF and at a standard theatre. Bill Wellman, who has seen so many Shakespeare productions in all manner of venues over the decades, originally avoided this topic. 'It's unfair to compare a national theatre production with a CSF one. Size of cast, resources, rehearsal time, prompters, understudies ... They are in a different league.' Yet when I pressed him to choose where he'd prefer to see a given Shakespeare play, he began by saying 'It depends on the actual production, the individual production ...' Then he interrupted his own train of thought and showed that his heart lies where mine does: '... but I would prefer to see it in the open, at the CSF, because I think it is more authentic Shakespeare'.

I have been using the expression 'conventional theatre' as a blanket term, and like most generalisations this is both useful but also overlooks the exceptions and the individual. There have been attempts in modern theatre to break down the infamous 'fourth wall' and there are all kinds of other theatres, many of which we are fortunate enough to enjoy in Cambridge alone, far less further afield. Close to where I live there is a church formerly known as the Leper Chapel of St Mary Magdalene. It was built around 1125, and some twelfth- century stone survives, as the chapel attached to a leprosy hospital on grounds that were then outside the city, although now are considered almost central. A history of performance there goes all the way back to 1199 when King John gave permission for the chapel to hold an annual three day fair with the proceeds going towards care for the lepers.

To move forward to current times, an avant-garde theatre group called *in situ* puts on Shakespeare productions there that also aim for a close audience ambience. The spooky setting of the Leper Chapel certainly brought interesting resonances to *Macbeth* a few years ago. The director, Richard Spaul, promoted the production, saying, 'By using such an evocative site for our performances, and combining that with imaginative use of voice and movement, *in situ* offers its audience a type of theatre that is more complex, more intimate and more atmospheric than most other theatregoing experiences.'

This is just one nearby example of the many other types of theatres where you can experience a Shakespeare play. There are also the many Shakespeare productions via audio and visual devices, and every leap forward in technology is immediately keen to ascertain its credentials by putting out the Bard's plays.

Audio

The means of delivering audio to us has gone through many developments – radio, gramophone, CD, mp3s, podcasts – and no doubt will continue to evolve. Whichever way you listen to a Shakespeare play, you are enjoying a significant benefit in that you are forcibly removing yourself from our now customary print- and visual-oriented approach.

Shakespeare's plays were written for listeners who depended on hearing words. His was primarily an oral culture; in everyday life as well as the theatre everything noteworthy was heard, not read. It is impossible for us to put ourselves in their position. They went out in the afternoon to hear a play, whereas we talk of going to see one. We go so far as to use the same phrase when we attend music concerts; we say we go to *see* a band. We cannot apprehend the same nuance, depth and sheer information as they could from the spoken word, or to take it in at the speed they could. Nonetheless, by listening to a spoken only version of a play, we can open our ears to many of these aspects that they took for granted. There are a tremendous number of splendid audio versions available to enjoy at the click of a computer mouse, and I often avail myself of their pleasures.

Nonetheless, while acknowledging that it can be invaluable training for our modern day sensibilities to appreciate the aural without the visual, relying solely on audio is, self-evidently, very limiting. If Shakespeare's art was mainly verbal, it was very far from being only so. Indeed, at times the visual was not only a sizeable component but the primary one. Think of Malvolio appearing cross-gartered in his yellow stockings, remember when you first saw the 'statue' of Hermione move and think too of the meaning evoked by the complex coming together and separating of couples and groups on stage. There are also the meaning and effect communicated in every facial or bodily gesture, and the whole rhetorician's school of communicating via hand and voice together. This was an art presumably taught to Shakespeare as a schoolboy and second nature to so many in his day that it is central to the overall effect.

It is not just sight that radio deprives us of but all other senses too; there is no smell or touch and you cannot taste the same summer air as the cast and fellow attendees at a CSF performance. All physicality is lost. Fine though audio is, on its own it leaves too much out of the picture.

Video

Film and television, although they have important differences, both throw the focus so far onto the visual that the verbal sense is dreadfully diminished, while the other primary senses named above are once again absent. You may see a garden but you cannot smell the flowers and feel the grass. Any filmed production is, by its very nature, very far from the spirit of Shakespeare's original theatre. At a very basic level the camera reveals where you are and what is happening. There is no need for description. Consequently much of the text is instantly rendered redundant. Famous cinema versions of Shakespeare's plays can feature a mere forty per cent, or less, of Shakespeare's words. These excised words conveyed not just portrayals of scene and narrative but were part of the web of imagery, metaphor and sub-text that conveyed overall meaning of great depth. That web is torn down and you have to accept what is thrust into your eyes as being the sole picture of the reality the film is expressing.

This inherent realism kills the main pleasure of experiencing a Shakespeare play, which is that of collaboratively engaging as a member of a crowd that is physically responding to real people acting the parts in front of you. In ideal settings, as you listen to those actors, the playwright's words are engaging your imagination to create your own individual mind's eye view of the play's version of reality.

In a similar manner to audio, visual media has gone through many changes: from cinema and TV to video tapes, DVD, Blu-ray, live streaming, video file downloads. In all cases the observer is isolated, passive and distanced from the action. With the exception of the cinema, we do not experience these plays as a member of an audience. Even in the cinema, audiences are very different from those reacting to live performers. As with all filmed versions, the absence of the physical bodies of the actors, along with all the sensory stimuli of sharing the same space and air as them changes everything.

To attempt to get closer to the real experience, live performances are now filmed and made available as DVDs and on other formats. The Globe Theatre's films of its Shakespeare productions are widely available, as are others. These can be terrific ways to experience a play, particularly if you have difficulties in attending theatres and they are absolutely outstanding for studying purposes. The Shakespeare students of today have a world of learning materials at their fingertips. As when reading a book you have the control over a recording to pause, to stop and start, to go back and revisit a particular incident as many times as you wish. Furthermore, you can switch on subtitles to combine reading and watching.

Nevertheless, even the magnificent Globe DVDs of *Henry IV* parts *I* and *II*, and *Twelfth Night*, for example, are a much weaker dramatic experience than you recieved when you were at the theatre watching those same productions. For one thing you are always watching the one performance that happened to be filmed. Whereas at the theatre, live plays change every time and being part of a communal audience changes how we react. The experience of being part of a crowd inevitably shapes our individual responses.

An additional drawback is that you watch these recordings in 2-D and they are therefore 'flat' in more ways than one. Even as the fledgling 3-D technology develops it will still miss the ambience and be restrictive in that your eyes can only follow what the cameras capture. You, as viewer, do not have the choice to change the angle of view, which actor to look at, how much of the scene to take in and so forth. A TV camera could zoom in on Ophelia as Hamlet watches the Mousetrap, or a cinema screen could be split in two so that I could see Ophelia and Hamlet on one side and Claudius watching the play on the other, but it still would not be by my choice or mere chance that I looked that way at that moment; I still can only see what is chosen for me.

Live Transmissions and Virtual Spectating

The closest you can currently get to the theatre-going experience without actually going to a theatre is via the increasingly popular medium of live transmissions from stage performances to selected cinemas. The Globe, the RSC and the National Theatre have all broadcast these, tending to focus, naturally enough, on the most famous plays in these initial stages.

Undoubtedly this set-up is a clever combination of modern technology and live stagecraft. You are watching a film, yes, but it is a film of a staged event and, unlike a DVD watched at home, you have a live audience around you so that part of theatrical experience is partially recreated. It is only partially so because it is not the same as an audience responding to real human beings acting in front of them.

Considerable distancing factors remain, however, to keep this audience passive and at arm's length. The viewpoint is always camera driven; you can still only see what you are shown albeit you get a theatre space on screen rather than a cinematic shot. You also have a huge screen, with unnaturally sized characters and electronically modulated voices. The audience, again seated in darkness, is alienated rather than embraced.

In addition to live transmission, the broadcasts are rerun at later dates in the same or similar picture houses. While the setting and performance remain the same everyone knows, and this makes no small psychological difference, that what they are watching is not live. One benefit of these replays is that you know that the play will be shown in its entirety. This is important because truly live transmissions are, like the CSF, hostages to the weather. It is noteworthy that inclement conditions are much more likely to cause an abandonment in their case, given the electronic equipment necessary for the undertaking. The downside of encore broadcasts, though, is that they share with regular cinema those pre-main feature adverts and mock-heroic voiced trailers at ear-splitting volume that assault your senses and propel you as far from Elizabethan theatre as is imaginable. It is completely the opposite effect to walking into one of the CSF venues.

Accelerating advances in technology may soon be providing an answer to many of the negative aspects of filmed performances. Developments in the field of allowing the viewer to perceive a concert, play, museum or art gallery as a virtual spectator are proceeding apace. The aim is that you will be able to witness everything from any angle, anywhere in the building you choose. This will give a whole new meaning to the phrase 'in the round'. You could attend a production of *King Lear* from your home sitting room. You could opt to be in a balcony box, or at the front of the stalls or view from a position on stage. You could move around. Perhaps you could stand beside an actor and view everything through his eyes, though it would be prudent not to choose Gloucester as your vantage point.

As with every other advance, such media will bring us closer to experiencing, via technology, the thrilling engagement we get when we are at an Elizabethan-style production. There will be a degree of control and choice on the spectator's part bringing the experience nearer to that of being there. Yet it will still be far from being the same as you will always know, no matter how convincing the illusion, that you are not really, physically among others nor in front of the actors. You will remain bereft of touch, taste or smell.

None of which is not to deny that many recorded or broadcast forms of Shakespeare are valuable additions to our viewing experiences, nor that technological developments hold tremendous potential for future audiences and will undoubtedly be a fantastic boon for anyone unable to attend the real thing. Such conjecture, however, takes me very far from my remit in this book, fascinating though I find it.

So, to return to the here and now, those of us fortunate enough to have access to the primary, authentic experience in rebuilt Elizabethan theatres or open-air festivals, such as the CSF, can also enjoy these supplementary recorded video and audio productions. We do not need to choose one experience at the expense of another. We can, depending on where we live, experience all of the many ways of witnessing a Shakespeare play. It is no surprise, though, that my overwhelming preference is for the kind of stage for which Shakespeare wrote. Those twin brothers, Bob and Bill Wellman, who have appeared throughout this book, feel the same. They wrote to me, saying,

> At the CSF we see Shakespeare performed in the open, as it should be, without modern technology and amplification. All the basic skills of ancient stagecraft are needed to project to the audience. Shakespeare's dialogue is never fully understood if delivered in the rapid conversation of today, or if it is subdued and mumbled as in much TV and film work.

I look forward to the CSF every year with the same feeling of excitement and sure anticipation of forthcoming joy as I used to have for my summer holidays from school, half a century ago. There is also a similar sense of desolation when summer ends. The loss of all that exuberance, delight, fun, anguish and insight, all that drama coming to an end, is felt very acutely. Thankfully, however, there is always next summer to look forward to and 2015 will include debuts for *Titus Andronicus* and *Timon of Athens*. I can hardly wait!

Notes

1 Shakespeare in Cambridge

1.   This was a commonplace book. These were not just popular but the very mainstay of Elizabethan literary reading. So much so that all the playwrights consciously put passages into their plays that were designed to be taken out of context and used in these collections of quotable, profound poetic passages.

2.   John Russell Brown, *Shakespeare's Plays In Performance* Chatham, W&J McKay & Co., 1966.

3.   Mark Rylance, interviewed in *Shakespeare's Globe* Illuminations, 2005.

4.   Charles W. R. D. Moseley, *Shakespeare's History Plays: Richard II to Henry V, the Making of a King* UK: Penguin, 1988.

5.   Styan, J. L., *Interview with Derek Peat* Shakespeare Quarterly: Vol. 31, No. 2, Summer, 1980.

6.   Charles W. R. D Moseley, *Shakespeare's History Plays: Richard II to Henry V, the Making of a King* UK: Penguin, 1988.

7.   Roland Mushat Frye, *Shakespeare: the art of the dramatist* London, Allen & Unwin, 1982.

8.   Styan, J. L., *Interview with Derek Peat* Shakespeare Quarterly: Vol. 31, No. 2, Summer, 1980.

9.   Linda Gates, *Shakespeare and Voice* Oxford University podcast.

10.   Sir Sidney Lee, *Shakespeare and the Modern Stage with Other Essays* New York, C. Scribner's Sons, 1906.

11.   Peter Brook, *The Empty Space* UK, Penguin Modern Classics, 2008.

12.   John, *Shakespeare's Happy Comedies* London, Faber & Faber, 1962.

13.   Lee, Sir Sidney, *Shakespeare and the Modern Stage with Other Essays* New York, C. Scribner's Sons, 1906.

2 Audience Proximity

1.   Leonni was taking part in a survey I ran for Cambridge Programmes' English Literature summer course at Churchill College.
2.   Mark Rylance in *Shakespeare's Globe: A Theatrical Experiment* Eds: Dr Christie Carson and Farah Karim-Cooper Cambridge University Press; 2008.
3.   *Ibid.*
4.   J. L. Styan: *Shakespeare's Stagecraft* Cambridge University Press, 1967.
5.   Harriet Walter in interview; Oliver Ford Davies, *Performing Shakespeare* Nick Hern Books, London 2007.
6.   Adrian Lester in interview; Oliver Ford Davies, *Performing Shakespeare* Nick Hern Books, London 2007.
7.   Michael Pennington, *Hamlet: A User's Guide* London, Nick Hern books 1996.
8.   Judi Dench in interview; Oliver Ford Davies, *Performing Shakespeare* Nick Hern Books, London 2007.
9.   J. L. Styan: *Shakespeare's Stagecraft* Cambridge University Press, 1967.
10.   Survey conducted by the author at Cambridge Programmes' English Literature summer course at Churchill College.
11.   Mark Rylance *Shakespeare's Globe* DVD, Illuminations, 2005.
12.   Dr Wright's website can be found here: http://people.ds.cam.ac.uk/elw33/

3 The Bare Stage

1.   Though there is an aural pun here too as "Ardenne" referring to a location in France sounds the same as "Arden" as in the "forest" near Shakespeare's birthplace and the surname of his mother. The text can support both France and England as the location and seems to do so, almost teasingly, while leaning toward "Ardenne" overall.
2.   Judi Dench in interview; Oliver Ford Davies, *Performing Shakespeare* Nick Hern Books, London 2007.
3.   Ian McKellen in interview; Oliver Ford Davies, *Ibid.*
4.   Ibid.
5.   Judi Dench in interview; Oliver Ford Davies, *Ibid.*
6.   John Barton, *Playing Shakespeare*, Bloomsbury Methuen Drama, John Barton 1984.
7.   Laurie Maguire and Emma Smith, *30 Great Myths about Shakespeare*, Wiley-Blackwell, 2012.
8.   J. L. Styan, *Shakespeare's Stagecraft* Cambridge University Press, UK, 1967.

9.   A spectacle of another kind, the gore-fest that is *Titus Andronicus* is an earlier, if less extreme exception to the norm in this regard also.

6 Communities

1.   Charlotte Ellen, who played Dromio of Ephesus to great effect in 2013's *The Comedy of Errors*, to which this refers. She followed it up with a memorable performance of Puck in *A Midsummer Night's Dream* in the second half of the year.

2.   Erin Weinberg's blog: http://thebardolator.com/tag/comedy-of-errors/

Bibliography

Constructing a bibliography is usually a straightforward task but it is not so in this instance. It is some forty years now since I read my first critical book on Shakespeare and it is impossible to remember the influence each of the many articles, documentaries, lectures, books and other studies has had upon me.

Similarly, those university lecturers I mentioned, who taught me Shakespeare between 1975 and 1979, further opened my eyes to his genius after my father, my first and greatest teacher in all things, had set me on the path of discovering the gifts that all writers, and especially the finest, bestow.

I would like to also acknowledge the undoubted impact of listening to radio documentaries and audio Shakespeare courses over the years. In time gone by Peter Sacchio accompanied me on a daily commute and, more recently, Emma Smith's splendid series of podcasts from Oxford University have kept me company on frequent round trips from Cambridge to Bedford. Delays at the infamous Black Cat roundabout and at the A14 roadworks became almost welcome, rather than infuriating, with Dr Smith for company.

The reader will have noticed that I quote J. L. Styan more than anyone else. This is not to deny the sterling work of others who have developed his work since, but rather when going back to Styan I realised how solid his work remains and he provides a direct link from Caldwell Cook. I also hope to counterbalance recent attempts to denigrate him for not taking into account the unpredictable and individual nature of each performance, albeit that nature is what I find most intriguing and stimulating.

The list that follows is of the books that I returned to or read for the first time specifically while writing this book.

The Shakespeare edition used throughout is *The New Cambridge Shakespeare* series of individually edited plays. General Editor 1984–90 Philip Brockman and, from 1990–94, Brian Gibbons.

Braunmuller, A. R. and Hattaway, Michael (eds), *The Cambridge Companion to English Renaissance Drama* (Cambridge: Cambridge University Press, 1999).

Brook, Peter, *The Empty Space* (UK: Penguin Modern Classics, 2008).

Brown, John Russell, *Shakespeare's Plays In Performance* (Chatham: W&J McKay & Co., 1966).

Carson, Dr Christie and Karim-Cooper, Farah (eds), *Shakespeare's Globe: A Theatrical Experiment* (Cambridge: Cambridge University Press, 2008).

Davies, Oliver Ford, *Performing Shakespeare* (London: Nick Hern Books, 2007).

Frye, Roland Mushat, *Shakespeare the art of the dramatist* (London: Allen & Unwin, 1982).

Goldman, Michael, *Shakespeare and the Energies of Drama* (New Jersey: Princeton University Press, 1972).

Gurr, Andrew, *The Shakespearean Stage 1574–1642 4th Edition* (Cambridge: Cambridge University Press, 2009).

Gurr, Andrew and Ichikawa, Mariko, *Staging in Shakespeare's Theatres* (Oxford: Oxford University Press, 2000).

Hansome-Reeves, Stuart and Escolme, Bridget (eds), *Shakespeare & The Making of Theatre* (Basingstoke: Palgrave Macmillan, 2012).

Lee, Sir Sidney, *Shakespeare and the Modern Stage with Other Essays* (London: Archibald Constable & Co., 1907).

Maguire, Laurie and Smith, Emma (eds), *30 Great Myths about Shakespeare* (Chichester: Wiley-Blackwell, 2012).

Palfrey, Simon, *Doing Shakespeare* (London: The Arden Shakespeare, 2005).

Styan, John L., *The English Stage* (Cambridge: Cambridge University Press, 1996).

Styan, John L., *The Shakespeare Revolution* (Cambridge: Cambridge University Press, 1983).

Styan, John L., *Shakespeare's Stagecraft* (Cambridge: Cambridge University Press, 1967).

Thompson, Peter, *Shakespeare's Professional Career* (Cambridge: Cambridge University Press, 1999).

Ward, Sir A. W. and Waller, Sir A. R. (eds), *The Cambridge History of English Literature Vol. VI Part Two* (Cambridge: Cambridge University Press, 1969).

Wells, Stanley, *Shakespeare, Sex, and Love* (Oxford: Oxford University Press, 2012).

Wells, Stanley (ed.), *The Cambridge Companion to Shakespeare Studies* (Cambridge: Cambridge University Press, 1986).

Wells, Stanley and Stanton, Sarah (eds), *The Cambridge Companion to Shakespeare on Stage* (Cambridge: Cambridge University Press, 2002).